cx

"You hired me to act the part of your wife,

"and that's what I'm doing—acting."

The oath Hunter muttered was succinct and ungentlemanly. Lowering his head, he crushed Gaylan's mouth with his, his mood suddenly savage. He plundered, needing to prove something.

Passion rose in him, a sleeping giant suddenly awakened. He would have denied his need for her with his dying breath, but he could no longer lie to himself. He wanted to take her, here and now.

Hunter told himself if he had her just once, then he would be free of her. He told himself she was no different than a dozen other women he'd known.

Then Gaylan sighed his name, and he told himself he was a damned liar.

Gasping for control, he pulled away from her. "Tell me again," he growled, "that you're *acting*."

Dear Reader,

Welcome to Silhouette **Special Edition** ... welcome to romance. This month we have a wonderful selection of books for you, and reading them will be the perfect way to get into that summertime spirit!

June is the month of brides, so this month's THAT SPECIAL WOMAN! selection is right in tune with the times. *Daughter of the Bride,* by Christine Flynn, is a poignant, warm family tale that you won't want to miss.

We've also got the action-packed *Countdown*—Lindsay McKenna's next installment of the thrilling MEN OF COURAGE series. And you won't want to miss *Always,* by Ginna Gray. This tender story is another book in Ginna's wonderful series, THE BLAINES AND THE McCALLS OF CROCKETT, TEXAS.

June also brings us more books by favorite authors—Marie Ferrarella, Pat Warren—as well as a compelling debut book by Colleen Norman.

I hope that you enjoy this book and all of the stories to come. Have a wonderful June!

Sincerely,

Tara Gavin
Senior Editor

Please address questions and book requests to:
Reader Service
U.S.: P.O. Box 1325, Buffalo, NY 14269
Canadian: P.O. Box 1050, Niagara Falls, Ont. L2E 7G7

PAT
WARREN
A BRIDE FOR HUNTER

Published by Silhouette Books
America's Publisher of Contemporary Romance

To my daughter, Jenny, who is every inch a survivor, with love and affection

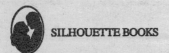 SILHOUETTE BOOKS

ISBN 0-373-09893-6

A BRIDE FOR HUNTER

Copyright © 1994 by Pat Warren

This edition published by arrangement with Harlequin Enterprises B. V.

® and TM are trademarks of Harlequin Enterprises B. V., used under license. Trademarks indicated with ® are registered in the United States Patent and Trademark Office, the Canadian Trade Marks Office and in other countries.

Printed in U.S.A.

Books by Pat Warren

Silhouette Special Edition

With This Ring #375
Final Verdict #410
Look Homeward, Love #442
Summer Shadows #458
The Evolution of Adam #480
Build Me a Dream #514
The Long Road Home #548
The Lyon and the Lamb #582
My First Love, My Last #610
Winter Wishes #632
Till I Loved You #659
An Uncommon Love #678
Under Sunny Skies #731
That Hathaway Woman #758
Simply Unforgettable #797
On Her Own #841
A Bride For Hunter #893

Silhouette Romance

Season of the Heart #553

Silhouette Intimate Moments

Perfect Strangers #288

PAT WARREN,

mother of four, lives in Arizona with her travel-agent husband. She's a former newspaper columnist whose lifetime dream was to become a novelist. A strong romantic streak, a sense of humor and a keen interest in developing relationships led her to try writing romance novels, with which she feels very much at home.

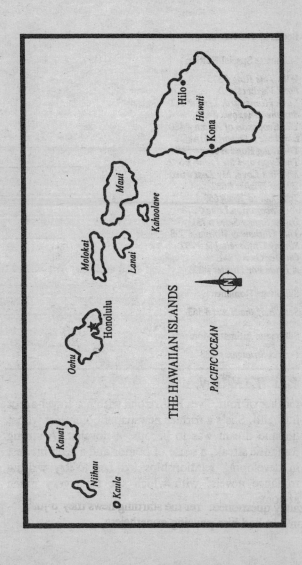

THE HAWAIIAN ISLANDS

PACIFIC OCEAN

Kauai

Niihau

Kaila

Oahu

Honolulu

Molokai

Lanai

Maui

Kahoolawe

Hawaii

Hilo

Kona

Chapter One

He needed a woman, fast. And not just any woman would do. She had to be bright, sophisticated, polished, beautiful. And needy. Very needy.

Hunter James II leaned back in his leather chair in his plush office suite on the top floor of the L.A. Towers on Wilshire Boulevard and studied the two men seated on the other side of his massive oak desk. On the right was Evan Porter, the corporate attorney for Compu West Corporation, the parent company for Hunter's vast computer business empire. Next to Evan sat Ross Weber, executive vice president and Hunter's personal righthand man and front-runner for many of his business transactions.

Both men were longtime trusted friends as well as business associates whose loyalty and judgment he rarely questioned. Yet the startling news they'd just laid on him had him pausing nonetheless.

Ross and Evan had told him he must acquire a wife by the end of the week.

"I don't see how what you suggest is possible," Hunter said, his mind already searching for alternatives. There had to be one. Marriage was definitely not in his game plan.

"There's no way around it," Ross countered.

"Otherwise you'll blow the deal," Evan stated emphatically.

Hunter unbuttoned his navy summer-weight sport coat and picked up his ebony Mont Blanc pen. He always thought better if his hands were occupied. Slowly rotating the pen between long, tan fingers, he considered the situation.

Evan and Ross had been working hard for months putting together a very important project of Hunter's, a link with a Japanese manufacturer of computer hardware and semiconductors that could house Compu West Corporation's extensive software programs. It was a business connection vital to his company's survival, the cheaper Japanese labor making the difference between a slim profit margin and substantially increased revenues.

His two trusted associates had just returned from Tokyo having thoroughly researched no less than six Japanese companies, ranging from large conglomerates to smaller, family-owned firms, in order to determine which would best suit Compu's requirements. And which company had greater need for all that Compu had to offer. They'd returned to report that Yamaguchi Systems, Ltd., was by far their best bet.

Ross had arranged for Hunter and Evan to join him in Hawaii next week for a series of meetings with the owner, Taro Yamaguchi, to work out the details and finalize the deal. But first they had to solve a potential problem that could squelch all they'd worked for.

The problem of finding Hunter a wife.

"This family image hang-up is ridiculous," Hunter began. "To determine before even meeting me that as a single man I'm not as trustworthy as a married counterpart is an archaic concept. How did the subject even come up?"

Ross, a stickler for detail, referred to his notes. "When we were making arrangements for Mr. Yamaguchi's accommodations at the Kalekiani in Kona. He asked for two suites because not only is he bringing his wife along for this meeting, but also his son and daughter-in-law."

"You mean the others will be vacationing while we do business with Mr. Yamaguchi?"

Evan jumped in. "Not exactly. This is a family company and although the women aren't directly involved, Taro and his son, Hiroki, *are* the company. They also have an executive assistant who will be joining us later, a woman whose name is Yasu Shigeta."

Hunter tossed down his pen. "Why don't they bring the whole damn clan including grandparents and cousins? They can frolic on the beach while we initial the contract changes. Are you sure we want to do business with these people? I prefer dealing with one man who has the authority to make decisions. And they have a female executive assistant, yet. You know how I feel about that."

Ross certainly did. Everyone at Compu knew that the boss liked women. They also knew that it was nearly impossible for a woman to get past middle management in his company. "Look, Hunter, you're going to have to play this their way. You have to try to under-

stand the Japanese way of doing business. They don't
trust easily and they're slow in making up their minds,
especially where no precedent has been set. And no
family-owned Japanese company has ever made the
kind of alliance we're suggesting with an American
firm.''

Patience he would somehow manage. A wife was another thing. "Just why is it that they insist I be married?''

"It's not a matter of insisting," Evan explained. "It's
more a matter of expectation. They're hesitant about
doing business with a single man. They feel married
men are more responsible, more committed. So when
they asked us if your wife would be joining you in
Kona, we hedged. It's your choice, of course, but Ross
and I feel strongly that this is a key issue with them and
one not to be taken lightly.''

Hunter had been married once, and if he'd have
stayed with Jolene, he'd be committed, all right. To a
rubber room. There had to be a compromise here
somewhere. "Let's just say, for the sake of argument,
that I'll go along with this cockamamie idea. Where am
I supposed to find a woman who's intelligent, sophisticated and suitable in one week?''

Ross was aware this was a sticky problem. He groped
for a possibility. "Don't you have a woman friend
who'd be willing to play along, someone you've dated
and would help us out in exchange for two weeks vacationing in the sun?'' Even as he said the words, he
had serious doubts. The boss played the field but love
'em and leave 'em was his motto.

A single man himself, Ross didn't find this odd. Both
of them were workaholics who were left with precious
little free time to devote to a meaningful relationship.

They were both thirty-eight, set in their ways, and liked their lives exactly as they were.

"No," Hunter stated somewhat defensively, "there's no such woman in my acquaintance. We'll have to hire one."

Ross's thick brows shot up. "Hire one?"

The more Hunter thought about it, the more certain he was that he'd found the solution. "That's right. I'm sure, between the two of you, you can locate a woman we could pass off as my wife for a week."

"More like two weeks," Evan commented. "As I said, the Japanese don't make big moves quickly."

Hunter sighed. He hadn't planned on being gone that long. However, they'd worked too hard to drop this now. He'd have to rely on the phone and fax machine to handle his other interests. "Okay, two weeks then." He'd always believed that with enough money, any problem could be solved. This one was no exception. "Offer the woman ten thousand per week. For that kind of money, I'm sure a dozen applicants will turn up."

Ross ran a hand through his unruly brown hair, feeling exasperated. "We can't exactly put an ad in the paper for this sort of thing." He shook his head. "We need more time. We'll have to postpone the Hawaii meeting."

"I don't want to do that," Hunter said quietly. "I want this deal to go through as planned. Go to a modeling agency. Or to one of the movie studios. Hire an actress we can rehearse."

"Hunter, women like that don't grow on trees." This whole discussion was frustrating Ross.

"I'm not for that, either," Evan said. "You're a wealthy man. There are too many potential lawsuits possible in hiring a stranger off the street. Let me think a minute here.''

Leaning back, the attorney studied Hunter. At fifty-five, Evan had worked for Compu for twenty-five years, having been coaxed aboard by Hunter's father, who'd founded the firm. Hunter, Sr., had been a cool, shrewd financial genius who'd started out as an IBM salesman and later formed his own company financed by a meager five thousand dollars. By the time his son entered Harvard, the man had become a multimillionaire.

Evan hadn't particularly liked Hunter, Sr., but he'd respected his business acumen. However, he did like the son, long ago having spotted a good sense of humor and a dormant vulnerability in Hunter II that had been missing in the father. That and a most generous salary had kept Evan with Compu. Divorced years ago and childless, Evan regarded Hunter almost as family. And as such, he was anxious to help him out of this dilemma.

"I think I may have an answer," Evan said into the silence.

Hunter looked up. "Let's hear it."

"I happen to know a young woman who might be interested in that kind of money. If she agrees, I know we could count on her cooperation and discretion."

"Who is she?"

"I'd rather talk this over with her before I tell you more about her."

Hunter hadn't gotten where he was by being impatient. "All right."

"Naturally, as an attorney, I wouldn't be a party to anything illegal," Evan stated for the record. "In any event, I'm not sure that the Japanese would buy into our deception."

Ross was more the impatient type. "Sure they will, if we prepare this woman correctly, rehearse her, dress her to fit the image."

"Evan," Hunter interjected, "I want you to know that although we'd be deceiving them about my so-called wife, there's no way we would short-change the Yamaguchis in any business transactions. Everything will be aboveboard and scrupulously honest and fair. You certainly know by now that that's the only way I do business."

Evan nodded. "But what happens afterward, if and when we carry this off and the deal is consummated?"

"We'll return to L.A. and I'll put a married vice president in charge of the Japanese operation." Having decided as much, Hunter checked his watch, anxious to get on to other things. "Talk to your young lady, check her out, and, if she meets our qualifications, make her the offer, contingent on my personal approval. Call me when you're ready for me to meet with the two of you." That settled, he opened the file in front of him. "If there are no more questions, I need to get to work."

Used to Hunter's abrupt dismissals, which they'd learned not to take personally, Ross and Evan left the room. On his way to his own office to use the phone, Evan thought that working for Hunter James was a lot of things, but boring wasn't one of them.

As soon as the door closed behind them, Hunter rolled back his chair and stood. Removing his jacket, he hung it on the back of his chair and stretched, easing the kinks in his shoulders.

Rearranging his muted paisley suspenders more comfortably, he strolled to the window and stood looking out on a sunny June afternoon. Of course, this being Southern California, there was residual smog that hadn't been burned off by the sun yet. He wasn't crazy about L.A., but this was where his executive offices were. Actually he liked to move around, to be on the go, although lately he'd developed a certain fondness for Hawaii. Just last year, he'd finalized the purchase of the Kalekiani Resort Hotel on Kona and had done over the Ocean Tower presidential suite to his specifications.

It was a good thing he liked Hawaii, for it would appear he'd be going back next week.

In his wildest dreams he'd never imagined he'd have need of a wife again, much less a paid imitation. How his father would recoil at the idea. Yet Hunter, Sr., had had a business credo he'd stuck to like glue: *Do what you have to do as long as it's fair to all parties.* So he was going to do what had to be done, but that didn't mean he'd have to like it.

Hunter studied his reflection in the polished glass of the window. He had a lean face, tan from the only recreation other than occasional running that he ever indulged in, golf. He liked golf because a man competed against himself, against his last best score. Avoiding doubles or foursomes, he usually played alone, carrying his own clubs, enjoying the exercise and solitude.

He had strong bones and deep-set eyes that ranged in color from cool pewter to warm gray, depending on his mood. His black hair was trimmed every week to ten days in an effort to control the curl no barber could ever quite tame. He favored wearing grays and blues, his clothes impeccably tailored, adapting beautifully to his tall, slim frame. He was a man edging toward handsome, comfortable with his looks but not one who dwelt on them.

A person of short acquaintance, if pressed to describe Hunter in one word, might easily choose intense. Those who knew him slightly better—and they were few—would probably say he was focused, a man who succeeded at nearly everything he tried, the one exception being close relationships. He was a man who didn't trust many, was friends with only a few, and liked it that way. Women? He had no trouble finding companions for a few hours or a few days. Since his divorce, or perhaps because of it, he had yet to meet a woman he wanted to linger in his life longer. He was vastly successful, busy, contented.

Why then, he asked himself, was he standing gazing out the window in midafternoon like a daydreamer when there was work to be done? Because of this rent-a-wife foolishness. He was rarely curious for long since he could usually get an answer to his questions with the flick of a button or the lift of a phone. But he found himself wondering about this woman Evan was probably even now arranging to interview.

What kind of woman would agree to play let's-pretend for two weeks with a total stranger? The kind who loved money and the things it could buy, of course. Like his ex-wife, Jolene. A woman who could never have enough. A woman of few scruples who'd do anything to get what she wanted. She would soon learn that if she completed her two-week assignment satisfactorily, she'd get the twenty thousand. And then she could hit the road.

Adjusting his gold cuff links, Hunter returned to his desk. Yes, that was how it would go and, as soon as possible, they'd wrap the Japanese deal and he'd be on

his way back home. Picking up his pen, Hunter began
to read from the open file on his desk.

She needed money, quite a lot of it, and quickly. In
her small condo in Glendale just northeast of Los An-
geles, Gaylan Fisher hung up the phone with a discour-
aged sigh. The fifth banker on her list had just turned
down her request for an equity loan. What on earth was
she going to do?

Rising, she walked across the kitchen, poured herself another cup of coffee and returned to sit at her
glass-topped table. She glanced through the archway
into her cozy living room and gazed at the bookcase,
where special mementos of her parents decorated the
shelves, along with a large collection of books. Invet-
erate travelers, Bob and Louise Fisher had purchased
many lovely things on their journeys. Although some
would probably be fairly valuable, Gaylan had no idea
how much she could get for them, should she even be
able to make herself part with the few keepsakes she had
left of her folks.

Did pawnshops take collectibles? she wondered.
She'd never in her life even been inside one. Or could
she locate a private collector? But where? Fighting
down panic, she brushed back a strand of her long,
blond hair and sipped her coffee.

How had she gotten into this mess? Just weeks ago,
her world had been on track, rosy even. She'd enjoyed
working as personal assistant to Reuben Cramer, a job
she'd gotten through an old friend of her father's, right
after she'd finished college. Evan Porter had introduced her to the seventy-two-year-old Reuben, a man
with a shock of white hair and a withering body, who'd

once been a wheeler and dealer in the electronics business.

Diabetes had cost Reuben one leg and damaged his other. Confined to a wheelchair, he'd been demanding and cranky. Gaylan had seen through to his fear of losing his clout in the company he'd founded, though he'd remained on the board of directors. The two of them had hit it off right from the start and she'd stayed with Reuben for six years until a sudden heart attack had taken him two weeks ago. She would miss him sorely, for despite his gruff demeanor, he'd taught her a great deal.

Although she never had done it before, perhaps she'd have been able to borrow the money she needed from Reuben, had he lived. He'd paid her a decent if not overly generous salary, always needing money himself for three ex-wives and two greedy sons. Though she'd managed to get along, she'd never been able to save much.

Because of Mel.

Gaylan raised her blue eyes and stared out the kitchen window, not really focusing on the pink bougainvillea trailing along her stucco fence but rather on the past. It seemed as if she'd been responsible for Mel all her life. She'd been a college junior at UCLA when her parents, who'd both worked for a local CPA firm, had been killed while driving home along the California coast one stormy night. At twenty, she'd been left with her twelve-year-old brother to finish raising.

After she'd paid the funeral expenses and bills, the small inheritance from the sale of the family home and her parents' insurance policies had allowed her to finish college with the aid of a scholarship, put a down payment on a condo and buy a used car. The rest had gone to keep Mel in a good boarding school. Even at that, from the beginning, he'd been a problem.

Gaylan finished her coffee and admitted to herself that she'd probably spoiled the motherless boy with the charming smile, blond hair so like her own and those huge blue eyes. Mel had been caught joyriding in a friend's father's "borrowed" car at fifteen, smoking pot at sixteen, and being drunk and disorderly at eighteen, totaling the convertible she'd bought for his graduation. He'd been kicked out of two colleges already, but the real trouble began last week when he'd been arrested for using and selling cocaine.

Where was she going to get the money for a defense attorney? The inheritance had been spent long ago and all she had left was the small condo she'd thought would give Mel a secure home base. The lawyers she'd queried had tossed out ten-thousand-dollar fees as openers. She'd taken out an equity loan on the condo for Mel's last violation when he'd been drinking and driving. She really couldn't blame the banks for not lending her more money on her already-mortgaged home when she had no job.

If only Reuben hadn't died, she'd have an income. The old man had often hinted that he'd leave something for her in his will, but already his family was contesting the document, each fighting for more. Gaylan was certain the estate wouldn't be settled for months, if not years. Too late to do her any good, even if Reuben had come through.

Gaylan got up and took her coffee cup to the sink. It was warm in the house because she hadn't turned on the air, trying to save money. Though she'd never been a big spender, she wasn't used to this enforced frugality, and it was making her cross and restless. Usually upbeat, she was suddenly depressed at thoughts of the future.

What could she sell to raise money? Her six-year-old Volkswagen had very low mileage, since she'd mostly ridden in Reuben's limo. But she'd need it to job-hunt. Which, she supposed, she'd better start doing immediately. Perhaps if she were gainfully employed at a new job, one of the banks she'd called would reconsider her loan application. It was all she could think to do in her present emotional state.

Finding the want ads, she spread the newspaper out on the kitchen table just as the phone rang. Her eyes on the Help Wanted column, she answered absently.

Minutes later, she hung up, a look of curious puzzlement on her face. She hadn't heard from Evan Porter in perhaps six months. Once a close friend of her father's, who'd done some legal work for the CPA firm her parents had worked for, Evan usually looked her up at Christmastime. They'd meet for lunch or dinner and she'd update him on her life and Mel's recent antics.

But just now, he'd sounded uncharacteristically serious. He said that he'd heard about Mel being in jail and that he'd like to come talk with her. As far as Gaylan knew, Evan was more familiar with corporate law than a criminal defense, but perhaps he could recommend an associate she could hire. And maybe that attorney would waive payment until she found a job.

Trying to tamp down the hope that suddenly flared, Gaylan hurried to shower and change. Evan had said he'd be over in an hour. Perhaps he would be the answer to her prayers.

Evan Porter sat back on the ivory-and-pale-green couch and crossed his long legs. "I was sorry to hear about Reuben's death," he told Gaylan.

Seated across from him in her favorite wing-back chair, Gaylan nodded. "So was I. He was difficult at times, as you probably remember, but he was good to me."

"You traveled with him a great deal, right?"

Gaylan wondered if this was just opening small talk or if Evan was deliberately going somewhere with his questions. "Reuben had business interests all over. We went to Paris, Rome, London, New York. He had a villa in Italy and a lovely apartment off Central Park. We stayed in the best of hotels in the other cities. We even flew to Hong Kong a couple of times. My passport pages are heavily stamped."

"Did he ever take you to Japan?"

"No, why?"

"I'll get to my reasons in a minute. And in addition to acting as his personal assistant, did you also take on the role of social hostess for Reuben during those trips?"

"Yes. He did a lot of business while entertaining. I'd work with the hotel staff or the housekeeper and caterers, arrange dinners often for anywhere from ten to twenty, hostess cocktail parties alongside him, attend receptions with him. All that." Curiosity as to the reason for this line of questioning had her shifting restlessly. Could Evan have another job in mind for her?

"I see." Evan unbuttoned his suit coat, finding it quite warm in the small condo. By contrast, Gaylan in her white slacks and deep blue silk blouse looked cool and comfortable. If he hadn't noticed the slight trembling of her hands as she'd served him a tall glass of iced tea, he'd have thought her relaxed, as well. "Tell me about Mel's recent difficulty."

"Difficulty doesn't begin to describe it, Evan," Gaylan confessed, not even trying to camouflage her disappointment in her brother. Glad that her father's old friend had finally brought up the subject most on her mind, she told Evan the whole story, including her frustrating search for an attorney to represent Mel, and her temporary lack of funds.

Evan listened intently until she finished. His heart went out to this young woman whom he'd admired for the strength of character she'd shown at such an early age and even to the present. "You realize that even though it's his first offense dealing, it's his second go-round with drugs, which is going to count against him."

Gaylan nodded wearily. "So I've been told. It cost me a lot of money to get him off the first time. I'm at my wit's end on this one. Mel's basically a good person. It's just that being orphaned at such an early age left him terribly unsettled."

Evan didn't buy that line. "You were orphaned at a tender age, as well, and left with an enormous responsibility for one so young. You didn't run amok."

Defending Mel had become second nature to Gaylan. "I was twenty, not twelve. That's a big difference."

"Have you ever considered the fact that letting Mel serve his time might be what he needs? Perhaps a stint in prison would shock him into straightening out."

Her eyes widened at the suggestion. "Being locked up for God knows how long with hardened criminals would harm him irreparably. I'm sorry, but I can't just abandon my brother. He's frightened now, and repentant, I'm sure. I know if I can just find a good lawyer who'll work hard to get him probation, he'll walk the straight and narrow from now on."

Evan wasn't convinced. He'd seen too many irresponsible young men like Mel Fisher never grow up, never take hold. But he knew that trying to convince his sister of that at this stage was futile. He'd had strong, almost paternal feelings for Gaylan for years. Perhaps he could help her through this, and provide Hunter with a solution to his problem at the same time.

"So, as I understand it, you need a job and you need some immediate cash to hire an attorney for Mel. Is that right?"

"That about sums it up." Gaylan struggled to find a small smile. "Any fairy godmothers on your list of acquaintances?"

More like godfather, Evan thought. "Maybe. Tell me, aside from Mel's problem, what plans do you have for another job? Surely, since Reuben was already seventy-eight, you'd thought about the possibility of his death or permanent retirement before all this happened?"

"Yes, I did." She studied Evan a long moment, wondering if she should reveal her somewhat ambitious plans. Did she have a choice? She needed his help, if indeed he was about to offer it to her. She hoped he wouldn't think her foolish. "I majored in business at USC, but I took as many art courses as I could squeeze in. My practical side knew I'd need a business degree to get a good job, but my heart's always been drawn to art."

"What kind of art?"

"Children's book illustrations. I've been sketching for years. And I have a friend, Helen Rankin, who's a natural storyteller. She's thirty-two, the divorced mother of two small children. She works in an insurance office and has sold several shorts stories to magazines. We've put together two manuscripts that we feel are salable. All we need is to find the right publisher."

"I see."

"For some time, I've been preparing for the possibility of Reuben no longer needing me. I'd planned to work part-time, even sell my condo if necessary so I'd have enough money to live on until Helen and I connected with a publishing house. I'd also like to take more art classes, but college is expensive."

Evan was impressed. She'd been willing to sell her one possession of value to gamble on her future. "But things changed."

"To say the least." Gaylan gazed off into middle distance, struggling to accept the postponement of her dream yet again. "Reuben's sudden death and Mel's arrest have altered my plans."

Evan saw in her expression what this setback was costing Gaylan, she who'd sacrificed too much already for her thoughtless brother. He'd needed to establish a strong motive in her before broaching his offer, certain that the idea wouldn't appeal to her unless her back was truly up against the wall. Knowing that his own motives were altruistic, he felt he could lay his proposition on the table finally and let Gaylan decide.

"Suppose I told you that I have a solution that not only would provide you with the money to hire a good defense attorney for Mel but would also leave you enough extra to live on for a while so you could concentrate on selling your children's books?"

Nerves had her stomach clenching in anticipation. "I'd say that you're Santa Claus and the Easter Bunny all rolled into one."

Evan leaned forward and took a long swallow of iced tea, then took a moment to study the young woman watching him with obvious interest. Gaylan Fisher was beautiful, which Hunter would undoubtedly appreciate. Standing about five-seven, she was slender, yet womanly enough to catch the eye of most men and set them to wondering. Her thick, dark blond hair had streaks of lighter shades, turning it a pale gold in the sunlight filtering in through the picture window. Her wide blue eyes reflected a keen intelligence, and her full mouth seemed to hint at a sensual nature not otherwise discernible. Physically she looked every inch the type of woman Hunter would have chosen for himself. Although she was dressed casually now, he knew she would need little guidance to carry off her role as Mrs. Hunter James II.

Her years working alongside Reuben had exposed her to many situations, business and social, that would be encountered by the wife of a successful executive such as Hunter. And her travels had undoubtedly taught her how to deal with many different kinds of people. Yes, she was as he'd expected, just right for this rather bizarre assignment. And needy enough to accept a proposal that under other circumstances she would reject instantly.

"Gaylan, my dear, I'm prepared to offer you twenty thousand dollars in return for two weeks of work."

She couldn't hide her interest at those words. Nor her skepticism. "Doing what?"

"Being the wife of millionaire Hunter James II."

Chapter Two

"You've got to be kidding!" Gaylan whispered.

The look of astonishment on her face had Evan smiling. "No, I'm quite serious. Do you know who Hunter is?"

Still in shock, she managed an answer. "I've heard the name, probably from Reuben. Electronics, I think."

"Computers, actually. Let me explain." Sitting back comfortably, he did just that, telling her about Hunter, his businesses, the Japanese affiliation, the sudden need for a wife. He told her nearly everything that Hunter, Ross and he had discussed yesterday. To be kind, he left out some of Hunter's more cynical remarks. "So you see, Gaylan, you'd be doing Mr. James a very important service and earning the money you need, as well."

"It's true that I need money, but there's a limit to what I'll do for it," Gaylan said, recovering somewhat slowly.

He'd expected as much and went on to reassure her. "You've known me a long time, Gaylan. I hope you understand that I would never suggest anything that would be harmful to you."

Intellectually she did know that. But what he was suggesting involved more than her mind. "You don't mean *legally* married, right?"

"Right. As I said, the Japanese are very family-oriented. We've worked hard to put this alliance together. It would be a shame to botch it because they feel an unmarried man isn't reliable. Hunter is the single most reliable man I know."

Questions, concerns, whirled around in her brain as she considered the proposal, wishing her present circumstances didn't force her to take it seriously. "But what you're suggesting is a deception, Evan."

Again, Evan leaned forward, his elbows on his knees. "In a way, it is. Hunter is presenting himself as a happily married man so they will trust him in this business endeavor. Now, I've worked with the man for sixteen years and with his father for nine years before that. I *know* he's trustworthy and honest in the way he conducts business. Yamaguchi Systems, Ltd., will profit from being tied in with Compu. If they need to think Hunter has a wife in order to discover that, so be it. I know that within a short period of time, they'll agree that the man who runs Compu would never let them down."

"Doesn't Mr. James know a woman who'd pose as his wife, someone familiar? Does he look like a toad? What's wrong with him?" Could she handle spending two weeks with someone who resembled the beast from *Beauty and the Beast,* even for that kind of money?

Evan's smile warmed. "Hunter doesn't like to be obligated to anyone. He feels that hiring someone to do a job is more preferable to asking favors. If you're concerned about his looks, don't be. Hunter's thirty-eight, tall, good-looking, a man who takes care of himself. He's well traveled, sophisticated, polished." However, despite their long association, he'd never seen Hunter warm up to a woman, not even to his wife, Jolene. Still, for twenty thousand, Gaylan could put up with a quiet, introspective man.

"Hard to imagine a man with all that, plus millions, not having a woman friend who would do him this favor. Doesn't he like women?"

Evan's nod was enthusiastic. "That he does. He's escorted some of the loveliest women I know. He was married once and it didn't work out, so he's gun-shy. But you'll find he can be very attentive."

Attentive. How attentive? "Evan, I need to know—would I have my own room? I mean, for that kind of money, if he expects bedroom privileges, I—"

"Absolutely, you'd have your own room and he doesn't expect you to be any more than his hostess, to be interested and polite to the Yamaguchis, to be friendly and charming at social dinners and the like." Evan could see that, despite her initial shock, she was warming to the idea. He decided to reveal the rest. "If you agree, Hunter will furnish you with a brand-new wardrobe and luggage suitable for the two-week stay on Kona. Afterward, you may keep everything except the rented jewelry."

It was beginning to sound too good to be true, yet Gaylan still hesitated. She'd always thought of marriage as sacred, recalling often the warm and loving union her parents had shared. Though she'd dated through the years when her busy life with Reuben had allowed, she'd not yet run across someone she felt strongly about.

But that didn't mean she didn't dream, didn't hope. A romantic at heart, even pretending to be married to a stranger didn't sit well with her. The whole thing sounded so bizarre, so ridiculous. On the one hand, she wished she could politely but firmly thank Evan Porter, turn him down and send him on his way. On the other hand, her more desperate self wondered if his offer might not be the answer—the *only* answer available at the moment.

With twenty thousand, she could hire a good attorney for Mel and go to work on her dream to see her illustrations finally in print. She thought of how she'd perused the want ads while waiting for Evan to arrive. Not a whole lot of job opportunities out there that she was qualified to accept. Of course, she did have a degree and years of specialized, on-the-job experience. She would find work again. But when?

And she needed money now.

Watching the play of emotions on Gaylan's expressive face, Evan saw that she was coming to a reluctant decision. Rising, he walked to her and touched her shoulder. "Gaylan, believe me, this would be a strictly business arrangement. Think of it as a two-week vacation in one of the world's loveliest resorts, with a few necessary dinners thrown in. Could you handle that?"

"I don't know." Rising, she walked to the side window and stood looking out on a jacaranda tree in full bloom, its purple blossoms shimmering against a blue California sky. Everything looked lovely and peaceful and normal. Only suddenly nothing felt normal. She was jobless and therefore dependent, Mel was sitting in a cell and she was faced with some difficult choices. Truth be known, she'd wrestled with many difficult decisions in her twenty-eight years, but the past two weeks had sorely tried her usually optimistic nature. "Could I think about this awhile?"

Evan shook his head. "I'm afraid not. We leave for Kona on Sunday and, if you agree, I need to take you to meet Hunter so you two can get acquainted a bit before the trip."

Her blue eyes turned cool. "You mean so he can look me over, approve of me?"

Rather than defensive, Evan seemed disappointed by her question. "I wouldn't put it that way. Hunter trusts my judgment. However, I think it's only natural he'd want to see the woman who'd be, for all intents and purposes, his wife for the next two weeks, don't you?"

She touched his arm in apology. "I'm sorry, Evan. It's just that . . . well, this is such an unusual offer."

"I understand. I wish I could give you more time. But after you meet with Hunter, then there's the shopping for clothes and—"

"I have clothes. I traveled all over with Reuben and I don't believe I ever embarrassed him by my appearance." She could justify accepting the money for her two weeks of playacting, but accepting clothes seemed too personal.

"I'm sure you didn't, Gaylan." Evan found he was uncomfortable with this aspect. He'd done his part, found a woman who qualified and was indeed needy. He would let Gaylan and Hunter work out the details about clothes and such. "I can't imagine you ever embarrassing anyone."

He was buttering her up, she thought. She had her back to the wall and he knew it. Gaylan sighed, wishing she could tell him to take his ludicrous offer and stick it where the sun never shines. But harsh reality didn't leave her with too many options. She looked up at him and saw he was waiting for her answer.

"All right," she said, hoping she wasn't making a terrible mistake.

Evan smiled encouragingly. "Please don't look like you're a lamb and I'm about to lead you into the lion's den. If you let yourself, you might even enjoy the two weeks. And you might find you like Hunter. He's not an ogre, you know."

She didn't want to hear what a wonderful guy Hunter James II was right now. If he was so damn wonderful, why didn't he have even one friend who'd help him out? Why did he have to hire a wife? She didn't want to think any more about him but rather concentrate on the details she needed to work out before committing totally.

"Evan, do you know a good attorney I could hire for Mel? And could I get an advance on this twenty thousand so I could get the ball rolling before we leave on Sunday?"

Now that he had her acceptance, he wasn't worried about the details. "I know a really fine criminal lawyer and I'm sure we can work something out. First, I think we should go meet Hunter."

She shot him a questioning look. "Right now?"

"As I said, time is of the essence. Why don't I phone Hunter and arrange a time while you change?"

Things were moving a little too fast for Gaylan, but she couldn't afford the luxury of time. "You can use the phone in the kitchen," she told him as she headed for her bedroom.

What did a woman wear when she was about to meet the man who would be her "husband" for the next two weeks? she wondered.

The whole damn building was intimidating, Gaylan thought. A huge high rise with revolving doors and silent elevators that whisked Evan and her to the tower suite. Of course, he'd be on the top floor. Nothing too good for a millionaire. Or was Hunter James II a zillionaire by now?

The doors slid open and they stepped out onto plush gray carpeting so thick her heels sank in a full inch. The dark-haired, thirtysomething woman seated at the ebony half-moon desk looked up, smiled at Evan and waved them on toward the double doors. Gaylan was annoyed to discover that her palms were sweating as she walked alongside the attorney. She'd been exposed to wealth for years with Reuben, but not on this scale. And not for this unsettling reason, a wife interview.

A discreet two knocks on the door and Evan swung one open. She entered the large room slowly, taking in the oil paintings on the walls, the smell of rich leather and finally the man seated behind the huge oak desk before a bank of windows overlooking L.A. As they neared, he stood, then walked around to greet them, his gray eyes assessing.

He wore Italian loafers polished to such a spit shine she could have counted her freckles in them. Silk shirt and tie, a crease in his gray slacks so knife-sharp that they could have sliced bread, and a jacket that had obviously been sewn to fit his broad shoulders then tapered to his slim waist. The overall effect screamed money. Lots of it.

Hunter held out his hand and she cautiously placed her small one in it while Evan made the introductions. Her skin was soft, warm and just a shade damp. Nerves, he decided, and was surprised. From Evan's hasty briefing, he'd expected a cool blonde completely in control. "I'm glad you could come on such short notice."

There was strength in his handshake, and a touch of impatience, Gaylan decided. He didn't like this any more than she did. Good. With any luck he'd require her presence only at a few dinners, and the rest of the time she could explore Kona.

"Have a seat," Hunter said, indicating the chair facing his desk as he went back around and settled himself again.

"Thank you." Apparently a man used to having his requests instantly obeyed, she thought as she sat down.

"I'll leave you two to get acquainted," Evan said, then touched Gaylan's shoulder briefly before quietly leaving the room.

She wished he'd have stayed. Probably they'd prearranged this scenario. What was it Evan had said about the lamb in the lion's den? She felt just like that, but she'd die before she'd let this cold fish see. Slowly she swung her eyes around the room. "Nice place you've got here. A bit stuffy, but nice."

Hunter frowned. "Are you always so outspoken?"

"Yes. But I can be diplomatic when necessary."

"If we agree to our business arrangement, diplomacy will definitely be necessary." The last thing he needed was a sassy woman to screw things up. Usually he could rely on Evan's opinion, but perhaps this time his attorney had misjudged the woman. "I understand you used to work for Reuben Cramer."

"Yes, for six years. Did you know Reuben?"

"I met him some time ago. I believe my father knew him."

"What did you think of him?"

"Irascible but honest and fair. Unlike his two sons."

"A good assessment." Although he'd inherited his father's business, Hunter II apparently was an astute judge of character. "Reuben was a good person."

How good? he wondered. She wouldn't be the first young woman who'd wormed her way into the affection of a rich old man rapidly going downhill. Well, she'd find no easy prey in him. "Evan told me you've refused our offer of the appropriate clothes."

Gaylan could tell that not only surprised but annoyed him. Not a man used to people altering his orders. "I've acquired a substantial wardrobe through the years as Reuben's personal assistant." All purchased from her own funds, but she saw no reason to go into that. She stood, holding her arms out at her sides. "For instance, this. Suitable?"

She had on a beige silk suit, the skirt falling just to her knees, the loose jacket worn over a chocolate-colored blouse and brown leather accessories. Her blond hair hung past her shoulders, looking a little wild and free-flowing, softening the severity of the business suit. Her face was oval with high cheekbones. Her makeup was subtle, her eyes an incredible robin's egg blue. He thought her stunning, but he kept his face blank. "If the rest of your clothes are in similar taste, then they'll do."

Lord, but he was as stuffy as his office, Gaylan thought as she sat back down. Crossing her legs, she met his eyes. "Evan told me some about your business and why you need a wife. But that's all. Tell me about you."

Hunter found his lips twitching. "I think that's my line."

Gaylan smiled at his first hint of human reaction. "You first."

Unused to discussing himself, Hunter shifted in his seat. "Well, I own Compu West and several other corporations. I have a duplex on Central Park West, a Tudor house in Beverly Hills that I have yet to redecorate and a permanent suite at the Kalekiani Resort Hotel on Kona. I keep a chauffeur and limo at each location as I dislike driving."

"Fascinating. But I'm not interested in what you own. If I'm to play at being your wife, I need to know *you*. What do you do when you're not being a business tycoon?"

Hunter's frown was back. "I don't think it's necessary that you know any more about me than you already do."

"You're wrong. Evan said I was to serve as your hostess at dinner parties and the like. What do I talk to the Yamaguchis about, your business holdings? Your chauffeur-driven limos?"

Openly annoyed, Hunter shoved back his chair and rose. "I don't think this is going to work, after all." Turning, he walked to the side window and stood staring out, struggling with his rising anger. What the hell had made him think he could fake it as a husband? He hadn't carried it off all that well when he'd been a real husband. It annoyed him that Gaylan was probably right, that she needed to know things about him in order to talk to the Yamaguchis, especially the women. The problem was that he didn't feel comfortable allowing her to invade his privacy.

"No, I don't think it is, either." Gaylan hated to walk away from the money that would save her. But she knew that unless he met her halfway, she could never carry off this stupid assignment. She got to her feet. "Sorry we've wasted each other's time."

"Wait." Hunter swung around and slowly walked back to his desk. The warnings that both Evan and Ross had uttered rang in his ears. Without a wife, a multi-million-dollar deal they'd already invested hundreds of working hours into would go down the tubes. Time was running out. It would be difficult if not impossible to find and rehearse another, possibly more suitable, woman before Sunday. Gaylan Fisher wasn't perfect with her sharp tongue and irreverent attitude, but she was the only game in town. And he needed her.

Taking a deep breath, he tried for a conciliatory expression. "You'll have to forgive me. I'm a very private man and not used to . . . to . . ."

"Sharing intimate details of your life with a stranger?" she finished for him. "Neither am I. But if we don't know something about each other, the Yamaguchis will see right through this charade the first day."

"You're right," he conceded, never an easy move for him. "Please sit down."

My, my. Not only a concession but a request that she sit instead of a command. Maybe there was hope here somewhere. Gaylan sat down.

He would go along with her suggestion, but first he needed to know something. "Before we begin, may I ask why you are willing to take this job?"

"No." She'd made the request for privacy to Evan and he'd agreed. "My reasons are my own and I'd like to leave it at that."

Money, Hunter thought. What else could it be? Another beautiful gold digger like Jolene. He should have known. It was better that way, really. A business arrangement and no more. If he knew exactly where he stood, there'd be no possibility of personal involvement, despite the fact that she was indeed a very attractive woman.

"Fair enough." Hunter picked up his brass letter opener and turned it over in his hands thoughtfully. "Let's see. I like to play golf, to go running early in the morning and to listen to classical music. I don't have much time for pleasure reading, but when I do I prefer biographies over fiction. I think most movies are a waste of time and I have no interest in team sports. Your turn."

Gaylan sighed. This was going to be uphill all the way. "Well, one out of six isn't bad, I guess. I play tennis, not golf. I'm an avid reader of fiction, love pop music and most movies. I'm mad about watching basketball and football. I do jog, however."

"Looks like the Yamaguchis are going to wonder what we have in common, aside from running." Two weeks with a total opposite. Ideally his business meetings would swallow up most of the day.

She shrugged. "Perhaps they'll figure that opposites attract."

All the way across his large desk, he could smell her scent, something clean and lightly floral, probably expensive. There was no question that he found her attractive, though he was a master at covering his reaction. However, it would take a lot more than costly perfume, a striking figure and wide blue eyes for him to drop his guard ever again around a woman who would use him.

His steady gaze made Gaylan a tad nervous. The quicker they finished this interview, the better. "Evan explained that I would act as hostess during dinners with the Yamaguchis. What else did you have in mind for me to do?"

"This job, should you decide to accept it, would involve very little more than that."

He was beginning to sound a shade too *Mission Impossible,* which was how Gaylan was beginning to view this whole arrangement.

"While Evan and I, along with my executive assistant, Ross Weber, are in business meetings with Taro Yamaguchi and his son, Hiroki, I'd like you to make yourself available to the women. I understand that Taro's wife, Yoshiko, is rather shy and quiet, but their daughter-in-law, Nari, is a less traditional, more modern Japanese wife. I've never met them so I can't say what they like to do. However, my resort offers just about everything imaginable so I'm sure you'll come up with something. I can see you're not in the least reticent."

He said it with a smile, but Gaylan was certain his observation wasn't intended as a compliment. "Do you prefer reticent women?"

Actually he did, but he knew that saying so wouldn't gain him points with her. "I'm drawn to women who are intellectually stimulating, well-groomed, socially savvy and... and..." He groped for the right words to express himself.

"And who know the score," she said, finishing for him. "Women who are fun to be with, good in bed, make no demands and know when to walk away with a smile."

He was annoyed to think she could read him that well this quickly. Annoyed enough to become defensive. "What makes you think that's how I feel?"

"Because I've met a lot of men like that over the past six years and you show all the signs." Suddenly feeling drained, Gaylan stood. "I think I know enough about you to play the role. Have we got a deal or not?"

His eyes never leaving hers, he came around his desk. "I find you acceptable, if that's what you mean."

Acceptable. What a perfectly lovely word. She wished she could say the same. It was going to be a mighty long two weeks. You can stand anything if you know there's an end in sight, her mother used to say. *I hope you're right, Mama.* "I'm terribly flattered."

"This is strictly business. Why would you expect flattery?"

"Why indeed. Where should I report and when?"

"My secretary Margaret has all the details ready for you, as well as a packet on the Yamaguchis including some background on their Japanese traditions that you might want to study. Ross will be in touch to update you on Compu so you won't be uninformed about our business. Will you at least allow me to buy your luggage?"

"No, thank you. I have a very *acceptable* set." She turned, thinking it was time to leave.

Hunter touched her arm, slid his fingers down the silk of her jacket and took her hand. He who had a built-in hesitancy about personal contact suddenly experienced an overwhelming need to touch her. "Since it's a business deal, shouldn't we shake on it?"

Gaylan's eyes searched his a long moment. She'd been wrong. Not a cold fish. The cool gray had turned hot and hungry just that quickly. The man was a chameleon. What was she getting into?

A beam of afternoon sun played on her hair, turning it several shades of gold. Hunter was jarred to realize he felt a primitive arousal that had absolutely nothing to do with business. Grasping her fingers, he felt her pulse scramble as his thumb grazed the sensitive skin of her wrist. As he watched, the blue of her eyes darkened with awareness.

"Understand something, Mr. James. A means to an end. That's all you are to me."

"I'll keep that in mind, Mrs. James." He let her go and took great satisfaction in the shocked confusion on her face at being referred to as his wife. He watched as she turned and forced herself to exit slowly.

Walking back to his desk, Hunter found himself smiling. He'd been dreading the trip, but Gaylan Fisher's visit had changed his mind. It might just prove to be an interesting two weeks, after all.

Gaylan tried hard not to be impressed, but it wasn't easy. Hunter's private jet was more luxurious than she'd imagined. Decorated in soft blues and a rich ivory, it had a full bedroom, bathroom with shower, compact galley and well-stocked bar. The midsection had four seating areas, two situated around tables. The lighting was muted, and soft music drifted from recessed speakers. She could just make out the three-man crew beyond the dangling navy curtain. An attractive uniformed flight attendant passed around drinks and munchies. A chef was preparing lunch. Yes, mighty hard not to be impressed.

Seated in one of the stretch-back lounge chairs, she watched Ross Weber as he scribbled notes on a yellow pad. She'd met with Ross several times over the past couple of days and had found it amusing that a man whose own clothes choices consisted mostly of mismatched slacks and jackets worn with loud ties had been sent to check out her wardrobe. He'd made a few subtle suggestions and brought her a stunning array of jewelry that Hunter wanted her to wear during the course of their stay. The fact that the jewels were rented didn't seem to decrease the dazzle. She'd insisted Ross lock them all in his briefcase, not wanting to be responsible.

She'd come to like Ross, finding him gentle and soft-spoken, undemanding and possessing a good sense of humor. He'd spent one whole evening telling her more than she ever wanted to know about the computer business and a good deal about the preferences and pet peeves of the man posing as her husband. It seemed that Ross and Hunter went back a long way and, although Ross respected and admired Hunter, Gaylan felt he also saw the man as he really was. And liked what he saw. That impressed her.

She glanced over at Evan on the opposite side of the plane, leaning back in his tilted chair, dozing in the morning sun streaming in through the window. She wished she felt comfortable enough to sleep, for the days before their departure had been hectic. Evan had introduced her to a friend who practiced criminal law and, after listening to both of them, Avery Woods had agreed to represent Mel. When she'd brought up his fee, Avery had said that Evan had made the payment arrangements. She'd been flushed with gratitude.

Her visit to Mel hadn't gone as well. Sullen and pouty, all Mel kept repeating was that he wanted out of the hellhole he found himself in. When she'd explained she'd hired an attorney who'd be interviewing him soon, he'd seemed more defensive than pleased. His attitude had disappointed her, but she'd tried not to let him see. She'd left him with a supply of cigarettes, a fierce hug and a breezy explanation that she'd be gone for a couple of weeks, but she'd come see him as soon as she could. She'd evaded his questions as to where she'd be, not wanting to explain her odd arrangement.

Gaylan sighed tiredly. Avery hadn't been terribly optimistic about Mel's chances. If he hadn't been dealing, the court would probably be more lenient on a first offender who'd been caught using. The best scenario would be that he'd get probation; the worst that he'd have to serve jail time. She'd done all she could by hiring Avery. The rest was up to the judge.

The real question rolling around in her mind was, had her brother learned his lesson? Would he come away from this and straighten out? She could only hope.

Needing to set aside that particular worry, Gaylan swung her eyes to where Hunter sat at one of the tables reading a stack of papers, his pen in his hand, occasionally making notations. Reuben had been wealthy, but his fortune couldn't compare to Hunter's vast holdings and affluent life-style. Yet Hunter didn't seem happy, didn't smile often, from what she'd seen so far. Money hadn't made Reuben terribly happy, either. There had to be a lesson there somewhere.

Just then, Hunter looked up and caught her watching him. She didn't blink, didn't falter, just locked her eyes with his. She'd caught him studying her peripherally now and then ever since they'd taken off two hours ago. His wide gray eyes were thoughtful, serious, unflinching. His hair looked freshly trimmed and shiny clean. As attractive as he was, she wondered why his marriage had broken up, why he didn't have someone special in his life.

But then, hadn't she learned how difficult rich men were? Gaylan turned away to gaze out the window. Maybe if she stared at the puffy white clouds she'd become sleepy.

Most women looked funereal in black, Hunter had always thought. Oddly, Gaylan didn't. She had on some sort of cotton jumpsuit with a multicolored sash tied at her waist, the black striking against her tan skin. On her bare feet she wore strappy shoes, her toenails painted a vivid pink. Her hair was pulled back today and tied with a scarf that matched her belt. In her ears were heavy gold hoop earrings. She looked very feminine, very appealing.

And he had to stop thinking along those lines.

Their arrangement was strictly business. At his insistence, he reminded himself. After this trip, she'd go her way and he'd go his. Even a brief affair would be out of the question. It would muddle things up. If he got her good and mad, she could screw up the deal. Or, God forbid, become clinging and demanding. No, platonic was the way to play it.

He went back to his reading.

But after ten minutes still on the same page, he gave up. He'd already been at it since takeoff. Tossing down his pen, he rose and stretched, then walked over and took the lounge chair next to Gaylan. She turned her head, surprised.

"You're not fond of flying?" Hunter asked. He'd noticed her white-knuckled grip on the hand rests as they'd left the ground.

"Just not crazy about takeoffs and landings. All this heavy equipment shaking and shuddering. So much could go wrong."

"But seldom does."

"True. You probably fly so often you never give it a thought."

"Statistically, more people die in auto accidents than in plane crashes."

As her own parents had. Still, flying made her nervous. "Statistics are small comfort when you're strapped in and you feel yourself leave the ground and your fate is out of your control."

"Is our fate ever truly in our control?"

She looked at him thoughtfully, surprised that he felt that way. "An interesting question."

"Isn't it." Hunter reached into his pocket and withdrew a small velvet case. "You'll need to put this on."

Gaylan took the box, opened it. Inside was a gorgeous wide gold wedding band circled with large diamonds that winked in the sunlight. More rented jewelry. She flipped the lid shut. "No. I can't."

"We're supposed to be married, remember?"

"I don't see a wedding ring on your hand."

With no small effort, he hung on to his temper. "That's different. I'm a man. My wife would wear a ring. The Yamaguchis will expect it."

She stood firm. "Then you'll have to come up with an explanation. I lost it or it's in repair. Whatever."

He saw the others were engrossed, but still he leaned

closer, keeping his voice low. "Dammit, why are you so difficult?"

"I don't mean to be." Her voice softened. "I'll pretend to be your wife and I'll do the things we agreed upon. But I simply can't wear a fake wedding ring. I...I just can't."

He shoved the box back into his pocket thoughtfully. "When I was growing up, we had a dog. A skinny, little brown mutt I'd found one day and dragged home. I named him Gypsy. I saw to it that he had lots of good food, his shots, a soft bed. Only every chance he got, he ran away."

Wondering where this was going, Gaylan watched his face, his unreadable expression.

"My mother or I would open the door just a crack and out Gypsy would dash on a run. I'd go after him and haul him back, lecturing him about the danger of cars and bigger dogs. But the next opportunity, he'd do it again. Finally, about the fifth time, I let him go." Hunter turned to her, capturing her gaze. "He'd pushed me too far. I loved that dog, but I figured if he was too silly to realize what a good deal he had, then he deserved whatever fate awaited him in the big, bad world."

She got the message, in spades. Keeping her features even, she didn't say a word.

Finally he looked away and slowly got out of the chair.

"Hunter?" She waited till he turned back to her. "Did you ever consider that it was nothing against you, that Gypsy just wanted to be free, to be the master of his own fate? The fastest way to kill love is to put restrictions on it."

He let out a ragged breath. "I don't know why I told you that story."

"Yes, you do. And I still won't wear the ring."

As Hunter resumed his seat, across the aisle, Evan, his eyes still closed, smiled.

Chapter Three

Gaylan had been in limos before, but never a stretch such as the white one whisking them to the Kalekiani Resort Hotel. Evan and Ross were seated in deep-cushioned comfort in the row facing the glass partition separating them from the uniformed chauffeur. She and Hunter were directly behind them facing a small television and bar. Two phones were nestled into side compartments, and champagne was chilling in built-in ice buckets. It boggled her mind to think that people really lived like this on a day-to-day basis.

She gazed out the tinted windows at the barren landscape on either side. The highway stretched ahead over flatland that seemed to go on for miles. Kona was built on volcanic ash so that the view she saw was mostly black rocks with a total absence of vegetation, since very little would grow in this area. Beyond the craggy hills the multihued Pacific could be seen shimmering in the early-afternoon sun. Gaylan marveled at the fact that any hotel owners would have chosen this moon-scape of an island to build a resort.

Alongside her, Hunter was reading another report from a seemingly endless stack. Evan had labeled him a workaholic, and from what she'd seen, she heartily agreed. Despite the monotony of the rocky terrain, the view was breathtaking. Yet Hunter seemed not to take notice. Of course, he'd been here often and this was her first visit.

Gaylan tried not to appear too touristlike, but her curiosity won out. "What are those clumps of white rocks every little while, some spelling out words?" There were names in an unfamiliar language, sayings and even ambitious sports slogans such as Go Blue. "Who on earth would take the time to come out to this deserted stretch and line up white rocks on the black ash to write out a message?"

Hunter glanced out his own window. "Some are college students. Others are Hawaiians writing their names in the language of their ancestors." They passed a cluster that read, Del loves Maggie. "Then there are the lovers that drive out to hike, maybe picnic nearby. Or tourists who want to leave a part of themselves on the island." He turned to her. "There's a saying that if you leave something of importance on one of the Hawaiian Islands, you'll return one day. Perhaps some travelers look on the rock messages as insurance that the gods will smile on them and they'll get a chance to come back."

It was the first fanciful thing she'd heard him say. He'd hardly spoken a word to her since his story of the runaway dog. He'd eaten his lunch alone at the far table, continuing to work while she, Ross and Evan had shared the other table, chatting about nothing in particular.

She'd napped a little, then stared out the window, fascinated by the changing colors of the sea, drifting from pale green to deep blue as the depth changed. With hardly a ripple, the big jet set down at the Kailua-Kona open-air airport and Gaylan gawked at the young men in their wild print shirts and tan shorts scurrying about to get their luggage. She'd scarcely had time to put on her oversize sunglasses before she'd been hustled into the waiting limo. Despite the three-hour time difference, she was wide-awake and alert, her interest in her new surroundings overriding her fatigue.

"And what do you leave behind to insure your return?" she asked Hunter.

"A lot of things. I hate packing so I keep a full summer wardrobe here. And books, records, that sort of thing."

Doesn't everyone? she thought. Did he also keep complete wardrobes in his New York apartment, his California house and other locations where he traveled frequently? Hard to imagine. "Well, that's a time saver, isn't it?" She went back to studying the scenery.

"Would you like a glass of champagne?" Hunter checked the bottle and determined it was sufficiently chilled.

Gaylan glanced at her watch. It was barely two, Hawaiian time. "A little early for me."

"It's five in L.A."

"I'm not much of a drinker." Even if she was, she'd have refused. She had all she could do to hold her own with Hunter James II without clouding her mind with alcohol, especially coupled with jet lag.

He offered the wine to Evan and Ross, but they also turned it down. "Do you like deep-sea fishing?" Hunter asked Gaylan, wondering why he didn't just let her be. Though he was reluctant to reveal information about himself, he was uncharacteristically curious about her. Perhaps because he'd rarely encountered a woman like her.

The difference between the women he was used to and Gaylan was that she stood up to him where most bent over backward to please him. He'd never been certain if it was his wealth or his dominant personality that caused that reaction. The reason he respected both Evan and Ross was that they also spoke their minds. In Gaylan, he both admired and was irked by the trait, yet he felt a need to discover more of her.

"I don't know," she answered without looking at him. "I've never been deep-sea fishing."

"My resort offers a great deep-sea fishing trip. Kailua-Kona is known as the Billfish Capital of the World. They take you out on this yacht, help you set up the equipment and even serve a fisherman's picnic lunch."

Was he trying to make up for his rather rude remarks on the plane? Gaylan wondered. "Sounds like fun."

"There's also a helicopter ride to a private island and a photographic safari."

She was turned toward him, but Hunter couldn't see her eyes through the darkened glasses. He fought an urge to whip them off her. And to ask her what scent she was wearing since it had the power to continuously distract him. Instead he kept his expression bland. "Do any of those sound like something you'd like to do?"

Was he offering to take her sailing, fishing or on a safari? It hadn't been in the original game plan. Gaylan's skeptical nature had her answering hesitantly. "They all sound interesting." Or was he suggesting these day-long trips to get her out of his hair? "But I thought I was along to entertain the two Yamaguchi ladies."

Of course. That was what he wanted, what he'd told her. He'd never done those touristy things himself, had never wanted to. He was surprised that he'd mentioned them now. He'd always considered day jaunts, such as the ones he'd described, as a waste of time. His father used to say that time was money and if you wasted it, you inevitably lost money. Hunter had more than doubled his inheritance by following that credo. It would be stupid to deviate now.

"You are," he answered, reaching for an explanation, one he'd believe as well. "I mentioned those outings as things you might want to do with the women."

Somehow Gaylan couldn't picture herself going deep-sea fishing with two Japanese women, one traditional and one not. She narrowed her eyes, trying to find the hidden agenda in Hunter's suggestion. "Why don't we wait and see what they like to do before we make any plans?"

Why didn't he stop talking to her since he kept inserting his large foot in his mouth? Hunter asked himself. Without another word, he resumed his reading of a report he was having a great deal of trouble concentrating on. The forty-five-minute drive from the airport to the hotel had never seemed so long.

Gaylan turned back to the view, coming to the conclusion that Hunter James II was as baffling a man as she'd ever met.

* * *

Hunter's personal suite on the top floor of the Ocean Tower of the Kalekiani was like a visual overload, Gaylan thought as she followed him in. There was a beautifully appointed living room complete with a grand piano and a stereo discreetly playing show tunes from *Phantom of the Opera*. The spacious dining room would seat ten comfortably, and, of course, there was a cook's pantry and complete bar. The decor was Japanese in shades of beige, black, rose and white. There were five connecting lanais all overlooking the Pacific Ocean. The view took Gaylan's breath away.

While Ross and Evan checked into their suite down the hall, Hunter showed her the smaller second bedroom with its own bath.

"This will be my room?" she asked.

"Yes." Then he led her to the master suite where a huge black lacquered canopied bed dominated the room. Enormous birds of paradise lent color to the large dresser alongside a heavy sculpture of a dolphin. In the corner sat a large desk complete with phone, computer and fax machine. The private bath included a sunken tub, shower and separate sauna. Two colorful Japanese robes hung in the double closet.

Nearly speechless, Gaylan turned to see Hunter watching her with amusement. "This is the most decadent layout I've ever seen."

He laughed and she watched with fascination how it changed his face. He seemed younger, suddenly carefree, finally approachable.

"I gather you like it."

"Like it? You'd have to be embalmed not to be impressed."

Her unadulterated enthusiasm pleased him. Perhaps he'd become somewhat jaded through the years. He'd come to look upon his various living quarters as comfortable and functional, although he'd helped design or refurbish each. Seeing it through Gaylan's eyes made him appreciate his surroundings anew. Yet her candor still surprised him. "Most women I know wouldn't be as honest."

She was certain he knew plenty of women, and she could picture the type. Leggy brunettes, elegantly dressed. Women who smelled of Joy and never sweat. And above all, who knew how to say, *Yes, sir.* "I guess I'm not like most women."

She had that right. He indicated her luggage stacked neatly in a corner. "The maid will be up to unpack for you."

Gaylan frowned. "They're in the wrong room. Didn't you just say that the other room was mine?"

"It is. But the Yamaguchis will be spending time in the suite, naturally. They'll undoubtedly be suspicious if they see your things in that bedroom. So, while you'll sleep in there, your things will be in here, next to mine."

She didn't like the sound of that. "I don't see why they need to inspect our bedrooms. Why don't we just keep the doors closed?"

"Appearances are important. Vital. We need to behave as husband and wife."

Semantics. "Just what does that include?" Nervous energy had her removing the scarf tied at her nape. She shook her head, loosening the thickness.

Hunter noticed her hair fluff out then settle around her shoulders, and felt his mouth go dry. What was there about her apparently unconscious gestures that unnerved him so? He took a step back and groped for an answer to her question. "Although the Japanese are not demonstrative in public, they're keenly aware that Americans are. Especially newlyweds, which we are purported to be. Knowing that, you should sit near me, be open to touching and hand-holding, to exchanging affectionate glances and remarks. That sort of thing."

He watched her wariness turn to chilly suspicion. "Touching is to be restricted to hand-holding, or I'm out of here. Understood?"

He, too, felt a flash of temper. "Look, I'm not about to attack you, most especially not in front of the very people I'm trying to impress. Ask Evan or Ross, or both. I'm very much a loner. I don't want you in my bedroom any more than you want to be here. So don't jump to conclusions and don't look at me as if I'm the big bad wolf."

Well, that certainly put her in her place. Gaylan relaxed. "All right. I apologize. I just want to make sure of the ground rules and that we both stick to our original agreement."

He liked that about her, Hunter realized. She was quick to anger, but when she was wrong, she backed down smoothly, without losing the ground she'd gained. He'd bet she'd be a hell of a negotiator across a business table. *If* he would ever allow a female to negotiate on his behalf. "Apology accepted. And I'm sorry if I automatically assumed you knew that I expected us to behave as newlyweds in front of the Yamaguchis. I'll try not to do that again. Assume anything, I mean."

"Okay." She threaded her hands through her hair, fighting a yawn. She hadn't slept well last night and it was catching up with her.

"Would you like to go down for a swim? The pool here is fantastic, winding and twisting under little bridges. And there are waterfalls, slides and a saltwater dolphin section where you can swim out and let one of them take you for a ride on his back.''

Gaylan smothered the yawn. "It sounds wonderful, but I think I'd be better off with a nap just now. Otherwise I might not be able to stay awake during dinner." The Yamaguchi clan was arriving around noon the next day, she knew. There'd be enough time to explore the hotel's facilities this evening or in the morning.

"I'll call down for the maid so you can change if you like."

"I think I'll just lie down like this, in my bedroom. I'll shower and change later." She walked toward the door, then remembered she wasn't exactly on a vacation here. "Unless there's something you need me for."

Hunter was a bit surprised that he'd liked to have shown her his hotel. He, who hadn't strolled the grounds or walked on the beach or eaten anywhere but in the dining room of his suite since he'd purchased the resort, was more than a little shocked that he suddenly thought of doing all three, and with a woman he'd just met. Perhaps he'd been working too hard.

"No, there's nothing I need you for at the moment." He waited till she left, called the maid then strolled out onto the lanai.

Frothy white waves pounded against moss-covered rocks, then slowed to roll onto sand made smooth by countless breakers. Sea gulls dipped low, looking for lunch. A chubby tourist, wearing a loud Hawaiian shirt over swim trunks, bent to gather shells. The scent of hibiscus and oleander sweetened the air. The sky was an incredible blue, almost the exact shade of Gaylan's eyes.

Damn.

Hunter loosened his tie and swore again under his breath. Where was the discipline that was as much a part of him as breathing? Where was the detachment that had served him well all these years? Thinking about a woman even for a short period of time went against his natural inclinations. Then why had Gaylan Fisher continued to pop into his mind and cloud his thinking since the day she'd sauntered into his office?

She wasn't all *that* gorgeous. Okay, she was attractive, but he'd known many attractive women. Then there was the indisputable fact that she was a shade too outspoken, a woman who told it like it was and let the chips fall where they may. Usually he steered clear of women like that. Unwittingly she aroused his curiosity and piqued his interest. Though he was certain she was in this for the money, in her eyes he saw an honesty he doubted she could fake. That puzzled him.

She threw him off center, and that intrigued him, for few could, male or female. And, getting around to the nitty-gritty here, she attracted him. She wasn't obviously sensual, but rather quietly so. All this and he'd touched only her hand.

Touching, as she'd moments ago made very clear, was not something she was going to permit. He'd never been a casual toucher himself. He didn't trust people who were. Still, despite the fact that he wanted no serious entanglements, he was a man in the prime of life with a healthy libido. And she'd managed to send it into overdrive.

Which was the last thing he wanted with someone he'd hired on a strictly business basis.

He'd have to work on himself, Hunter decided. First, a refreshing shower. Then he'd dig into the mountain of paperwork he'd brought along, as usual. Habit, control, moderation. That was the ticket, he thought as he heard the doorbell.

It took the maid twenty minutes to unpack his and Gaylan's things in the master bedroom suite and quietly withdraw. It took Hunter almost as long to stop staring at Gaylan's feminine things hanging next to his suits and shirts. He was equally fascinated with the jars and bottles that smelled so like her in the medicine chest alongside his shaving gear.

On an oath, he quickly undressed, stepped into the shower and turned the handle to cold.

He was late. Hunter wrestled with his tie in front of the mirror, hurrying because he knew the Yamaguchis were due any moment in the suite for dinner. There'd been a problem in his Virginia plant, so he and Ross had been on the phone back and forth for hours, trying to straighten out the mess. Time had gotten away from him.

Gaylan had interrupted him only once to ask if he wanted to confer with her and the hotel catering staff regarding the menu. He'd been preoccupied and had told her to handle it. He fervently hoped he hadn't misjudged her capabilities, though Evan had insisted she'd hostessed much larger dinner parties.

The door chimes sounded just as he shrugged into his jacket. Leaving his room, he saw that Gaylan was already greeting their guests.

"I've so looked forward to meeting you," Gaylan said as she swung wide the door.

"We're pleased to be here, Mrs. James," Taro Yamaguchi said with a slight bow. Just over five feet, the Japanese businessman wore a dark business suit that was beautifully tailored to camouflage a slight paunch.

Behind his glasses, intelligent brown eyes studied the woman he'd only recently learned was Hunter's wife.

"That's a Sakamura, isn't it?" Gaylan said, admiring his tie. "He's one of my favorite designers."

Taro's broad face registered a surprised smile. "Mine as well." Moving inside, he looked up at Hunter, who'd joined Gaylan and acknowledged her introduction. "You honor us with your invitation, Mr. James."

"The honor is ours," Hunter said smoothly. He turned slightly, indicating the two men who strolled in from the lanai. "I believe you already know Evan Porter and Ross Weber."

While the men greeted one another, Gaylan smiled down at the delicate lady with the warm brown eyes who was leaning rather heavily on a cane. "Mrs. Yamaguchi, may I suggest you sit here?" she said, leading the older woman to a short-back easy chair. "I understand you've recently had knee surgery."

"Yes," Mrs. Yamaguchi said, sitting down somewhat awkwardly and arranging her print dress primly about her legs. "I don't want to be a bother, but I'm a bit slow these days."

Gaylan was impressed with the woman's perfect English. "I know what you mean. I tore a ligament in my leg awhile back playing tennis and it seemed to take forever before I could walk comfortably again."

"You play tennis?" Nari Yamaguchi asked from the doorway.

Gaylan turned to the daughter-in-law, admiring her red silk blouse worn over white designer trousers, the shiny black hair that hung down to the middle of her back. She nodded. "Yes, I love the game."

"Wonderful. I hope we can get in a set some morning."

"I'd like that." As Nari moved to shake hands with Hunter, Gaylan greeted the son, Hiroki, who was considerably taller than his father and handsome enough to be in the movies with his jet-black hair, full mustache and dark eyes. "So glad you could come."

Hiroki chose a handshake over the more traditional bow, grasping her fingers warmly. "My pleasure. I wasn't aware Mr. James had a wife until my father mentioned you this afternoon. I must say you're lovely."

"Thank you." Gaylan wondered what Ross had told the Yamaguchis about her. She would have to wing it. Her years of training at Reuben's side kicked in. "This is my first visit to Kona," she said, realizing her comment was a bit of a non sequitur. "It's very beautiful."

Hunter watched Gaylan get everyone comfortably seated in the spacious room. He'd reserved a space for her next to him on the couch beneath the wide windows that opened on to the sea. Before sitting down, she nodded to the waiter in the dining room who quickly brought in a tray of sparkling champagne in chilled fluted crystal stemware.

He couldn't help but be impressed with Gaylan's performance so far. She'd obviously done her homework. He'd never heard of the Japanese designer, Sakamura, nor could he have recognized one of his designs. And in short order she'd managed to find something in common with both women, a leg injury with one and tennis with the other. Evan had been right. Gaylan Fisher was a born hostess. But then, this was how she made her living, he reminded himself. At a salary of more than a thousand dollars a day, she ought to be good.

Rising, Hunter offered a toast. "To a most profitable alliance."

"To friendship," Taro returned, then sipped as everyone else followed suit.

"Gaylan plays tennis, Hiroki," Nari informed her husband, then turned to their hostess. "And here I thought I'd have little to do other than sit in the sun and miss our little boy while Hiroki's in meetings."

Settling back on the couch, Gaylan was aware of Hunter's watchful eyes on her. "How old is he and what's his name?"

"His name is Taro, after me," the boy's grandfather spoke up. "Taro means first-born male. Our little one's four years old."

"Nari wanted to bring him, but I thought we needed some time alone," Hiroki explained.

"He's with my parents," Nari added. "Do you have children?"

Unruffled, Gaylan shook her head. "Not yet," she said, sending a mischievous glance at her "husband." "But we hope to have three or four, right, darling?"

Hunter cleared his throat. She was enjoying this, he thought as he stretched his arm along the couch back and settled a hand on her shoulder in a husbandly gesture. "I'd been thinking more like two."

"Children are a blessing and a pleasure," Yoshiko said as she adjusted a pin at her nape, where her dark hair streaked with white was coiled into a bun. "In our country, we're urged to limit our families."

"Even though some of us would like a dynasty of sons." Hiroki reached for the cigarettes in his pocket, then remembered his manners. "May I smoke?" he asked, looking at Gaylan.

"Certainly." They hadn't discussed this one, but she saw an ashtray on an end table.

"Mother, look, your favorites." Hiroki passed a pale blue dish containing macadamia nuts to her.

Yoshiko smiled shyly. "My weakness," she admitted, taking several.

"How was your flight over, Mr. Yamaguchi?" Ross asked politely.

"Very comfortable." From behind his glasses, his eyes shifted to Hunter. "I understand you have your own plane."

"Yes. We find it far more convenient."

"A business expense that pays off," Evan added.

Gaylan sat listening as the men launched into a discussion on the pluses and minuses of a company having its own plane. Taro, Evan and Hunter all had on dark business suits despite the tropical climate. Ross appeared not to notice what a contrast his plaid sport coat and wide floral tie was to the dark conservative look of the other men. She wondered if Hunter slept in a suit since she'd never seen him when he wasn't wearing one. His eyes when he'd come out of his room had skimmed appreciatively over the pale yellow dress that accented her tan, but he hadn't commented. She hoped she was dressed "acceptably."

Very aware of his warm hand on her shoulder, she tried to keep her mind on the conversation, steering it this way and that, unobtrusively jumping in when there was a lag. Reuben had taught her well. The secret to being a great conversationalist, the old man had often said, was to discover the other person's strongest interest, ask questions about it, then sit back and listen intently. The one doing the talking would inevitably walk away thinking the other person was wonderful.

The catering servers caught Gaylan's eye, indicating that dinner was ready. Nodding, she waited for a lull in the discussion, then ushered everyone to the oval table. Things seemed to be going well, she decided as the clear broth was served, yet her stomach was jumpy with nerves. Perhaps after this initial evening, she'd be able to relax.

Though she'd taken an instant liking to Nari, the young woman seated on Gaylan's right was full of questions that had her on edge. Gaylan was deathly afraid she'd slip up. On her left, Hunter was taking part in the talk around the table, but she could feel his attention focusing on her frequently.

"I'd just love to visit California," Nari went on. "Whereabouts do you live?"

One of the easy ones, thanks to Ross's briefing. "We've just purchased a Tudor home in Beverly Hills, but we haven't had a chance to decorate it yet."

"You haven't been married long then?"

"No." Gaylan bent to her soup, deciding she needed to follow Reuben's advice. "Tell me what it's like to live in Tokyo," she said to Nari. The friendly woman grabbed the bait and went into a lengthy description of her home life as the others talked among themselves.

"Taro, Ross tells me you like to play golf," Hunter said across the table. "Perhaps we can get a round in one day."

"I hope so," Taro answered. "Does your wife play?"

"I'm afraid not," he answered easily. He saw Gaylan set down her spoon. Casually he reached over and took her hand in his. "However, we do jog together mornings," he said, looking into her eyes.

Gaylan felt heat move into her face. This phony intimacy was disconcerting. Smiling sweetly, she extricated her hand and reached over to pat his flat stomach. "It's the only way to keep the pounds off, right, dear?" To Taro, she said, "He sits behind a desk too much."

Taro laughed. "I struggle with weight myself," he confessed. He glanced at his wife. "Because Yoshiko feeds me so well."

"Do you like to cook?" Yoshiko asked Gaylan. "Our Nari doesn't."

Undaunted, Nari shrugged. "I'd rather eat out."

"I like to cook, when I have the time," Gaylan answered.

"Do you work outside the home?" Hiroki asked.

Gaylan froze. This was one they hadn't touched on.

Hunter came to the rescue. "She keeps quite busy traveling with me. I'm like a full-time job." He smiled boyishly.

"I love your hair," Nari told Gaylan, who was still looking at Hunter's smile.

"And I've always wanted dark hair," Gaylan confessed, recovering.

"Such light hair is rare in our country," Taro commented. He raised his wineglass in a salute toward Hunter. "I compliment you on your lovely bride."

"Thank you," Hunter said, holding up his glass as his eyes moved to Gaylan, who seemed suddenly to have a lot of color in her face.

The stuffed sea bass arrived just then, along with a generous assortment of vegetables, brown rice and warm rolls. Gaylan picked at food she couldn't later recall and hoped that the conversation would center on business or the weather or just about anything that didn't include her.

This charade was turning out to be more difficult than she'd imagined. She didn't know whether to be pleased or upset that lying didn't come all that naturally to her.

Hunter yawned, glad that everyone had gone. He'd opened the lanai doors off the living area to air out the smoke. Removing his coat and tie, he walked outside and breathed in the scented night air. It really was lovely here, as Gaylan had pointed out. Odd how he'd never taken much notice.

He rolled his shoulders, comfortably tired. He and Taro had an 8:00 a.m. tee-off time, then after lunch they'd be meeting with Hiroki, Evan and Ross. The Japanese didn't like to rush things, didn't trust anything fast, but Hunter wasn't concerned. Four or five hours a day hammering out their differences should easily bring them to a finish well within the two weeks. Meanwhile, a little leisure time wouldn't hurt. He couldn't remember his last real vacation.

Hearing a noise, he turned to see Gaylan come out of his room. Since all her things were there, she'd asked for a little privacy to change in his bathroom. Stepping inside, he inhaled her elusive scent. The moonlight wrapped around her pale green floor-length robe. He fought an urge to touch her, then wrestled with a rush of anger that he wanted to.

"It's all yours," she said, indicating his room.

Perversely he didn't want her to leave him just yet. "What do you think of the Yamaguchis?"

She sent him an uncomplicated smile. "I like them."

"Do you always decide so quickly, take people at their face value?"

He seemed to want to fence with her again, and she wondered why. It had been a long day. Still, she couldn't just walk away. "Is there some reason I shouldn't?"

"You could get hurt by trusting too easily."

She gave a careless shrug. "Life's full of risks." She faked a yawn. "I'm really tired. See you in the morning."

He stepped nearer, touched her arm. "I need to ask you something. Your scent. I can't figure it out. What brand of perfume do you use?"

"I don't use any."

Her hair beckoned his touch as he imagined the silky feel of it. He gritted his teeth. "You must use something. I—"

"Baby soap. That's all."

"Soap? The one babies use?"

"That's the one. Good night, Hunter."

He watched her walk to the opposite bedroom and shut her door. Baby soap. That was a good one. Smiling, he went into his room.

Chapter Four

The sun woke Hunter before six. He pulled on his gray cotton sweatpants and a white T-shirt, then walked to the small pantry and poured himself a generous glass of orange juice. Drinking, he noticed that Gaylan's door was closed. He debated only until his glass was empty about whether to ask if she'd like to join him for a run.

He knocked softly on the door. Nothing. He rapped again, harder. Not a sound. He took a chance and cautiously opened the door. Her bed was empty. She'd mentioned she was an early riser, but few ever beat him out onto the jogging trail. Grabbing a towel, he looped it around his neck and hurried outside.

The beach was some distance from the Ocean Tower. Walking briskly, Hunter wound his way across two bridges and along an overgrown path through a copse of trees before moving into the sandy clearing. The morning sun was warm but not burning hot, the sky a clear blue with only a few wispy clouds. Drawing in a deep, salty breath, Hunter set out to the right because most other early risers chose the left. He liked his solitude.

He was into his rhythm quickly, enjoying the feel of his running shoes pounding on the hard-packed, damp sand on this nearly deserted stretch of beach. He heard a gull screech, then turned his head to watch the bird swoop down into a breaker and zoom upward with something in its beak. An early breakfast, he imagined.

Pacing himself, he estimated when he'd run about a mile and slowed a bit, using the towel ends to wipe his face. He passed a woman in a vivid pink bikini lying on a towel, sunglasses on her eyes. Hunter hoped she'd remembered sunscreen since her skin looked winter-white although it was June. Hitting his stride again, he moved into double time, feeling the pull and tug of muscles that hadn't been exercised in about a week.

Back in the States, he didn't always take the time to run. He had yet to map out a route he was comfortable with around his new house. There was a gym with state-of-the-art equipment in his building, but he seldom found the time to use it. What was it Gaylan had said at dinner when she'd reached to touch his stomach—that running was the way to keep off the pounds? He believed that, too, which was how he maintained a flat belly at thirty-eight.

After another mile or so, he slowed to a walk, then stopped to wipe his damp hair and blot his face. Squinting, he gazed off toward a pile of rocks on the edge of the sea not far ahead. Someone was sitting on the highest one, staring out at the water. She had a lot of blond hair tied back off her face and she wore green shorts and top. So this was where she'd come.

Hunter approached quietly, but she spotted him anyhow. He was a dozen feet from her when she turned, and again he was struck at the pure blue of her eyes.

Gaylan looked him over for a long minute, then smiled her approval. "I was beginning to think you never appeared in public without one of your dreary dark suits. You look terrific. Pull up a rock and sit down."

He was red faced and sweat stained, yet she said he looked terrific. A hard woman to figure, Hunter thought as he sat down on the smoothest rock just below her. "Nice out here, isn't it?"

"Mmm." She brushed back strands of hair that the breeze insisted on tugging free of the green yarn she'd tied at her nape. "I love the sea. One day I'm going to live on the ocean. I don't care if it's a shack as long as it's on the water."

It was hard to imagine her making do with a shack, this lady who'd worked for years for a millionaire and was currently earning ten thousand a week. "I like it, too."

"Yet you don't own any oceanfront property?"

"I do, but I've never built on it. Up in Big Sur."

"Oh, that's gorgeous up there. And so private."

Uncomfortable in his damp T-shirt, Hunter pulled it off over his head and tossed it on an adjacent rock. "Is privacy important to you?" She'd practically lived in Reuben Cramer's pocket all those years. Of course, she'd undoubtedly been well paid for her time.

"Very important. As I know it is to you." Gaylan reached down for her plastic bottle of ice water and inserted the straw. "Would you like a drink?" He looked parched.

"Thanks." He drank deeply, letting the cold water slide down his throat.

She watched his throat work, then slid her eyes to his chest matted with dark hair, the skin damp from his run. He was built nicely, not muscle-bound like a bodybuilding fanatic, but more like a man who took care of himself.

It seemed an act of intimacy to share a straw with someone he'd met but a few days ago, Hunter thought, yet it didn't seem to faze Gaylan. He handed back the bottle. "I always forget to bring something cold along."

She took a drink, then set down the bottle.

"Gaylan's an unusual name," Hunter said, leaning against the rock sideways so he could look at her.

"Irish, on my mother's side. My father was English. The two aren't supposed to get along, but my folks sure did."

"Did?"

"They died in a car accident eight years ago."

He remembered Evan's short briefing on her. "I'm sorry. That must have been hard on you."

He didn't know the half of it. "Does your mother live in California?" Evan had told her that Hunter, Sr., had died a long time ago. It was Ross who'd filled her in even more by revealing that Hunter's father had been a harsh, ruthless businessman, disliked and feared by many. And that his mother had divorced him some time before his death. She was curious what Hunter would say.

"No. She remarried and lives in Georgia. Pete raises peaches and they're happy. So she says."

She almost laughed out loud at how impossible he made it sound that *anyone* could be happy living on a Georgia peach farm. "Different strokes for different folks, and all that. Do you see much of them?"

"Not much." Hunter gazed out to sea. He'd never understood his mother. For that matter, he hadn't understood his father, either, but he'd had to admire a man who'd built an empire from nothing. He'd offered to buy his mother the house of her choice in California or anywhere else she wanted. She'd told him she wanted to stay with Pete in Georgia. Hunter had trouble accepting that.

Gaylan had been watching his puzzled expression and guessed that he was thinking of that peach farm. "Maybe she loves him," she suggested quietly.

Slowly he turned to look at her. "I wouldn't have thought you'd be a romantic." Women who worked for wealthy men were usually pragmatic and practical, he'd found.

"But I knew you'd be a cynic."

"A realist," he corrected.

"Semantics, Hunter. You do that a lot." She shifted to face him. "What's your life like? I mean, day to day. I spent six years around a rich man, but Reuben was old and wheelchair-bound, which made him crotchety. But living like...like this..." She waved her arm to include the magnificent hotel somewhere behind them, the beach, the sea, all of it. "What's it like to live like this daily?"

The question took him by surprise. "It's hard to explain since I've lived like this most of my life. That probably sounds boastful—which I don't mean it to be—but it's a fact. Until I was about ten, we lived in Glendale in a nice three-bedroom house on a shady street. By the time I was in my teens, we moved to a bigger place in Thousand Oaks and later to a sprawling ranch in San Clemente. We had cooks and gardeners and chauffeurs. After college when I went to work for the company, I set up the same life-style for myself that I'd always known."

She found that kind of affluence hard to imagine. "Don't you sometimes long for privacy, to just be alone without servants and business associates around you, to just take off and drive somewhere and be yourself?"

He shrugged. "I am myself. I'm doing exactly what I want to do. I have boards of directors, of course, but I own controlling interest in all my companies. So I pretty much call the shots. I go where I want, do as I please." Why did his life sound somewhat shallow and empty when put into words? He was happy with the status quo. Men from all walks of life would love to change places with him. What was she getting at? "Does that sound so terrible?"

"Not terrible. It's just that you spend all your time acquiring money and more money. Where's the fun, the pleasure in little things—a sunset, a baby, a walk on the beach?"

Hunter draped his arms on his bent knees and dismissed those things with a wave of his hand. "You don't understand. To me, business *is* fun. Nothing I know gives me greater pleasure than to close a particularly difficult deal. It's no longer just the money. It's winning."

"Then it's like a game to you?"

"Sort of." He warmed to his subject, trying to make her see. "One of the reasons Compu West has gotten this far with Yamaguchi Systems is that I did a lot of research and learned that Japanese firms consider business as war. They figure out their strategy and move in for the kill, taking advantage of their opponents' weak points. Knowing that, I've been careful not to expose any of our vulnerabilities, which are few anyway. In each negotiation, there's a winner and a loser, occasionally a compromise. I don't mind compromising some, but I definitely want to come out a winner."

"And that's your way of having fun?"

Picking up his shirt, Hunter used it to blot his damp face. "You make it sound like a perverted pleasure."

"Not perverted, but certainly single-minded. It's as if you live to do business. Haven't you heard that all work and no play makes Jack a dull boy?"

He'd had enough analysis of his methods, his personality. In a remarkably smooth move, he got to his feet, put both hands on her upper arms and pulled her up to him. He did it so quickly that she had no chance to protest or to resist. Holding her close to his chest, his face inches from hers, he stared into her eyes. "Do you think I'm dull, Gaylan?"

Her legs felt rubbery and her heart began to pound. Residual effect from her run and the sun, Gaylan told herself. She could feel his warm breath on her flushed cheeks, and the heat of his bare chest through the thin cotton of her top, could smell the sea mingled with his hot male scent. His eyes were the color of old pewter as he held her gaze. She wasn't afraid, but she wasn't unmoved, either. "I don't believe I said that," she managed.

He loosened his grip on her, but only slightly. "Tell me the reason you wouldn't wear the ring. The *real* reason."

She eased out of his hold and shook her head. "You wouldn't understand."

Frustrated, he jammed his hands into his pants pockets. "How can you know that?"

"Because you don't understand why your mother would choose to live with a mere peach farmer rather than with your wealthy and powerful father."

"And you do?"

"I think so."

"Would you care to educate me?"

She sighed. He wasn't going to like her answer, and she wasn't thrilled about giving it. But she could tell he was nothing if not persistent. "You labeled me a romantic earlier, and I probably am. But it's more than that. I won't wear that ring nor *any* ring on the fourth finger of my left hand, not until the right moment. It's reserved for a special ring from the man I have yet to love and who will love me in return. I don't know your mother, but I understand her. She'd rather live on a peach farm, even if she has to work hard alongside a man she loves, than live in grand style with a man who loves his work more than her."

"You're too pragmatic to believe all that romantic nonsense."

She frowned up at him, squinting against the rising sun. "Is that how you see me?"

He shrugged. "You're here, aren't you? Opportunity knocked and you answered. I'm not criticizing you for that, but I think you ought to accept the fact that your argument doesn't wash and that you're more like me than you care to admit."

Gaylan felt the heat rise, and it wasn't from the sun. "The day that pigs fly," she told him, then bent to grab her bottle and scamper off the rocks.

Before Hunter could react, she was running along the sand in the direction of their hotel. Tucking his T-shirt into his pocket, he smiled. He'd hit a nerve, he decided. Yes, he'd definitely hit a nerve with Miss Gaylan Fisher.

"You are unbelievably good," Nari said to Gaylan as she came around the net, her racket tucked under one arm, her other outstretched in congratulations. "Three out of four sets. I should hang my head in shame."

"Don't be silly," Gaylan answered as they walked off the tennis court. "You said you rarely play singles and prefer doubles. Next time, we'll get Hiroki and maybe Ross to play with us."

"Or perhaps your husband."

That word nearly stopped Gaylan in her tracks. She couldn't get used to hearing Hunter referred to as her husband. "Hunter doesn't play tennis, just golf."

They reached the outdoor bar with its umbrella tables and sat down in a shady corner, ordering two iced teas from the waiter who seemed to materialize from nowhere. Nari lifted her long ponytail off her neck, letting the slight breeze cool her heated skin. "Thanks for a great workout."

"I should be thanking you. I haven't had a chance to play lately and I've missed it." Reuben had had a tennis court in his huge backyard and he'd urged Gaylan to play afternoons while he napped. She'd recruited the cook's daughter and the chauffeur, both better players than she, and they'd improved her game.

"Last night at dinner, Hunter said that you didn't work outside the home because you traveled with him and he kept you busy. Did you ever hold down a full-time job?"

Gaylan acknowledged the arrival of their tea and bought a little time. How could she answer Nari without lying, yet not revealing their little deception? She took her time squeezing lemon into the cool drink. In the end, she opted for the truth, or at least part of it. "I majored in business in college and I worked for a while as personal assistant to a man who was in the electronics business."

Nari sipped her tea. "So that's how you met Hunter, since your employer was in the same business as he?"

"More or less. Actually, we met through Evan, Hunter's attorney." So far, so good. Gaylan hated being on guard during what should be casual chats, but she supposed there was no way around it. "Do you work outside your home?" She didn't imagine Nari did with a wealthy husband and a small child to raise, but she wanted to shift the focus.

Nari sighed somewhat dramatically. "No, and I want to badly." She leaned forward, lowering her voice. "You see, in Japan, it isn't considered good form for a wife to work if her husband can easily support the family. She would take away a job from someone in need. But more important, a wife is expected to care for her husband's every need, as well as those of their children, the household and, when it becomes necessary, both sets of aging parents. This leaves little time or energy for outside work."

Surprised, Gaylan leaned back. "I knew that was the case with the older generation, but I thought that modern sophisticated young Japanese women were changing all that."

"I wish that were so. A career is permitted *before* marriage, but frowned upon after. Look at our new Princess Masako who recently wed the Crown Prince. She resigned from the foreign ministry as soon as she agreed to the marriage."

"But that's royalty. Surely the average Japanese woman..."

"Gives in eventually to our male-dominated society," Nari interjected. "Conditions have improved somewhat, but it's a rare Japanese man who feels confident enough to allow his wife to hold down a meaningful position *and* help her with the home and children so she can. Unable to do it all, she inevitably quits her job."

Gaylan smiled her understanding. "Many men in the States feel the same way. Although the women's movement has changed things, chauvinism is still alive and well. Tell me, if you were able to work, what would you want to do?"

Nari looked up, her dark eyes shining. "Promise you won't laugh?"

"Of course."

"I want to do fashion work. I design and sew all my own clothes. And I've so many ideas. I fill all these books with sketches, but I must keep them to myself." She took a deep breath, trying to explain herself. "Don't get me wrong. I love taking care of my husband and son. But I feel I have something to contribute. I want badly to be taken seriously. Is that so wrong?"

Gaylan brushed back her hair, amazed at how the two of them from such different cultures longed for the same independence and recognition. "Oh, Nari, I don't know. It's an age-old discussion. Some women would vote yes and others no. It's an individual interpretation. It isn't always chauvinism but tradition that dictates these decisions. If you feel this strongly, why don't you discuss your need with Hiroki?"

"Because I know what his answer would be." Nari swallowed more tea thoughtfully. "Did you know that even as we speak my father-in-law's personal assistant has arrived? Her name is Yasu Shigeta, a very bright Japanese woman who is thirty-two and unmarried. Apparently she's decided to go against tradition and work her way up in the business world. Of course, she was educated in your country at Yale. She'll also probably remain single."

"Do you think it's the American influence that made her decide which way to go?"

Nari shrugged. "Perhaps. She's attractive enough to have had proposals, but she has a few traits men are uncomfortable with."

"Such as?"

"She's outspoken and quietly aggressive, assertive in meetings, I hear, and somewhat opinionated. I doubt if Yasu would take a back seat to any man."

Gaylan waited until the waiter had poured their refills. "I don't see why she needs to, not in business nor in a personal relationship. What's wrong with a fifty-fifty arrangement?"

"Is that the kind of marriage you and Hunter have, where you share the running of the household and, eventually, the raising of children equally?"

A stumper. Gaylan knew Nari was no dummy and would by observing Hunter and her together quickly determine who was making most of the decisions. She forced a small laugh. "I'm saying that that is the ideal situation. Not many of us have it, at least not yet."

Nari nodded in agreement, then willed herself to brighten. "I hope you don't mind my bringing up this discussion. It isn't often I feel an immediate kinship with another woman, especially one who isn't Japanese."

"Thank you. I feel the same."

"We should be grateful our husbands are kind, considerate men, even if they don't jump to grant our every wish. It was obvious to me the other night at dinner that Hunter is very pleased with you."

Pleased that she was fulfilling the terms of their agreement, Gaylan thought. "I hope so," she said, unable to think of a better reply.

"It's also obvious you're newlyweds. I noticed that he often finds reasons to touch you, to hold your hand." Nari sighed longingly. "Five years of marriage has cooled Hiroki's romantic inclinations."

"Didn't I hear him say he chose to leave your son home so the two of you could be alone part of this trip? That sounds romantic to me."

"Perhaps. Hiroki is difficult to evaluate at times."

Gaylan smiled. "Of course he is. He's a man, isn't he?" As Nari laughed, she rose. "On that comment, I think it's time to grab a quick shower before lunch." Gaylan signaled the waiter for their check.

Gaylan dropped the smile from her face as Hunter closed the door on yet another group dinner in their suite. It seemed as if she'd been smiling for hours, but it had been worth it, for the evening had gone well, with their Japanese guests complimenting her with what appeared to be genuine sincerity. Though Hunter hadn't said, she thought she detected approval in his manner, his eyes straying to her frequently.

Three days down and another eleven to go, she thought as she slipped off her pumps. She'd actually enjoyed this evening, mostly because of her conversations with Yasu Shigeta, the small-boned, slender woman with a pixie haircut that made her look much younger than Gaylan knew her to be. Perhaps that was deliberate, her youthful facade causing others to underestimate her intelligence and experience. Yasu appeared to be shrewd enough to have figured out that ploy and use it to her advantage.

Gaylan watched Hunter remove his jacket and tie, and unfasten the top button of his shirt. He'd seemed quieter tonight than usual and she was curious why.

But before she could ask, Hunter spoke up from the corner of the couch where he'd dropped his tired body. "What do you think of Yasu Shigeta?"

She walked over to sit opposite him, wondering if he was asking to be polite or if her opinion had some value to him. "I like her. Why?"

"Just curious, since you were a personal assistant for quite a while."

"Our jobs aren't really comparable. I worked for a semi-retired executive who hated the limitations age and poor health forced on him. Reuben traveled often out of boredom, presumably to check on his investments, although I suspect he felt if he didn't keep an eye on things, his two sons would bankrupt the company. Yasu works for a man still very much in charge of his company with his son being groomed to take over one day, but not yet."

Her observations, he'd come to realize, were usually on target. "You're right. Hiroki is *kohai* to Taro, which means second in command."

She raised a brow. "Are you studying Japanese?"

"I've picked up a few words. Did you get the impression that Yasu is earning her keep?"

"I couldn't say after observing her through one dinner and never seeing her in action in a business meeting. Apparently Taro and Hiroki think so or she wouldn't be their right hand, so to speak."

"Would you like to sit in on one of our meetings and watch Yasu in action?" The minute the words were out of his mouth, Hunter wondered where the thought had come from.

Gaylan sent him a skeptical look. "You're kidding, right? I can't imagine your placing serious importance on a woman's opinion. Certainly you'd never put a woman in a power situation in your company."

He stretched his long legs out. "Maybe you're wrong. Maybe I value your opinion."

She studied him a long minute, then shook her head. "I suspect not. I think you have to accept Yasu as part of the negotiations since Taro brought her along and because of her titled position. *But* you wouldn't hire a woman to fill a similar position in Compu West."

He felt a flash of anger. She was right, yet she made him feel suddenly defensive about his belief. He decided to hedge. "You're not sure about that."

His eyes were evasive and she was sure. "Okay, how many women hold key positions in your companies?" She watched him turn to stare out the open lanai doors, a muscle twitching in his jaw. He was silent but she had her answer. "Tell me, do you have a poor opinion of women in general or just in business?"

Hunter ran a hand over his face wearily. He never should have started this discussion, he realized belatedly. "I happen to like women and I even respect their various abilities in business. It's just that I don't care personally to do business with them."

Somehow, hearing it out loud even though she'd suspected as much made it worse. "Women belong in the kitchen and the bedroom, is that it?"

He tried not to grind his teeth. "It's been my experience that women infect business dealings with their own agenda, using whatever means necessary to get their way, for their own good, not always the good of the company."

Infect? Half a dozen rebuttals sprang to her mind but, as she was choosing which to lay on him, he turned and she saw his eyes. Something there stopped her—a residual pain, a vulnerability he quickly masked. Gaylan tamped down her annoyance and remembered Ross's telling her that Hunter's wife had worked at Compu West. "It's your wife, isn't it? She did something to make you feel this way."

Carefully Hunter unclenched his jaw. "My *ex*-wife, you mean. Yeah, you could say she did something." Feeling restless, he rose and walked out onto the lanai. The moon filtered through the swaying palms, casting dancing shadows as the breeze rustled the fronds. A peaceful night. He wished he felt peaceful.

Jolene had seemed so sweet when he'd first met her, fresh out of college, eager to learn. She'd been an assistant to one of his vice presidents when he'd begun dating her. Six months later, they'd been married.

For the first time, Hunter had allowed himself to dream about something other than business. A wife and later, maybe children. Together he and Jolene would make a home such as he'd never known with his workaholic father and unhappy mother.

But he'd soon discovered that Jolene had ambitions, hidden agendas that slowly crept out. She didn't want children, but rather to become a viable force in his company. She wanted to be his right hand, be named vice president, replacing Ross, who clashed with her often. She'd wanted equal power and equal say.

When Hunter refused her requests, saying that she hadn't earned a right to such a position, that she wasn't knowledgeable enough, nor experienced at all, she'd decided to show him. She'd skipped with three patents Compu West had been working on and gone over to their strongest competitor. Naturally they'd been delighted to hire her on, and then she'd filed for divorce.

Shortly after, he'd heard that Jolene had made vice president. Hunter felt sorry for the men who worked with her.

Responding to the defenseless look she'd momentarily glimpsed in his eyes, Gaylan followed him out. She lay a hand on his arm and waited for him to look at her.

It was the first time she'd touched him, without others present, when they weren't pretending to be husband and wife. When she asked him to tell her the story, he did. Quickly and unemotionally.

"Did you go after her, sue to get your patents back?" she asked as he finished.

He shook his head. "I just wanted to be rid of her. A messy court case would have dragged things out. I never wanted to see her again. And I haven't." He let out a huff of air. "So you see why I have a little trouble putting a woman into a power position in any of my companies?"

He wasn't such a tough guy, Gaylan decided. Just a man who'd been hurt and was still reacting to having his trust trampled on. Coupled with the sort of father he'd had, she wasn't surprised that he showed little outward signs of a warm, loving nature.

Acting purely on instinct, her fingers tightened on his arm in a reassuring squeeze. "I do understand. But perhaps you shouldn't judge *all* women by that one woman."

Hunter didn't want her sympathy, could never accept it. He studied her hair made silver by the moonlight, her eyes a luminous blue as they searched his. Her fragrance wrapped around his senses, weakened his resolve. No, not sympathy. What he suddenly wanted was her.

He stepped closer, his arms encircling her, bringing her closer to his body. Her hands flew to his chest as if to push him away, but she didn't push. He felt her breath flutter out between her parted lips.

"The Japanese have a phrase they use," he said softly. "*Dai rokkan.* It means sixth sense. A sudden intuition. I feel *dai rokkan* nudging me right now. It tells me that you want me to kiss you." And before she could protest, his mouth took hers.

He wasn't in the least hesitant, nor particularly gentle, Gaylan noticed. He tasted powerful, merciless, impatient. Instinctively she should be turning from him, but instead her lips opened under his. At her acquiescence, his hand moved down her back, drawing her nearer.

Trapped. By the hard muscular feel of him, the heady male flavors, the raw masculine scent of him. Trapped by her body, which she'd too long denied this wild explosion of feeling. Trapped high atop the seventh-floor tower under a smiling moon with the warm evening air swirling about them.

With his hands, Hunter aligned her soft body so it fit perfectly with the hard planes of his own. She sighed softly into his mouth at the contact, and he felt a shiver skitter up his spine. Like this, he'd wanted her just like this, since she'd first strolled into his office. His mind had warned him to keep her at bay while another more insistent part had urged him to pull her close.

Caught. He was caught by his own helpless need, by her warm willingness, by that hint of surrender that precedes seduction. Her mouth, clever and agile, moved under his, accepting enjoyment, giving pleasure in return. When his tongue touched hers and she moaned softly, he knew he was lost.

But he couldn't allow it to happen, couldn't lose control. He was paying her ten thousand dollars a week to pretend, he reminded himself. Was she pretending now, too?

He drew back, breathing hard, searching her face. Her eyes were hazy with the beginnings of passion, her breath as short as his. If she was pretending, she was a damn fine actress.

Yet he still had to let her go. She was like Jolene, one of those women who used men to climb the ladder to whatever suited their fancy this week. To fall into Gaylan's trap could destroy him. He didn't really want her, he told himself as he took a step back. It was just that he'd been celibate too long and she was here. Yes, that was it.

"I'm sorry," he muttered.

She stood quietly watching him, confusion on her face, a flash of pain in her eyes. Sorry was for doing something wrong, for overreaching your bounds, for taking what was not freely offered. The kiss hadn't been wrong and she'd participated without persuasion as much as he. Perhaps more. Sorry was a cop-out to evade facing feelings that overwhelmed.

He took her hand in apology, not wanting to mess up their whole relationship over one kiss. "I shouldn't have done that. I'm sorry," he repeated.

"Are you?" she asked softly. Pulling free, she went inside and closed her bedroom door behind her.

Her hand had been small in his, her skin incredibly soft. About as soft as he was getting in the head, Hunter thought. Gaylan Fisher had an uncanny way of getting under his skin, of making him lose control, without doing much.

He stared up at a clear night sky. And he had eleven more days of this to endure.

Chapter Five

Taro Yamaguchi bowed ever so slightly to Hunter, as he did each time he entered and left the James suite. "We had a most productive meeting, wouldn't you say, Hunter-san?"

"Yes, indeed," Hunter lied, seeing Taro to the door. The others had left moments ago.

"Would you and your lovely wife join us in our suite for lunch, say in half an hour?"

"Gaylan went for a walk on the beach some time ago. She should be returning any minute. I'll check with her."

"Good. We hope to see you then, Hunter-san."

Taro had begun using the more familiar form of address—Hunter-san—since getting to know his American counterpart better. Hunter wasn't sure if he cared for the liberty taken, or perhaps he was just short-tempered these days.

He wasn't sleeping well and his nerves were jumpy. He would have been overjoyed to finish these negotiations immediately so they could all go home. The "most productive meeting" Taro spoke of hadn't been nearly as productive as Hunter would have preferred. The cautious Japanese and their slow way of doing business were beginning to chip away at his patience.

The most they ever put in was five hours, usually from eight to one. Then the Yamaguchi tribe would have lunch, golf or go swimming, and even take touristy jaunts to local points of interest. It was Nari and Hiroki's first visit, and the older couple enjoyed showing them around. Dammit, Hunter thought, they could finish up a week earlier if they kept at it for a normal ten-to-twelve-hour day such as he was used to working.

But, as Yasu was prone to reminding him, it was important to take their time working out the details of such an important merger. Yasu, it turned out, also had a law degree. Both Evan and Ross were impressed with her, but Hunter wasn't. She hammered away at nitpicky points until it was all he could do to keep from throwing things. Perhaps tomorrow he'd work by phone with his California office and leave the details to Ross and the others.

He glanced at his watch. Where was Gaylan? He'd personally asked her to be back here for lunch with the Yamaguchis at one. Yoshiko had spent the morning getting her hair done and Nari had gone snorkeling. Gaylan had set off alone walking. Was she sitting on her favorite rock, daydreaming about romance as she probably did, letting the time get away from her? Hunter marched out onto the lanai, trying to see her. He hated being late.

She'd been wearing white shorts and a loose blue shirt. His eyes, as she'd come to tell him where she'd be, had lingered on her incredibly long legs. They were tan and well shaped and . . .

And he was surely losing his mind, Hunter decided with disgust. One little kiss and she had him nuts. All right, so it had been a pretty long kiss. She hadn't fought him, had instead kissed him back. That had surprised him.

He'd had a weak moment. He couldn't allow that to happen again. He needed to maintain a businesslike attitude toward Gaylan when they were alone, and a friendly, married manner when in the company of the Yamaguchis.

Right now, he needed to find his so-called wife.

The sun was high in the sky and it was hot by now. He took off his jacket and tie, then left the suite, slamming the door. He would find her and remind her that he was paying her to show up at certain events and she'd damn well better do just that.

It took him a while. Like twenty minutes. Even then, she didn't see him approach because she was engrossed in a volleyball game in the sand with nine or ten young men and women, all looking like ads for suntan lotion in their skimpy suits and cutoff shorts. Hunter stood on the sidelines near a hotel snack stand, trying to control his simmering temper. He watched as she returned a fast ball, lunging up toward the net, socking it a good one with her small fist. It sailed over two heads and a third person swung and missed.

Gaylan scored, jumped up and let out a victory shout as her teammates cheered her on. Acknowledging them, she turned and . . . and lost her smile. Standing on the grass edging the sand was Hunter with a scowl on his face. Quickly she checked her watch and frowned. Damn.

Slowly she left the impromptu court and walked to his side. "I lost track of the time. I'm sorry." He just looked at her, unsmiling. "You could have just eaten without me. I'm not very hungry anyway."

Why didn't he say something, instead of just standing there looking irritated? Gaylan felt like a schoolgirl caught playing hooky. Why had he come all the way out here after her? He was as out of place on a Hawaiian beach in his black silk slacks and hand-stitched leather loafers as a nun in a brothel. She felt her temper rise. "Don't you own anything but formal clothes and jogging pants? I mean, this is *Hawaii,* for heaven's sake. Do you have to dress like an undertaker?"

Hunter wished he could take the time to count to ten. "I don't believe I hired you to tell me how to dress. I hired you to be present at certain functions, one of which is lunch in the Yamaguchi suite this very moment."

He was right and she was wrong. "I said I was sorry." She held up her watch. "We're already late. Why don't we skip lunch today and have some fun? We could use another player on our team."

Just then, the ball came flying toward them. Instinctively Hunter caught it to keep from getting hit in the head.

"Out-of-bounds," someone shouted.

"Hey, man, bring the ball back and join us," a barrel-chested, redheaded man called to Hunter. "We're short one player over here."

"I've never played volleyball in my life," Hunter muttered to Gaylan. He tossed the ball to the redhead.

"It's an easy game," Gaylan said, taking his hand. "Come on, Hunter. Loosen up."

"You two in or what?" a young woman with a blond ponytail asked.

"Yeah, fella, get a move on," another voice piped up.

This was ridiculous, Hunter thought. Loosen up! Men his age didn't play games in the sand. Why was Gaylan looking at him like that, as if he were the biggest stick-in-the-mud she'd ever seen? Didn't she know that executives couldn't waste time playing?

"Let him be, Gaylan," the redhead called. "He's too old to play anyhow."

"Are you?" she asked softly.

Too old! Angry now, Hunter stepped over to the snack stand and asked to use the phone. He begged off lunch with Taro, explaining that something had come up. Then he slipped off his shoes and bent to remove his socks. Old, indeed. He'd show these muscled beach boys that he wasn't exactly over-the-hill quite yet. If he made a complete fool of himself, well, he'd never see these people again anyway. Quickly he rolled up his pant legs and followed a smiling Gaylan onto the sand.

He'd never played any sport as a kid, never had the time or the friends who'd have coaxed him to play. He'd watched a lot, but that wasn't quite the same. Turning up his shirtsleeves, he walked with no small amount of fear and trepidation to the back area where Gaylan positioned him.

All too briefly, she explained the game to him as he nodded, wearing a look of confidence he was far from feeling. His height was an advantage, Hunter soon realized, and his morning runs kept him limber enough to make some good jumps in order to whack back the ball. He was both embarrassed and pleased when his team members cheered him as the other side missed his serve and he scored.

He turned to Gaylan with a cocky grin. Nothing to this game, it said.

It was all she could do to keep from rushing over and hugging him. He was so pleased with himself, his smile so genuine. She hadn't seen him look truly happy since she'd first met him. But he did now.

She wondered what Ross and Evan would think if they saw their employer barefoot in the sand, and smiled at the thought.

Their side won the game and, to Gaylan's surprise, Hunter suggested another go-round. By the end of that game, he was red faced and damp, looking thoroughly disheveled with his white shirt sweat stained and his dress pants full of sand from when he'd fallen returning a fast serve. Never had she seen him look better.

As the players broke it up, they slapped one another on the back and gave out playful arm punches before going their separate ways. Several came over to Gaylan and Hunter, smiling and clapping them on the shoulders, reminding them to be out here tomorrow, same time, for a rematch. She knew Hunter wasn't a toucher, yet he took the good-natured jostling well.

"You're not as old as I thought," Eric, the redhead told Hunter. "Good job. See you tomorrow?"

"You never know," Hunter answered, slipping his shoes back on.

Inching her feet into her sandals, Gaylan smiled up at him. "We deserve a reward." She took his hand and drew him along the grassy path.

"What did you have in mind?" he asked, feeling good. Feeling oddly like a truant who'd gotten away with something. He also felt the exhilaration that comes after a good workout. The sun was shining, he had a beautiful woman holding his hand, and the world suddenly seemed like a friendly place.

"Over there." Gaylan pointed to a lunch wagon with a red-and-white awning shading the vendor. "Hot dogs and beer. Nothing better on a hot afternoon."

He patted his back pocket. "I didn't bring my wallet."

"My treat." She reached into her shorts pocket where she had her key and a folded ten-dollar bill.

"I'll pay you back when we get upstairs."

"No," she said firmly. "A simple thank-you will do." She stepped up to the vendor.

Hunter hadn't had beer since college. He rarely drank anything except an occasional glass of wine with dinner, as he often worked afterward and needed a clear head. But as they settled down under a palm tree on the grassy slope and he tipped his head back for the first taste, he decided she was right. He had never tasted anything better. He bit into the huge hot dog covered with mustard and sauerkraut and found it delicious.

"New York style," she said, watching his face. "Almost as good as strolling down Fifth Avenue, window-shopping on a chilly afternoon and buying one of these hot off the grill."

He'd never done that, either. Not that he'd been longing to. After all, he could have if he'd wanted to. When in New York, he'd mostly hustled from meeting to meeting, eaten business lunches at Twenty-One and dinners at The Four Seasons, or been served late suppers in his own apartment by the small staff he kept there. It had never occurred to him that he'd been missing anything.

Until Gaylan.

"Is that what you did when you accompanied Reuben to New York, go window-shopping while he was in meetings?" Suddenly he wanted to know what her life had been like those six years.

Gaylan swallowed a chewy bite, then shook her head. "I attended the meetings alongside him, took notes that I later typed up and filed, made suggestions occasionally, kept track of his schedule and reminded him of appointments. I wandered off on my own during his naps, which were getting more frequent toward the end. I love walking around that city, looking in the fabulous stores, observing the people."

"What's the pleasure in window-shopping? I would think it would make you feel like a kid with his nose pressed against the candy-store window and not a nickel in his pocket."

"I had a few nickels in my pocket. But the point of window-shopping—the pleasure—is the opportunity it affords you to dream. Even if I had pots of money, I wouldn't buy half the things I saw, but it's such fun to fantasize, don't you think?"

He'd rarely fantasized about anything that he couldn't go out and buy. "I guess I'm not much of a dreamer." Finishing his hot dog, Hunter sipped his beer.

"That's a shame. You miss a lot if you don't dream."

Stretching out, he propped himself on one elbow and studied her. She had her hair caught back off her face with a gold clip, but several insistent curls had escaped and brushed her cheeks in a light ocean breeze. She'd removed her sunglasses and he saw that she hadn't bothered with makeup. He noticed several faint freckles on the bridge of her nose. She didn't look hot or rumpled, despite playing several volleyball games. And then there were those incredible legs, tanned a dark gold.

He watched her wipe her mouth with the paper napkin. The same mouth that had felt so soft, so giving, under his. Slowly she turned to look at him, her eyes bluer than the sky. Clearing his throat, Hunter decided he'd better jump back into the conversation or she'd find a reason to go back. Uncharacteristically he wanted this lazy afternoon to go on.

"Tell me what you think I miss by not dreaming."

She gave herself a moment, wondering how best to explain a dreamer to a pragmatic. "Possibilities. Like that TV ad says. Edison was a dreamer who envisioned a lighted world without candles. Flights of fancy via imagination. Michael Crichton brought to life a whole assortment of dinosaurs in *Jurassic Park*. Hope for a better future. The young person who stares into a shop window at beautiful clothes she wants and determines that one day she'll be able to do more than just look."

Gaylan shifted her gaze to him and saw he was listening with furrowed brow, honestly trying to understand. "And romance, with all its accompanying excitement and adventure that turns a tedious life into a thrilling one."

He was amused by her recitation, but knew better than to let her see. "Would you describe your life as tedious?"

No, but she rather thought his was. "Not at all. I'm luckier than most." Despite the early loss of her parents and her difficulties with Mel, she'd traveled widely, had good friends, and, after these two weeks, she'd have the resources to again be self-supporting and beholden to no one. Yes, she was lucky.

Lucky? Hunter wondered. Or had she just used her friendship with Evan to wangle an introduction, first to Reuben and then himself, two millionaires who'd hired her? But he didn't want to alienate her by pointing out all that. "If not tedious, then is your life thrilling?"

She frowned, wondering where he was going with this. "Define thrilling."

He sat up and drained his beer can. "Well, that was your word, but I'd define thrilling as exciting, stimulating."

She'd have to be careful on this one. "I'd say that certain aspects of my life are stimulating."

"Not exciting?" Leaning to her, he reached to wipe away a dab of mustard trapped in a corner of her mouth, taking her aback with the unexpected gesture. "Your life isn't exciting?"

Easing back from him, Gaylan scrambled to her feet. "On a scale of one to ten, I'd say I'm hovering around four in the exciting department." Squinting, she gazed out to sea at a sailboat skimming along the calm surface. "We'd better be getting back. I think I've had enough sun for one day." And enough questions.

Rising, Hunter stepped closer, aware that her back was mere inches from the palm tree that prevented her from moving away. "I think you underestimate yourself. In the exciting department, I'd label you at least a nine."

"We aren't talking about me, per se, being exciting, but my life in general," she corrected, looking around for a trash can.

"Now who's employing semantics?" Taking her beer can from her, he tossed both into a nearby metal container. "Thanks for lunch." On the path, he turned back toward her. No one was around that he needed to impress with their marital unity. Yet he wanted the contact anyhow. He held out his hand to her.

Without hesitation, Gaylan put her hand in his and they started back toward the Ocean Tower.

He was loosening up around her, she thought with satisfaction. This afternoon had definitely been a step in the right direction, despite their word skirmishes. As in his business dealings, Hunter had this insatiable need to outmaneuver the other person in conversations. Apparently he had to feel like a winner even in casual chats, because if he didn't, he'd be a loser.

And, from what she'd observed about Hunter James II, that was one thing he'd never consider himself.

"It was a fine performance," Taro commented as he accepted a cup of tea from Gaylan. "I wouldn't have thought, in this remote place, they'd have such a talented opera company."

"I agree," Yasu said, politely refusing the refreshment with a shake of her head. "Thank you for taking us, Mr. James."

Hunter acknowledged her appreciation with a nod as he watched Gaylan serve their guests. They were seated in the living room of the suite, discussing the production of *Madame Butterfly* they'd all attended that evening. He wasn't much of an opera buff, but he'd thought his guests would enjoy the show, which apparently they had.

"It was every bit as good as the performance I saw last summer in New York," Gaylan interjected as she took her seat alongside Hunter.

"How do you think the two compare?" Nari asked Hunter.

Oops, Gaylan thought, glancing at him. She'd slipped up, for, of course, he hadn't been with her in New York.

"The voices in this production were better than any I've heard," Hunter said smoothly. He turned to Gaylan, noting the apology in her eyes. "Wouldn't you say so, sweetheart?"

A close call. She smiled with relief. "Absolutely." When his arm resting on the seatback settled on her shoulders, she felt he was undoubtedly playing the devoted husband role to the hilt, especially when his hand squeezed her shoulder affectionately. But then, he'd warned her that, as supposed newlyweds, they'd be expected to display a few tender gestures in public.

"Of course, the opera takes place during World War II," Taro went on, "yet I wonder how much has changed in Japanese-American relations since then."

"A great deal, I think," Ross said. "People have begun to realize that Eastern and Western philosophies have more in common than they'd originally thought. Intermarriage has helped ease tensions, as well."

"Are you in favor of intermarriages?" Yoshiko asked, surprising the others as she so seldom joined in the conversation.

"Yes," Ross answered immediately. "In America, we believe in blending cultures. It leads to better understanding among nations as well." He loosened the knot of his wide polka-dot tie.

"You must understand that we have less enthusiasm for intermarrying than Americans," Taro explained. "The Japanese have centuries of culture behind them and a basic purist outlook, whereas America is a melting pot. It is taking us longer to accept other philosophies."

"But we're coming along," Yasu said, directing her words at Ross as she ran a hand through her short, black hair. "We have strong feelings about family values and the importance of generational ties. We can relate to Americans who also feel that way, who are proud of their heritage, whatever it may be."

"For instance," Hiroki chimed in for the first time, "businesses being passed down from father to son. And including the entire family when we travel, even on business trips." He smiled at Hunter as he stroked his thick mustache. "Apparently you share our philosophy since your wife is here with you. My father and I have noticed in our dealings that this isn't always so, which is why we're so pleased you and Gaylan have strong family values."

Hunter wasn't thrilled with the direction of the conversation, but he didn't want to be obvious in changing the subject. Discussing families and family values always made him uncomfortable since he'd been raised in an autocratic household where his parents had agreed on very little. Still, he'd gone to a lot of trouble and expense in hiring Gaylan in order to present a strong family image to the Yamaguchis. If only he didn't feel so damn hypocritical, a factor he hadn't considered when he'd begun this deception. His glance at Gaylan told him she, too, was uneasy with tonight's discussion.

"As newlyweds," Hunter began, hoping to find a way out of this dead end, "we naturally want to spend as much of our time together as possible." He sent Gaylan a loving look and saw her concerned frown disappear, to be quickly replaced by a warm smile. She was quick on the uptake, he was pleased to notice.

Catching the hint, Ross got to his feet. "Why don't we let the newlyweds have a little privacy," he suggested. "Yasu, would you like to go for a walk on the beach with me? It's a lovely night."

Hunter was grateful for Ross's assistance and yet surprised that he was suggesting time alone with the young Japanese lawyer. In their long association, he'd never once seen Ross show interest in a woman they worked with.

"I would enjoy that, yes." Yasu rose and again thanked her hosts for the pleasant evening.

The others followed suit and in minutes, Hunter and Gaylan were alone. As Hunter closed the door, Gaylan let out a relieved sigh, glad the evening was over. More often now, the strain of this make-believe marriage was taking its toll on her. She began to gather up the tea things to place them in the pantry.

"Leave those," Hunter said. "The maid comes in the morning."

"I know, but I don't want her to think we're slobs."

Hunter took off his jacket and undid his tie. "I'm sure she's seen worse."

At the buffet, she automatically stopped to check the soil in a potted plant. Finding it too dry, she filled the sprinkling can with water in the pantry kitchen and returned to give the wandering jew a drink, unaware that Hunter was watching her, genuinely puzzled.

"Why are you doing that? The hotel staff takes care of the plants."

"It takes but a moment. The cleaning people are busy—they might forget."

Slipping off his tie, he walked over to her, not bothering to hide an amused smile. "Do you talk to them, too?"

Gaylan didn't take offense. The man was so accustomed to having others do for him that he could scarcely imagine someone getting pleasure from tending a plant. "Sometimes. Plants thrive on love, just like people and pets. Take this one. See the yellowing leaves? That's a sign that it's been neglected in the past, allowed to get really dry, then overwatered to compensate. Careless attention is as bad as no attention. Again, just like with children or puppies."

He didn't quite see the comparison as clearly as she.

Finishing, she looked at him. "Do you have plants in your house?"

"Yes. A plant service maintains them on a regular schedule."

She looked genuinely shocked. "You're serious? What a shame. Gardening and working with growing things is nourishment for the soul. You ought to try it sometime."

He shook his head, rubbing the back of his neck. "You're beginning to sound like a fortune cookie."

Gaylan laughed. "So I am. Time to get some rest. Good night."

He searched for something, anything, to prolong the evening, no longer questioning why. "You want a nightcap?"

"Thanks, but no. See you in the morning."

"Right." Hunter watched her close her door, then turned and walked to the sideboard. An impressive array of bottles containing everything from fine wines to expensive liquors and exotic liqueurs were lined up on the glass shelf. He'd have sipped on one if she'd stayed. Alone, he didn't much feel like it.

Strolling to his bedroom, he wondered why lately being alone had somehow lost its appeal. Taro and Yoshiko were in their room, as were Nari and Hiroki, undoubtedly enjoying a second honeymoon. Even Ross and Yasu were out there somewhere walking on the beach. Only Evan had begged off early with a headache.

And, on the other side of the suite in the smaller bedroom, Gaylan was undressing, preparing for bed. While he was doing the same in his room, although he wasn't in the least bit sleepy. He could, of course, get his briefcase and do some work, which in the past he often had until the wee hours. Or he could read one of several books he'd brought along, something he rarely had time for.

Slipping off his shoes, he stared out through the glass door to the lanai that faced the ocean. Too nice an evening not to enjoy fresh air. He slid open the door and inhaled the scent of the sea. Turning, he gazed at the huge king-size bed.

Unbidden, his mind pictured Gaylan lying on the dark blue sheets, her blond hair spread on the pillow, her arms inviting him to come to her. Where had that thought been born?

Shaking his head in an effort to clear it, Hunter went into the bathroom to finish undressing.

She couldn't get to sleep. No matter how much she tossed and turned, sleep eluded her. Though she'd had trouble resting since the day Evan had come to her with Hunter's offer, it had never been as bad as tonight. The luminous digital clock showed 2:00 a.m. and she was still wide awake.

Giving in, Gaylan rose, pulled on her pale green robe and pushed open the door of her lanai. She stepped out, looking up at a nearly full moon in a cloudy sky, letting the salty breeze caress her warm cheeks. She felt slightly flushed, oddly restless. From below, she could hear the waves rolling in to shore. Listening to the ocean was supposed to be calming, soothing. Moving the lounge chair out of the way, she walked to the chest-high ledge. Perhaps some fresh air would pacify her restlessness and clear the cobwebs.

Hunter heard a noise, like something scraping on cement, and sat up in bed. He hadn't been asleep and he was certain the sound had come from the direction of his lanai. Hunter rose and walked outside, his bare feet quiet.

She was standing on her balcony, alongside the one next to his. The breeze lifted her hair and tossed it about her head, but she seemed oblivious to the capricious play. She stared out toward the sea, lost in her thoughts. As she shifted her stance, he caught a glimpse of her face and realized her thoughts weren't happy ones. Her expression appeared haunted and inexplicably sad.

Soundlessly he stepped through the connecting gate and walked over until only one small railing separated them. So quiet was he that she didn't hear him, or perhaps she was too involved in her troublesome thoughts. The long, pale robe whirled about her bare ankles, the silken material clinging to her delicate frame, causing his mouth to go dry. She was so lovely and yet so melancholy. What had caused her usually cheerful facade to slip? he wondered.

Letting out a shuddery sigh, Gaylan turned, then gasped as she saw Hunter standing in the shadows. Her hand flew to grasp her robe together. "You...you startled me."

"I didn't mean to." He opened the gate and stepped across.

There was enough moonlight for her to see that he wore only a pair of silk paisley shorts, his bare chest all too near. She took a step back only to find herself against the ledge just behind her.

"Are you all right?" Hunter asked. Surely she wasn't frightened of him.

"Yes." Her voice was throaty, low, one she hardly recognized. His eyes stayed locked on hers and she felt herself drowning in their gray depths. She wanted so badly to tell him that she wasn't all right at all, that she was lonely and frightened of an uncertain future. She was afraid for her brother and wondering how long she could justify this crazy deception she'd agreed to. She hated the lying, hated fooling the Yamaguchis, whom she'd grown to like a great deal.

How could she tell Hunter that she longed to have strong arms hold her for just a little while, arms that would be a comfort, not a threat? So used to being the supportive one, always there for Mel, on her own at an early age, sometimes it all got to be too much a burden for her to carry alone. Unable to say the words, Gaylan let her eyes speak for her.

Something was wrong, Hunter knew, something she couldn't put into words. Not one to easily confide his own worries, he understood that and respected her for her silent struggle. He could see she was trying to remain brave, trying to carry the load alone. He could also see a need in her that she likely couldn't define. Acting instinctively, he pulled her close to his chest as his arms encircled her.

Gaylan closed her eyes, accepting what he offered, unable to resist the strength she was seeking. Inhaling his heady male scent, she absorbed this moment of comfort. She was in the wrong place with the wrong man, but for now, she would welcome the solace he offered.

His heart beating steadily beneath her ear gave her a peaceful feeling. His hands on her back gently rubbing sent pleasant waves through her. Always she'd known that there was a time to give and a time to take. Gratefully Gaylan took.

How long they stood like that, Hunter later couldn't have said. The gentle sea breeze made an effort at cooling his heated skin, yet her small hands spread heat wherever they touched. He rested his cheek on her head, breathing in the by-now-familiar scent of her hair. And his heart picked up its rhythm.

She felt the change, in his breathing, in his heartbeat, in the way his hands stilled, then shifted to press her nearer. As if in slow motion, Gaylan eased back and raised her eyes to his. She should move away, she knew. Only two wisps of filmy cloth stood between her and Hunter's chest. If he kissed her now, when she was so filled with inexplicable longing, there'd be no mistaking her desire. The wise thing would be to just say goodnight.

Wise moves were rarely satisfying. Gaylan rose on her tiptoes until her lips were inches from his, and paused, waiting.

Stronger men than he would have difficulty refusing such an invitation, Hunter thought as he lowered his head a fraction and took her mouth. He heard her make a small sound deep in her throat and tightened his arms around her. Pliant, her lips moved against his. And his head began to swim.

She tasted like moonlight and summer rain and sweet surrender. Her slender body molding to his shouldn't feel so good, so damn right. Needs grew, expanded, clamored for attention. Shaken, Hunter struggled for the control that so seldom eluded him.

He was big, strong, powerful. There was no mistaking that Gaylan was drawn to that strength, that power. She felt as if there was a storm brewing in him, one he fought against. He wanted her, of that she was certain. His hands skimming down her back, pressing her closer, made certain she knew how much he wanted her. All her life she'd searched for a man who'd want her so fiercely, who'd make her feel so much.

He shifted, taking her deeper, his tongue possessing her mouth. She'd never thought a kiss could blow the top of her head clean off, but that's how she felt now.

She wasn't completely innocent. She'd felt desire, had known passion. But not like this. Dear God, not like this when every part of her yearned for more. And still more. When every pore seemed alive and capable of intense feeling. When every muscle was made weak and her brain turned to mush.

His hands shifted to thrust into her hair, his breathing labored, his mouth loath to separate from hers. He was throbbing, aching, consumed with need. He wanted to drag her into the bedroom, to make love with her till neither could move, till the sun rose high in the sky.

The sun that would bring morning. And reality.

Hunter wrenched himself from her, moving back a step or two. Breathing hard, he turned from her, could not look at her. He called himself every vile name he could think of to have led her on—led them both on—only to have harsh reality intrude.

He hated being sensible. But their arrangement was a professional one and he had no business changing the rules in midstream. He brushed a shaky hand over his face. "I'm sorry, Gaylan. I can't seem to mind my manners around you."

Manners! Did he think he'd committed a breach of etiquette by kissing the hired help?

Drawing her robe tightly around her, she held her head high. "It's all right. I'll try to remember my place in the future." Turning, she reentered her bedroom.

Her remark made him feel worse than ever. "Wait! That's not what I meant."

But before he'd finished, she'd closed the heavy glass door.

Swearing ripely under his breath, Hunter stomped back to his own room.

Chapter Six

Hunter sat at the head of the dining room table conducting their usual morning business meeting in his suite, for all outward appearances looking completely in control. But his thoughts wandered and he was getting worried.

Gaylan had been gone since 6:00 a.m.

The sun hadn't been up long when he'd come out of his room dressed for running, tapped on her door and found she'd already left. Since that first morning he'd found her sitting on the rock gazing out to sea, they'd run together by mutual agreement. Always in the same direction, always returning after about an hour.

Today, he'd followed their usual path and she was nowhere to be seen. Although he had a morning meeting scheduled, he'd run for a while in the opposite direction, trying to catch a glimpse of her. To no avail.

Annoyed, he'd returned, showered and gone right into the morning session at eight.

As Evan and Yasu discussed a legal point, Hunter snuck a peek at his watch. Eleven. Where the hell was she?

With her fair coloring, even with a previous tan, if she'd been out in the sun for five hours, she'd likely have a burn by now. She didn't strike him as careless. Had she wanted to get away from him so badly after last night's scene on her lanai that she'd risk skin cancer to avoid him? No. She didn't strike him as stupid, either.

Early on, he'd told her that for the most part, the mornings were hers to do with as she saw fit, since he'd be tied up in meetings till about one. Several times, after their run and a quick shared breakfast, she'd gone to play tennis with Nari. He'd checked the courts on his way up and she hadn't been there, either. Nari had slept in this morning, Hiroki had mentioned in answer to Hunter's deliberately casual inquiry. Yoshiko was attending a lecture on Hawaiian flower arranging given by the hotel, her husband had volunteered. Everyone else was here. Hunter tried to look unconcerned as he caught Ross studying him curiously.

It wasn't that he needed her for anything. It's just that because of the way they'd parted last night, he wanted to talk with her, to make sure she understood why he'd said what he'd said. After all, it was important to his relationship with the Yamaguchis that Gaylan and he present a picture of marital bliss. That's what he'd hired her to do, pose as his loving wife. If she was still angry with him, she'd likely be unable to hide it. He needed to remind her of her commitment.

It wasn't that he was worried about her, but rather concerned about their working relationship, he told himself.

Volleyball, he suddenly remembered. She'd probably run into those muscled beach boys who never seemed to have anything to do other than play in the sun. Even as he sat here seething, she was probably out there jumping around, whacking the ball like the carefree coed she sometimes resembled. Then again, as when they'd attended the opera, she could look cool and sophisticated wearing a long black dress that left one shoulder bare and clung in all the right places.

He'd had trouble keeping his eyes from her that night. As he was having trouble keeping his mind from straying to her now.

He shouldn't have gone to her last night. When he had gone out on his lanai and seen her standing there, he should have just let her be. After all, she was his employee, not his responsibility. If she was troubled, they were *her* troubles and not his concern. But she'd drawn him to her like a magnet.

All right, so she'd needed comforting, for whatever reason. Why hadn't he just let it go at that, released her and left her? Because, when she'd risen on tiptoe and looked up at him with those huge, vulnerable eyes, comfort had turned to desire. There it was again, the simple if painful truth: he wanted her.

And he couldn't have her.

Which was why, after kissing her breathless, he'd found the strength from somewhere to turn away, to apologize. But it was that very apology that she'd misinterpreted. If only she'd stayed a minute or two longer, he'd have explained. He was unused to having to justify his actions. He was rusty at male-female relationships, not having had many beyond fleeting encounters.

The women he was used to knew better than to expect more than he was willing to give. Hunter liked it that way, clear-cut, everything out in the open. Each knew what to expect from the other and no one got hurt.

But Gaylan was different. She was a romantic through and through, by her own admission. She was a dreamer who undoubtedly envisioned a bright future with Mr. Right. Probably a wealthy Mr. Right, if her past work history could be considered a factor. Had her mother once told her it was just as easy to fall in love with a rich man as a poor one? So she worked for millionaires in the wild hope that she'd meet a rich man who'd whisk her away on his white horse and they'd live happily ever after.

What hogwash! How could any intelligent person believe in such an obvious fairy tale? And Gaylan was intelligent. But she was setting herself up for a big fall. There *was* no happily-ever-after. Marriages weren't made in heaven, but rather more likely put together in a lawyer's office, where they also all too often ended a short time later in divorce.

He wasn't jaded, Hunter insisted to himself. He'd just learned the hard way. He'd believed once, too, though observing his parents' indifferent marriage should have been a warning. Of course, he was ten years older than Gaylan. She, too, would learn. But he didn't want to be her teacher.

He wished fervently that she didn't attract him, didn't muddle his mind, didn't distract him so repeatedly. Her beauty, her wit, her genuine warmth had him wanting to pull her closer, even though his experience told him he should be keeping her at arm's length. Because no matter the attraction, when these two weeks were over, he would go his way and send her on hers. He had no intention of a permanent alliance with any woman.

Especially a woman like Gaylan. Instinctively he knew she could weaken him, could even destroy him. He'd vowed after Jolene that he'd never allow another woman to get close enough to hurt him. It was a vow he meant to keep.

Perhaps he hadn't explained himself fully to her, Hunter decided. He would, at the next opportunity. He didn't want her to get hurt, either. He actually liked her, enjoyed her. If only she wasn't a forever woman, they could have shared a pleasant interlude during this stay. But he could spot the happily-ever-after types a mile away. Religiously he avoided them.

Until Gaylan.

Yes, he would set her straight this very day. As soon as she returned and they were alone. He looked at his watch again. Where in hell had she gone?

"We've examined a number of possibilities regarding shipping," Ross was saying. He picked up a thick report from his folder and handed it to Taro, then passed copies to Hiroki and Yasu. "This is the comparison study and we think you'll agree with our conclusions." He glanced at Hunter and found him toying with his pen, his eyes downcast. It was so unlike him to be distracted during business meetings that Ross wondered if his employer was feeling well.

"Our recommendation is quick, efficient and reasonable in cost. It's the same method we've used with our East Coast affiliate, and that whole operation's run very smoothly. Hunter can tell you more about that."

Again, Ross looked over at Hunter, who seemed not to have heard him. In the silence, everyone seated around the table glanced up from the report, their eyes sliding to Hunter, waiting. Ross cleared his throat somewhat noisily. "Hunter?"

Suddenly aware that his name had been spoken, Hunter straightened in his chair and noticed everyone looking at him. He sent a questioning look to Ross.

"Would you please explain how our shipping methods have worked with our East Coast affiliates?"

Long ago, Hunter had schooled himself to keep a poker face at these meetings. His discipline came through as he quickly picked up the ball and launched into the requested explanation. He couldn't help noticing the relief on Ross's face and the worried frown on Evan's.

Never had he wished this badly for a meeting to end.

Gaylan got off the Ocean Tower elevator on the top floor and walked slowly along the outdoor hallway carrying her zippered case under her arm. Needing to be alone this morning, she'd left the suite earlier than usual and run in the opposite direction from her usual jogs with Hunter. Finally, comfortably tired, she'd gone to the lower-level pool area and had two glasses of juice at the outdoor stand.

Hunter wouldn't think to look for her there, for it had been already crowded despite the early hour. He didn't like crowds. Children inevitably rose with the sun, and swimming was a good outlet for their energy. Finding a shady tree, Gaylan had tugged over a lounge chair and happily wiled away the hours sketching youngsters on floats, rushing down a short waterfall slide, struggling to swim wearing bright orange water wings.

She'd guessed that Hunter might be searching for her. Not to explain himself, for Gaylan felt that he embraced Henry Ford II's philosophy of "never complain, never explain." No, he'd be looking for her to make sure she remembered for the rest of their stay that she was the employee and he the employer. And never the twain should meet, at least not on a romantic level.

Oh, she knew he wanted her physically. That much was unmistakable, not just when he kissed her; she could read it in his eyes. Yet he didn't *want* to want her. She wasn't suitable in his eyes, not for a millionaire executive of Hunter James II's caliber. Gaylan wondered if there existed a woman he'd consider suitable.

Jolene had scarred him, and scared him. Gaylan couldn't help but wonder what his marriage had been like really. Could she believe his version? Or had his wife simply tired of Hunter's unflagging devotion to acquiring more and more money, to "playing the game and winning," as he'd put it? Perhaps Jolene had wanted love and affection at the outset, and had had to settle for a business relationship.

The rich and powerful *were* different. Gaylan had learned that long ago as she'd watched Reuben wield his unsteady authority from his wheelchair and seen his two sons swagger and scramble, competing with each other to be the main heir apparent. Hunter had inherited millions at an early age, then doubled his father's wealth, according to Evan. That sort of potency was bound to affect a man, to make him arrogant and something of a control freak. Though Hunter would deny her assessment.

The man needed humanizing, needed to see that people were more important than possessions and power, and that, especially as he grew older, money and stock certificates would make lonely bedfellows. On the afternoon they'd played volleyball and shared hot dogs and beer, she'd begun to think that he was teachable. Then, last night, he'd denied his desire and turned from her, remembering belatedly that she was hired help, albeit a well-paid one. Gaylan cringed at the memory.

She shouldn't have gone up on tiptoe and blatantly offered herself to him. Chalk it up to loneliness and a longing for closeness that had overcome her good sense. She wouldn't make that mistake again. She would remember her place and not let him see that he'd hurt her. She would play her role, be the laughing, affectionate "wife" he'd hired her to be whenever the Yamaguchis were present.

But in their private moments, she would try to steer clear of probing or intimate conversations. She had to guard her heart, which was reluctantly softening toward the goodness she saw in him, the unprotected part he fought against revealing to others. If she didn't take some protective measures, she'd find herself in that loneliest of all places, in love all alone.

Reaching the double doors of the suite, Gaylan took out her key and put on her friendly, wifely face, for she knew the meeting would still be going on. Entering, she noticed the conversation dwindle around the table as people looked up. Everyone gave her some sort of greeting. Everyone except Hunter, who watched her with a closed expression.

Smiling, Gaylan stepped closer. "Hello. Isn't it a perfectly gorgeous day?"

"Yes, indeed," Taro remarked, pushing his glasses higher on his nose. "I'd rather be out on the golf course than in here."

"Have you been walking?" Ross asked, guessing that Hunter's restlessness might be related to Gaylan's long absence.

Gaylan removed the gold clip that had held her hair pulled back. "Some. And I sat at the pool watching the children. There're quite a few staying here."

"Yes," Taro agreed. "It's a family facility. Something for everyone. I only wish my grandson were here."

"Gaylan," Hiroki said, "Nari asked me to tell you she's made a reservation on the helicopter picnic to the hotel's private island for the four of us. I guess you two discussed the outing yesterday. We leave at three from the heliport."

She was taken aback. "The four of us?"

Hiroki nodded. "You and Hunter, she and I."

Gaylan had discussed the trip with Nari, along with several other jaunts the hotel offered, as Hunter had once suggested. But she'd meant that Nari would go alone with her husband, never considering the woman would go ahead and include her and Hunter. "I don't know..." She glanced at Hunter.

"I think that's a great idea," Hunter said. Maybe this trip, with Hiroki and Nari along as buffers, would get him back on track with Gaylan. And chances were they'd find some time to talk alone, as well.

She saw no way out since both men were looking at her expectantly. "All right," she said, finding a smile.

Hunter wondered what was in the case she was carrying, but decided it was none of his business. He turned to Hiroki. "Good, then we'll meet you both at the heliport at three."

"I need a shower," Gaylan said, deciding it was time to take her leave. She started toward her bedroom, then realized the Yamaguchis thought she was sharing the master suite with Hunter. All of her things were there anyhow. Covering her tracks, she stopped at the small refrigerator in the pantry for a soft drink, then continued on to Hunter's room, closing the door.

She prayed the meeting wouldn't end until she'd freshened up. Then all she'd have to do would be to avoid being alone with Hunter until it was time to join the others at three.

The helipad was a wide circle of cement on the far side of the hotel. As Hunter and Gaylan arrived, they saw Hiroki pacing and the pilot already seated in the helicopter, about to start the engine.

"Where's your wife?" Hunter asked above the noise.

"I tried calling you," Hiroki explained, "but you must have been on your way here. Nari's got one of her bad headaches. She tried lying down to get rid of it, but she simply doesn't feel well enough to take the trip. I'm sorry."

"I am, too," Gaylan said, wondering why Hiroki wasn't his usual smiling self. Surely he wasn't that disappointed over one small outing. "Please tell her I hope she feels better soon. We'll go another day."

"Nonsense," Hunter said firmly. "We're here, the picnic dinner's on board and the pilot's ready to roll. We'll go alone." He patted Hiroki's shoulder. "Our best to Nari." He held out his hand to help Gaylan aboard.

Gaylan tossed her head back to get her hair out of her eyes, blown about by the whirling blades overhead.

"Are you sure you don't want to wait a few days and go with them?" she asked Hunter hopefully.

"Go on and enjoy yourselves," Hiroki interjected. "It's already paid for. Our treat." He stepped back and waved, looking as if he were anxious to be on his way. "Have fun."

There seemed no easy way out. Gaylan stepped aboard and took her seat, fastening the belt firmly around her. She'd never been in such a small helicopter, just the larger ones that flew between airports in New York. She wondered if her sudden queasiness was due to fear of flying or fear of being alone with Hunter.

"Hiroki seemed worried about something, didn't you think?" Gaylan commented.

"Maybe he and his wife are squabbling," Hunter answered, taking his seat and fastening his belt.

The pilot leaned over and pulled the door shut, locking them in. Sitting down behind the wheel, he looked over his shoulder at them. "My name's Jim. Welcome aboard. I hope you brought your camera because I'm going to give you a dazzling tour of the big island before I drop you at Kalekiani's island for your private picnic."

"How long does the tour last, Jim?" Hunter asked, guessing that the pilot had no idea that he owned the hotel, and meaning to keep it that way. He'd never tried out most of the hotel's facilities, and this would give him an excellent opportunity to check out at least one trip.

"About an hour."

"What's the weather report? I see some pretty dark clouds off in the distance."

"Not uncommon late afternoons. Don't worry. If it starts to rain, we'll head back here real fast." He prepared the helicopter for lift-off. "I've been doing this for five years and haven't lost a passenger yet. Relax and talk among yourselves."

They could talk, they just couldn't hear each other very well over the sound of the motor and blades coupled with the wind. Gaylan clutched the armrests as they climbed upward, their ascent a bit shaky. Soon they were over the ocean, looking down at the changing colors of blue and green, the moss-covered lava rocks and the whitecaps.

She was watching a boat with a bright yellow sail billowing in a hefty breeze, when Hunter's hand closed over hers. She jumped, turning to look at him.

"Beautiful, isn't it?" he asked, close to her ear.

She nodded, then turned back to the window. She'd managed to avoid him by lying down fully dressed on his bed on top of the spread and feigning sleep after her shower. She'd heard him come in, check on her, then quietly leave. She hadn't come out until it was time to go to the heliport. He'd been quietly watchful, but hadn't initiated a real conversation. She could relax during the tour, but what about when the pilot plunked them down on the picnic site and left them there for a "secluded rendezvous" as the brochure had called it?

Gaylan was pretty sure neither of them wanted anything of the sort right now. Why, then, had Hunter insisted they go on this picnic? The pilot spoke into his headset microphone and she tugged her attention back to what he was saying.

"We're approaching the north coast of the island," Jim said in his tour-conductor voice, "which is inaccessible any other way due to the sheer sea cliffs made mostly of lava rock. As we move along, we'll be seeing part of the famous Parker Ranch and farther on around, the Kilauea volcano. If we're lucky, she'll give us a fiery show with a little explosion or two.''

Gaylan thought she'd just as soon skip seeing a fiery volcano explosion, but she didn't think either man aboard shared her opinion. Hunter seemed surprisingly fascinated, glued to his window and leaning forward to ask Jim an occasional question. She hadn't pegged him as the typical tourist, yet here he was, awestruck just like everyone else. She wondered why he usually tried to cover up such a purely human reaction. Lessened his sophisticated image, most likely.

For the better part of an hour, they dipped between huge cliffs rising impossibly high from the foamy sea, dodging rock outcroppings and tilting crazily at incredible angles. They rose straight up at times, then bobbed downward. Gaylan was left feeling dizzy as they spiraled along a deep gorge, then rode so low she thought for a minute Jim was going to land along a small stretch of pure white sand.

But he soon soared upward again and finally they were approaching a small strip of land seemingly all alone in the middle of the ocean.

"There it is, folks, Kalekiani's island. The only way in or out is by helicopter. The hotel also offers sailing excursions over here by reservation. There's a grassy picnic area, a ramada and functional if not elegant bathroom facilities.'' He pointed off to the side toward a thick forest. "That's where the pandanus trees grow. They produce lauhala leaves, which the Hawaiians make into baskets, the finest you can buy. You'll find rubber plants and flowering bushes, as well as palm trees. As you can see, on this side there's a steep cliff, but if you like to walk, there's a secluded sandy beach about a quarter of a mile across, and some interesting lava caves."

"Look at that," Hunter said, leaning over and pointing out Gaylan's window.

A series of cascading waterfalls raced down the black face of the cliff in pale blue stripes. Stunned by the beauty, Gaylan looked around, trying to take it all in.

Maneuvering the vehicle deftly, Jim had them hovering over the small landing spot at the leveled-off top of the cliffside. Gaylan was certain the pilot could have landed on a dime, so expertly did he put her down. He slid open the door and pointed to a large cooler alongside a picnic basket. "There's your dinner and supplies. I'll be back for you in a couple of hours, around six."

Hunter had enjoyed the tour, but he was still a little concerned about the weather. Several lingering heavy clouds looked to be dark with rain, and the sky had shifted from a bright blue to a pale gray, unusual for only four in the afternoon in Hawaii. "What if we get a storm?"

"I'll be back early if it begins to rain." He pointed vaguely to the left. "There's a makeshift thatched hut near the tree line over that way in case the rain beats me. But it shouldn't. This isn't our rainy season."

"That's a comfort," Hunter said, stepping out. He helped Gaylan alight, then hauled out the cooler and basket. They ducked low to avoid the blades and walked to a grassy area surrounded by pandanus and palm trees. Together they watched Jim lift off and head back in the direction of their hotel.

Gaylan listened to the disappearing sound of the motor, then the sudden silence. It felt somewhat spooky to be all alone on an uninhabited island with the only accessibility the helicopter quickly moving away from them. Alone with the elements, capricious tropical weather patterns and no real shelter.

She rubbed her forehead, wondering how she'd allowed herself to be talked into this silly trip. She, too, could have claimed a headache. As a matter of fact, she just might develop one real quick all alone here with Hunter, who was already looking at her oddly.

Hunter set down their things and opened the basket. On top was a plaid blanket and a blue checkered tablecloth. "Are you hungry?"

"Actually, I am," Gaylan answered, helping him spread the blanket and cloth on the long, silky grass. She hadn't had either breakfast or lunch, although she'd drunk a lot of juice and iced tea.

Sitting down on the blanket, Hunter opened the food cooler. "Let's see. We have cold chicken, lobster salad, tomatoes, assorted cheeses. A loaf of French bread."

Her mouth beginning to water, Gaylan leaned over for a peek. "Here's a can of liver pâté and a jar of caviar. The brochure did say this would be a gourmet picnic."

"I've never liked caviar. Very plebeian of me, I know."

"I don't like it, either. Too salty." They both laughed, and Gaylan felt some of the tension ease. She dug back into the basket. "Look at these huge strawberries. And chilled grapes. They look luscious." She popped one into her mouth.

Hunter returned his attention to the basket. "Ahh, here's the best part. A bottle of white wine in a chilled container. And a bottle of red." Hunter examined the labels. "Not bad. Which would you like?" He dug out two glasses.

"The white, please. Two bottles. Are they trying to get us drunk?"

"They packed enough for four, remember?" He got the bottle open and poured them each a glass. He started to take a sip, but her hand on his arm stopped him.

"We have to toast," Gaylan insisted.

He'd forgotten her romantic streak. "What shall we toast?"

Thoughtfully she gazed up and saw a gray cloud block the sun. "How about to sunny skies?" It seemed bland enough.

"Not to the future or to happiness always?"

She supposed she deserved his teasing. "Are you making fun of me?"

The cloud moved on and sun poured down on her, turning her hair golden. Hunter fought not to reach out and touch it. She was sucking him under again, making him forget his resolutions to have that talk with her. Looking into her clear blue eyes, he forgot what he'd planned to say. "No," he answered seriously. "I think I'm making fun of me." He clinked his glass to hers. "To sunny skies."

Gaylan lay down on the blanket on her stomach, propping up on her elbows, staring into her wineglass, wondering what he meant by that.

Hunter decided it was time to take the bull by the horns. "About last night..."

She looked up. "What about last night?"

"That kiss. I..."

"Oh, that." She forced a laugh. "No big deal. I've forgotten it already." She gazed off at the distant water, not wanting him to read the lie in her eyes.

Forgotten it? The memory kept revisiting him and she'd forgotten it. From her profile, he couldn't tell if she was lying or if she meant it. Well, hell, isn't that what he'd wanted, Gaylan's not making a big deal out of a little kiss? He hadn't wanted her to misinterpret his momentary lapse, to start thinking romantically about something that had been merely a surge of moonlight madness.

Why, then, was he just a little hurt that she was so easily dismissing a kiss that had rocked him to the soles of his feet? He cleared his throat. "Right. Me, too," he lied. "I'm glad you feel the same. You left so abruptly that I wasn't sure. It was just that we were both feeling restless and—"

"And there was moonlight and we just reacted to the moment. It was nothing more than that." She took another sip of wine and hoped he didn't notice that her hand was trembling.

"Exactly." Hunter let out what he hoped sounded like a relieved sigh. "I'm glad we had this talk. I wouldn't want you to get the wrong idea."

"Certainly not. What we have is a strictly business arrangement." If her feelings had shifted, if her attraction to him had increased, it wasn't his fault, Gaylan told herself. He was still sticking to the game plan and she would, too. If it took every ounce of strength she had.

"Yes, strictly business. Attraction aside, we're very different, you and I. We don't want the same things out of life."

She turned to study him as he sat cross-legged, reaching for a cluster of grapes. He had on navy slacks and a blue striped shirt. She wondered if he'd purchased the casual outfit in the hotel shop after she'd commented on his ultraconservative taste. His boat shoes were new, but at least he hadn't worn wing tips. How she'd love to liven up his wardrobe. She pictured him in a pair of well-worn jeans, the material soft, hugging his thighs. He had a great body, but he hid it behind layers of dark, dreary clothes. You'd think the man had been born in London instead of California.

It was none of her business, Gaylan reminded herself. If he chose to wear Nehru suits or an Indian loincloth, she could not care less. Their arrangement didn't include anything personal, anything intimate. Why, then, did she want to move closer, to touch him, to see if what she'd felt last night was a fluke of moonlight or a soul-wrenching sensation she'd never felt before?

He seemed unusually introspective today, and she wondered why. She'd told herself she wouldn't get into anything but superficial conversations with him when they were alone, but her curiosity outweighed her caution. "What is it you think I want from life?"

Hunter lay down on his back, shielding his eyes from the sun and from her probing gaze by an upraised arm. "What most women want. Money. Things to go your way. Your future assured."

She frowned. "I thought you said we didn't want the same things. That sounds more like your list than mine."

He'd walked into that one. "All right, tell me your list."

"I want to be self-sufficient, to make my own way, to earn my own living and not have to answer to anyone."

His face registered surprise, then he nodded approvingly. "You must have a nice nest egg set aside since working for Reuben Cramer. Along with what you earn on this trip, you should be able to strike out on your own. What line of work are you planning on going into?'' And wasn't it going to be difficult for a woman who'd lived in the style of a millionaire for over six years to plod along in a new venture?

She knew exactly what she'd do, if only it would work out, Gaylan thought. As soon as she completed this job, she'd contact Helen and query several literary agents until they found one who believed in their efforts. Then they'd let the agent find the right publisher. But first, she had to get Mel out of prison, and had to have enough money to live on until she and Helen established a strong reputation in the business.

A nice nest egg put away, indeed! If only he knew. Mel's disregard for the law had taken up everything she'd been able to set aside, and then some. All she had was her small, mortgaged house and her six-year-old Volkswagen. Still, if all went according to plan after these two weeks, she'd make it work somehow. But she wasn't about to tell Hunter about Mel, her financial worries or her own dreams. He was a man who believed in hard reality, not dreams. She couldn't stand the thought of his laughing at her.

Gaylan sat up. ''Oh, something will turn up when the time's right.'' She tore off a piece of bread. ''Say, let's eat. I'm starving.''

Hunter rose and reached for the plates at the bottom of the basket. Something will turn up, she'd said. Good Lord, how could she pin her future on such a vague thought? She'd never get ahead at that rate. The money he'd pay her would drift away as she waited for something to turn up, as the money she'd earned with Reuben probably had. Pipe dreams. He'd thought her smarter than that.

They ate mostly in silence, each lost in their own thoughts. Occasionally they commented on the quality of the food or the peaceful place. Gaylan found she wasn't as hungry as she'd thought, their disturbing conversation having chased away her appetite. She sipped her wine, wondering why she felt so melancholy when nothing had really changed.

Or was it that she had?

Hunter packed their leftovers in the cooler. Only half an hour had passed. It would be a while before Jim returned. The tension between them had returned twofold. He stood, thinking they'd have to do something to fill the time.

"The island's only a quarter of a mile across, Jim said. We could go exploring a little through those trees and see if we can locate the beach."

Gaylan didn't feel adventurous. A thicket of trees in this remote area represented too many surprises. Little furry creatures, unknown slithery things, bugs. "I don't know. What about snakes?"

"There are no snakes on any of the Hawaiian islands."

"Nowhere?"

"Not a one."

"Well, what about bugs and—"

"The sea breezes keep bugs to a bare minimum." He held out a hand to help her up. "Come on. If we run into anything, we'll turn around and come back." He glanced up at a darkening sky. "I'm more concerned about the weather than bugs."

Gaylan saw what he meant. The shadowy clouds were nearly overhead and churning restlessly all around them. It wasn't even five yet and already it was getting dark.

They left the basket and cooler under a tree and started walking. It was still quite warm, the humid air thick and smelling of tropical vegetation. On the far side of the landing pad, they ran across a heavy growth of pandanus trees. Hunter led the way, keeping an easy pace.

After about ten minutes with no break in the trees evident, Gaylan grew concerned. "Where are we going?"

"Just a little farther."

The large leaves overhead kept most of the light from getting through. The wind had begun to pick up and the branches swayed in a brisk breeze, batting the green fronds against their faces. The idea of getting lost in an uninhabited area held no appeal to Gaylan. After another ten minutes, she'd had it. "Let's go back."

Hunter stopped. He supposed there wasn't much point in continuing. He'd wanted to see the beach, but he couldn't see an opening ahead. He turned around on the narrow path. "Okay."

They'd gone only a few feet when a sharp honking sound split the still air.

"My God, what's that?" Gaylan peered through the treetops.

"Sounded like a wild goose or banshee."

"Banshees aren't real. They're in Irish folklore and—"

The sudden heavy flapping of wings had them both ducking toward the protection of a tree trunk. Something large with a huge wingspan fluttered overhead, honked fiercely again, then took off.

Through a sliver of space between leaves, Hunter watched the huge bird fly off. "Well, I'll be. If it's not a goose, it sure looks like one. I've sure never seen a sea gull that big." As he continued to stare upward, he became aware of another sound—droplets falling onto the flat surface of many leaves. "Damn, it's raining. We'd better head back toward the helipad. Jim's probably on his way."

In what seemed like only mere moments, the rain became heavier and found its way through the thick foliage. Keeping her head low, Gaylan followed Hunter along the path. Water dripped onto her white tennis shirt, and her green cotton slacks were dampening quickly. The ground beneath her sandals, so dry just ten minutes ago, was turning a muddy brown. In the distance, she heard a low rumble and wished it was the helicopter. But it proved to be thunder, moving closer. How had this storm worsened so quickly?

Hunter cleared the copse of trees and could see the helipad still empty, the rain quickly drenching the area. His mouth a thin line, he realized he should have followed his earlier instinct and not left the hotel with the storm a possibility. But he'd wanted to talk with Gaylan. As she emerged from behind him, he saw that her hair was already plastered to her head and her clothes were soaked.

"Jim's not here yet," he said.

Gaylan brushed damp hair off her face. "Do you think he can take the helicopter up in a storm?"

Hunter doubted it, not with high winds. But he didn't want to alarm her further. "Let's wait and see what happens."

Just then, a huge bolt of lightning streaked alongside the cliff no more than thirty yards from them and disappeared into the restless sea waters. Gaylan grabbed his arms with frantic fingers as a clap of thunder reverberated along the ground so fiercely that they felt the tremors through their shoes. Then the murky sky turned into a wild kaleidoscope as streaks of lightning danced at various intervals and shot into the churning ocean. Answering bursts of thunder echoed all around them.

One directly overhead nearly shattered Gaylan's eardrums, so close was it. Letting out a scream, she threw herself into Hunter's arms and clung to him.

HOW TO VALIDATE YOUR
EDITOR'S FREE GIFT "THANK YOU"

1. Peel off gift seal from front cover. Place it in space provided at right. This automatically entitles you to receive four free books and a lovely Austrian Crystal Pendant.

2. Send back this card and you'll get brand-new Silhouette Special Edition® novels. These books have a cover price of $3.50 each, but they are yours to keep absolutely free.

3. There's no catch. You're under no obligation to buy anything. We charge nothing—ZERO—for your first shipment. And you don't have to make any minimum number of purchases—not even one!

4. The fact is thousands of readers enjoy receiving books by mail from the Silhouette Reader Service™ months before they're available in stores. They like the convenience of home delivery and they love our discount prices!

5. We hope that after receiving your free books you'll want to remain a subscriber. But the choice is yours—to continue or cancel, anytime at all! So why not take us up on our invitation, with no risk of any kind. You'll be glad you did!

6. Don't forget to detach your FREE BOOKMARK. And remember...just for validating your Editor's Free Gift Offer, we'll send you FIVE MORE gifts, *ABSOLUTELY FREE!*

NOT ACTUAL SIZE

YOURS FREE!
*You'll look like a million dollars when you wear this lovely necklace! Its cobra-link chain is a generous 18" long, and the multi-faceted Austrian crystal sparkles like a diamond! It's yours **absolutely free** — when you accept our no-risk offer!*

THE EDITOR'S "THANK YOU" FREE GIFTS INCLUDE:

- ▶ Four BRAND-NEW romance novels
- ▶ An Austrian Crystal Pendant

THE SILHOUETTE READER SERVICE™: HERE'S HOW IT WORKS

Accepting free books places you under no obligation to buy anything. You may keep the books and gift and return the shipping statement marked "cancel". If you do not cancel, about a month later we will send you 6 additional novels, and bill you just $2.89 each plus 25¢ delivery and applicable sales tax, if any.* That's the complete price, and—compared to cover prices of $3.50 each—quite a bargain! You may cancel at any time, but if you choose to continue, every month we'll send you 6 more books, which you may either purchase at the discount price...or return at our expense and cancel your subscription.

*Terms and prices subject to change without notice. Sales tax applicable in N.Y.

Chapter Seven

Ross Weber hung up the phone and walked over to stare out the window at the electrical storm lighting up the sky. "Damn, I wish Hunter hadn't chosen today to go on some silly helicopter ride."

Yasu came over to stand beside him. "What did the pilot tell you?"

"That he'd given them an hour's tour, then dropped them on the hotel's private island about four. He was to pick them up at six, but with these high winds and the lightning, Jim doubts he'll be able to leave for hours. Maybe not until morning." Ross thrust his fingers through his brown hair that would never quite stay in place. "Imagine Hunter and Gaylan stuck out there all night in this."

Yasu's chuckle was low. "Yes, imagine."

He turned to her. "What's so amusing?"

Yasu drew him away from the window. "Do you always worry so much? Hunter doesn't strike me as a man who panics easily. And from what I've seen of Gaylan, she's sensible as well. I suppose it's a little frightening at first, but it's also very romantic."

"Romantic? Lightning could strike them, a tree could fall on one of them, or—"

"Oh, really, Ross. You're sounding like the distressed parent of a teenager. These are two mature adults. *Married* adults. So they're marooned on a remote island all night. We know it's temporary. The storm will pass and Jim will go get them."

He supposed he was overreacting. What Yasu said made a lot of sense. Ross knew that Hunter was not only careful but very resourceful. "I guess you're right."

"Of course." Taking his arm, she led him over to the table room service had wheeled in just a short time ago. Her accommodations weren't anywhere as large as the suites, but there was a spacious sitting area off the bedroom. The tablecloth was pale peach and the waiter had lit the tall white candles. The soft glow fell on their covered dishes where dinner waited. If only she could calm down her fretful guest.

Yasu liked Ross and admired the no-nonsense way he conducted business. After just a few days, she had to admit that she was attracted to him and more than a little curious as to where this attraction might lead. But first, she had to get his mind off his employer. "We should remember that they're newlyweds. Most likely, they've found shelter and are watching the storm in each other's arms. That can be quite exciting."

He wanted to buy her version, but it didn't quite compute. They weren't newlyweds and no one he knew was less romantic than Hunter. Although, Ross had to admit that his friend had been acting a little out of character lately. Lingering looks aimed at Gaylan, hand-holding, tender touches. Even though Hunter was supposed to be playing the role of the happy husband, Ross didn't think he was that good an actor.

The only other answer had to be that Hunter was falling for her. He grinned suddenly. Wouldn't that be something, Hunter falling for his hired wife? Evan, the matchmaker, would undoubtedly be pleased.

"Does that smile mean that you agree with me?" Yasu asked as he pulled out her chair for her.

"You could be right," Ross answered as he slipped off his jacket before sitting down opposite her.

He was wearing a pink shirt with what could only be called a psychedelic tie in vivid shades of blue, red and yellow. Yasu, whose taste ran to conservative pastel solids, was surprised that she found Ross's clothing choices quite endearing. He seemed like a small boy who dressed in a hurry, paying little attention to what he grabbed, and never bothering to comb his unruly hair.

She smiled at him as he poured their wine. "I'm glad you think so. Now can we relax and enjoy our meal?" He'd invited her to dinner at one of the hotel's dining rooms, but she'd persuaded him to eat in her room instead. After a long day, she didn't want to dine surrounded by a lot of people.

"They're probably not in danger so I guess I can relax."

"I went to that island on my first visit here on an evening sailing trip. It's lovely, with a sandy beach, several interesting lava caves and beautiful flowers. And they have food and blankets, right?"

"So Jim said." Ross looked at the petite woman across from him, her skin a pinkish gold in the candlelight. She was lovely, and he was glad she'd suggested a private dinner. Despite their vastly different backgrounds, he found himself more comfortable with Yasu than with any woman he'd met in a long while. "It may sound romantic to be stuck on an island together, but I'd rather be here with you." He raised his wineglass to her.

Yasu clinked her glass to his, then sipped. She guessed that Ross wasn't any more romantic than she imagined Hunter was. Yet he was coming around. She removed the silver covers and set them aside. Succulent shrimp on a bed of rice nestled next to steamed broccoli. "I hope you approve of my choice."

Ross picked up his fork. "Smells wonderful."

Outside, the storm still raged, slinging torrents of water against their window despite a small overhang. Thunder moaned in the distance, and an occasional flash of lightning bounced off the swirling sea. If it was this wicked here, it must really be wild on the island. But not terribly dangerous. There were no animals on the island and no life-form other than vegetation. They'd be drenched, of course, but there were rock shelters and it wasn't cold.

Tasting her shrimp, Yasu decided she envied Hunter and Gaylan their little adventure. She'd bet they were having the time of their lives.

"Are you all right?" Hunter asked as Gaylan clung to him with a death grip.

Gaylan sucked in a shuddering breath and eased her hold on him. "I'm sorry. The thunder. It—"

"No apology necessary. A lot of people are afraid of storms."

She blinked rapidly against the rain that seemed to pour down her face like a fountain from above. "I'm *not* afraid of storms. Usually. But this one seems so...so close."

"Yeah, it is. We can't stay here. Too close to the trees. Lightning might hit one of them." Shielding his eyes, he looked in all directions. The sky was gray but it wasn't dark out yet. There was no way of telling how long the storm would last. "I think we should pick up our supplies and see if we can find some sort of shelter."

"Do you think we should leave the area of the helipad? What if Jim returns?"

"Not in this, he won't. At least not for a while. And if he does land, he'll come looking for us. He knows there's no other way off this island." Hunter walked over to where he'd placed the basket and cooler and picked them up. "Let's walk that way. Hopefully it leads to the beach. Maybe we can find that hut Jim told us about."

Since Gaylan couldn't think of a better suggestion, she went with him. "I can carry one of those," she told him.

"It's okay. I've got 'em."

There was no point in bending low against the rain. It slammed into them from all sides. Besides, they were about as wet as it was possible to be. Still, Gaylan had to admit she wasn't chilly except when the wind gusted into them occasionally.

She felt as if her feet, in wet and muddy sandals, weighed twenty pounds each as they finally reached the sand and slogged along, picking up more sludge. Up on a small rise, she saw the ramada that had been constructed to offer some shade to sunbathers. It would do them no good today. The thatched hut Jim had mentioned lay crumpled on its side, apparently a casualty of an earlier storm. Wearily she followed Hunter.

It seemed as if they'd been walking a long while when Hunter stopped abruptly. He set down their supplies and peered intently at the rock formations that bordered the beach at this point. "Maybe one of those openings leads into a small cave or overhang large enough to shield us. You wait here. I'll climb up and check it out."

A cave. Visions of dark, dank, smelly caverns jumped into Gaylan's mind. And bats. Didn't all caves have bats? She'd rather sit down here in the sand and let the rain fall on her than crawl into a cave where unknown creatures probably lived.

Waiting for him, she wrung out her hair, even though it wouldn't stay dry long. Carefully she removed her sandals one by one, let the rain wash them off, rinsed her feet and put the shoes back on again. Glancing down at her clothes, she decided there was nothing to be done at the moment. Her white knit shirt clung to her, vividly outlining her breasts as a cooling wind shook her. She could only hope Hunter was too busy playing caveman to notice.

He returned, looking pleased. "I found a cavelike space that's big enough for both of us." He grabbed the handles of the cooler and basket. "Come on."

Gaylan wasn't quite so eager. "Is it dirty? I mean, what about rats or mice? I read that bats live in caves."

Hunter looked at her, more amused than exasperated. "It wouldn't pass the white glove test, but it's the only game in town. Mice live in fields, not caves. I didn't see any rats or bats. I'm going up. Are you coming?''

Put that way, she guessed she'd at least go have a look. She could always scramble back down if it was truly repugnant. Reluctantly Gaylan followed him up the hill.

It wasn't steep, just drenched and slippery. Lava rock, when wet, was slick as glass. She nearly slid back down several times and wondered how it was that Hunter scampered up like a mountain goat. Finally they reached a fairly wide ledge and she followed him along it until the small opening could be seen.

"It's wider once you get inside, but you have to scoot in on your bottom. Or crawl in, if you'd rather."

What she'd have rather done was skipped the whole experience. Just then another shuddering explosion of thunder sounded nearby, changing her mind quickly.

"I'll go first, pull in the supplies and then reach for you." Sitting down with his back to the cave entrance, Hunter wiggled himself inside, then dragged in their things. Finally he held out his hands. "Sit down, bend your head low and scoot in."

She'd kill for a flashlight to examine the cave floor and walls before entering, Gaylan thought. She'd have to suggest to the hotel management that they add one to the basket for future outings. Sort of a survival kit in cases of being marooned.

She sat down and felt Hunter's hands close around her waist. She squirmed and inched until she was alongside him. In the dim light, she saw that the so-called cave was really a rocky outgrowth of lava accumulation that had probably been there for a century or so, worn smooth by time and weather. Their ceiling was perhaps three feet high, the width only about as wide as a double bed and the depth barely six feet. Hastily she scrutinized the inside for signs of any living things. Finding none, she breathed a sigh of relief.

"Will it do, madam?" Hunter asked, having watched her inspection with a look on her face that indicated she felt as if she'd been forced into a snake pit.

"Under the circumstances, I suppose so."

"I'm going to have to get after the staff, have them erect a shelter with hot and cold running water for future emergencies." He brushed rain from his head and face.

"All right, so I'm a little picky about my caves." Again, Gaylan removed her sandy shoes and placed them just outside the opening so they'd rinse off. Then she shifted her attention to her hair—wet, tangled and straggly. She'd opted to leave her purse back at the hotel, thinking she'd have little use for it. Ah well, the light inside was dim at best. Who cared how she looked?

"I have a comb," Hunter said, pulling one from his back pocket. He held it out to her.

"Great. Thanks." She pulled it through her long hair, smoothing out the snarls, and immediately felt better. She shifted to seat herself more comfortably on the hard rock floor. "Not exactly a feather bed, is it?"

"Let's see if we can soften it a bit." Hunter found that the things inside the basket had barely dampened. He pulled out the blanket. "Lift up and I'll spread this under us."

She did and helped him arrange the folded blanket beneath them. A definite improvement. Now if only she had a dry change of clothes, she might even be content to sit here and watch the storm play itself out. She turned to Hunter and saw he'd removed his shirt.

Hunter felt better without the sodden material clinging to his skin. He shifted to look at Gaylan. Her soaking wet shirt stuck to her uncomfortably. "Don't take this wrong, but you'd feel better if you'd do the same."

Right. "Thanks, but I'll manage." She shifted her gaze to the opening and watched another swatch of lightning flicker and disappear.

Hunter dug out the tablecloth. "All right, how about this? Take off your wet shirt and slacks, then wrap this around you. It's clean and dry. I'll turn the other way."

She studied his eyes. He looked merely helpful. She *was* uncomfortable, and she was probably being immature. "Okay."

It took her only a few moments. Wrapped in the generous tablecloth, she could feel it absorbing her dampness. He turned back to face her, an amused smile playing on his lips. Ignoring him, she drew the fabric tighter around her.

His slacks were soaking the blanket. Hunter reached to undo his belt.

Her head swiveled to him. "What are you doing?"

"Removing my pants. They're drenched." Quickly he unzipped and struggled out of them in the tight quarters, bumping his head once and swearing under his breath. There was a small ledge above and behind them. Squirming around, he spread out their clothes there, though he had little hope they'd dry anytime soon.

Terrific, Gaylan thought. Here they were, down to their underwear, in a darkening cave, with rescue unlikely till daylight. Fully clothed, with just a look, he often had her blood heating. A few evenings ago on her lanai, when she'd had on only a thin nightie and gown and he'd worn those sexy silk shorts, she'd all but jumped his bones. How would she get through the long night with Hunter inches from her and wearing only dark blue briefs?

How had she allowed herself to get into this fix? Closing her eyes, Gaylan lowered her head to rest on her bent knees.

Hunter reached into the cooler and drew out the wine they'd barely touched earlier. "Here's something that'll warm us."

Her eyes flew open. Just what she needed, wine to further muddle her mind. "I'll pass, thanks."

"Don't be silly. Do you want to catch a cold?"

"I've never read that wine is a cold preventive."

"Well, it is." He filled a glass and held it out to her. "Drink this."

It was easier to comply than to argue with him. She sipped.

He poured his own and drank it down quickly, feeling the warmth spread almost immediately. They were out of the rain, drying off, warming up. He supposed that was about the best he could hope for until morning.

Hunter dug around in the basket again to see if he'd missed anything they could use. "Aha! Look what we have here." He held out two candles, each in a small brass holder, and a book of matches. "Let there be light."

"Shouldn't we save them until it gets really dark?"

It was dusk by now, just after seven by his watch, with the sky a muddy gray. They could see the outer area clearly and make out each other quite well. He set the candles back into the basket. "Good idea. Are you hungry?"

Gaylan shook her head, then flinched and shuddered when a heavy clap of thunder echoed through the cave.

She looked small and miserable. He wasn't altogether comfortable, either, but he wasn't frightened. He'd seen these sudden electrical storms come up in the islands before, albeit from the dry comfort of his suite. He also knew that in a couple of hours, it would wear itself out and move on. It seemed likely that Gaylan had never experienced a storm up close before. Hunter moved a couple of inches closer to where his thigh was just touching hers. "Are you all right?"

She nodded.

"Cold?" She hadn't finished her wine.

"A little."

Shifting nearer still, he put his arm around her and tried to draw her closer to his body. She immediately stiffened. "Ease up, will you? I'm only trying to keep us both warm."

She felt contrite. He was sitting there bare-chested and bare-legged while she at least had the tablecloth. She forced herself to relax against him.

Hunter rubbed his hand along her covered arms in a further attempt to warm her. A side benefit was that he was also warming himself. And it wasn't necessarily the wine or finally drying off. It was the womanly heat of her spreading to him.

Gaylan's mind scurried about, looking for a safe topic of conversation. Because if they didn't talk soon, she'd find herself struggling with another dose of unwelcome desire. "Do you remember on the flight over from L.A. when we talked about fate being in control? This storm is one of those times when the gods are definitely in charge, and it makes me uneasy."

"But we're out of harm's way now. Lightning doesn't strike inside a cave, even one this small. Thunder is upsetting, but it can't hurt us. We're drying off and we'll be safe until Jim comes for us, which he'll do as soon as he's able to fly. Nothing to worry about." To emphasize his words, he gave her arm a squeeze.

Nothing to worry about. Safe. Not quite, Gaylan thought. She had him to worry about, and her confused feelings every time she was near him. And she was very near him, near enough to feel his warm breath on her face as he snuggled in closer. Safe? Hardly. It wasn't the storm she feared, but rather the man who'd found shelter for them from the storm.

Think, think, she commanded herself. *Talk. Conversation is diverting.* "Did you always want to be a tycoon?" she finally managed.

He chuckled close to her ear, sending shivers through her. "I don't imagine too many little boys say to themselves that they plan to be a tycoon when they grow up. It's not exactly like wanting to be a fireman."

"What were you like as a little boy?" She had trouble imagining Hunter as anything other than grown, confident, in charge.

"Lonely, mostly." Hunter realized it was the truth, though he seldom thought about his childhood and certainly hadn't planned to disclose information so private. It was the situation they found themselves in. Stranded, isolated, intimate. The combination lent itself to confidences that would rarely be shared in sunny daylight. "I hardly saw my father," he found himself confessing. "He was always working or traveling. My mother was so disenchanted with him and with their marriage that she wasn't your average cookie-baking, fun-loving parent, either."

Gaylan shifted so she could see his profile. "Who did you have in your life that you were close to?" Surely there had to have been someone.

"A housekeeper," he admitted finally. "Mrs. Mertz. You know, like Ethel on the *I Love Lucy* reruns. Only my Mrs. Mertz was named Mary. She used to help me with my homework and make me my favorite cupcakes. Chocolate with white icing and sprinkles on top. And she'd sit for hours and build model airplanes with me."

The picture he painted was of a sad, solitary child. Gaylan's heart went out to the boy he'd been. "Where did your mother spend her time?"

"She escaped into bridge. She played four or five days a week at the club." He shrugged. "Better than escaping into a bottle, I guess."

From bridge enthusiast to peach farmer, Gaylan thought. Must have been quite a transition. And why did the housekeeper have to spend time building airplanes with him? "What about your friends?"

Hunter frowned, as if he'd suddenly realized the conversation was revealing far more than he'd intended. "I didn't have a lot of friends. My father thought that a boy growing up should be involved only in educational things. Visits to art galleries, museums. Season tickets to the symphony for juniors. Not surprisingly, most of my classmates preferred sports or movies or just plain hanging around." He looked over and saw that her face was soft, empathetic. "Hey, it wasn't so bad," he insisted. "I was the only twelve-year-old kid who could tell the difference between a Rembrandt and a Dali." He laughed to show that such a revelation no longer had the power to hurt him.

There were many ways for a child to grow up deprived, Gaylan thought. By comparison, her childhood had been normal, loving, boisterous, though they hadn't had nearly as much. Her parents had taken her and Mel swimming, fishing, to ball games and on Disneyland excursions whenever they could get some free time. She put on a smile, knowing he'd hate to be pitied. "You survived. That's the main thing."

"Yeah, I'm a survivor." He met her eyes, found them warm and suddenly bright. "Like you. You were left all alone at an early age. That's tough."

She took a deep breath, wanting to tell him a little since he'd been so painfully honest with her, but not reveal everything. "Not exactly alone. I have a brother." It was time to change the subject. "Do you think I could have some grapes? I'm hungry, after all."

Hunter shifted over and opened the cooler. She didn't want to talk about her background and he understood. He wished he hadn't revealed as much as he had. He removed the fruit and set it in front of her, then spread pâté on several crackers.

They ate a little, glancing out through the cave opening, hoping to see the storm abating. It didn't seem to be moving away, Gaylan noticed uneasily. And it was growing darker by the minute. No lights for miles, and two skimpy candles. The hours before daylight stretched before her, seemingly endless. She drained her wine, then held out her glass for more. Maybe a little vino would make her sleepy.

It did. As she helped him repack the cooler, she stifled a yawn. "Do you think there's enough room in here to lie down? Might as well try to get some rest."

He'd been thinking the same thing. The thunder was reduced to low rumblings rather than loud crescendos.

They could blot the lightning out by closing their eyes. "I think so, with a little rearranging."

Gaylan helped him spread out the blanket. Hunter lit one of the candles and propped it on the far corner ledge, and they both lay back. The walls on either side were quite close, which meant mere inches separated them. He was too tall to stretch out fully, so he lay on his side, his legs bent at the knee. She felt quite lethargic from the wine, yet very aware of the man lying a hairbreadth from her who, with but one small touch, could set her skin fairly humming.

Deliberately she turned her back to him, closing her eyes, shutting him out. She dozed for a while, she didn't know how long. Restless movement alongside her brought her eyes wide open. She couldn't have been asleep long for the candle hadn't burned all the way down yet.

Gaylan became aware of a light rain outside, but otherwise there was silence. She lifted her head and could see no lightning, hear no more thunder. Perhaps the worst of it was over. At least the winds had stopped that awful howling. She wondered if Hunter was asleep as she carefully rolled onto her back.

A sharp protrusion of rock poked him uncomfortably just under one shoulder. Hunter turned again, cushioning his head on his upraised arm. He'd been moving around restlessly for some time, unable to settle down. He hadn't wanted to disturb Gaylan, yet he simply couldn't lie still.

In the candlelight he could see that her eyes were open and focused on their low ceiling. He'd been wanting to know something. No time like the present. "Will you answer something for me?"

Her heart skipped a beat, wondering what was coming. "I'll try."

"You're very attractive, intelligent, accomplished. Why is there no one special in your life?"

"What makes you think there isn't?"

"Evan didn't mention anyone when he told me about you."

She turned to face him, her eyes suddenly blazing. "You had me investigated?"

"Hardly that. But I did ask a few questions since Evan's known you for some time. I didn't want some jealous lover to show up and make trouble." His attorney had said he knew of no one man in Gaylan's life at this time.

A jealous lover. Gaylan almost laughed aloud. She wasn't worried he'd learned about her past lovers, for there had been few. Her concern was that he'd stumbled across Mel's problems. "And what did you learn, Sherlock?"

"Not much." He eased up, resting his head in his hand, wondering why her expression was pinched, worried. "Is there someone?"

"No." Gaylan adjusted the tablecloth, tucking it under her arms, freeing her hands. She was feeling suddenly warm.

"I didn't think you'd kiss me the way you did if there was someone else." She didn't respond to his baited comment, so he decided to come at her from another angle. "You don't strike me as the type who needs one special person in her life, despite the fact that you're drawn to romance."

She stared up at the ceiling again. "Don't I?"

"Well, do you?" And why did he want to know?

"I think you've got us confused again. It's *you* who claim you need nothing but work to focus on."

"And it's the truth. I don't want a long-term relationship. Never again."

Well, that was certainly crystal clear. But what wasn't clear was the reason he felt the need to hammer that fact home to her again and again. "I don't see anyone trying to talk you out of your firm stand."

"You do, Gaylan." He rolled closer to her, his arm going around her waist, and noted the surprise leap into her eyes as the candlelight flickered over her features. "Every time you look at me with those huge eyes, when your hand takes mine, when you kiss me back like there's no tomorrow. It's subtle, insidious even, but it's there. You're trying to show me what it would be like if we were together."

She felt a rush of anger. "That's crazy. I'm not trying to show you anything. You hired me to *act* the part of your wife and that's what I'm doing—acting."

The oath he muttered was succinct and ungentlemanly. Lowering his head, he crushed her mouth with his, his mood suddenly savage. His tongue moved inside and he plundered, needing to prove something, to her, to himself.

Her anger left as quickly as it had come. Gaylan felt heat flooding her as she kissed him back with all the pent-up longing of two days of abstinence. Her hands bunched on his bare back, then roamed freely. The smoky male taste of him exploded on her tongue and she sighed his name.

He heard and increased the tempo. Passion rose in him, a sleeping giant suddenly awakened. He would have denied his need for her with his dying breath, but he could no longer lie to himself. He wanted to take her, here and now, in this damp cave on this remote island with the storm outside dying and the one inside just coming to life.

He told himself if he had her just once, then he would be free of her. He told himself she was no different than a dozen other women he'd known. He told himself he was a damn liar.

He raised from her, gasping for control. "Tell me again that you're acting."

She struggled to slow her breathing. "I've never denied wanting you. You're the one who winds up apologizing every time you kiss me. Why is that, Hunter? Is it because you want me, but you think I'm not good enough for the great Hunter James II?"

"No, dammit. This isn't about 'good enough.' It's about commitment. I want *no* commitments. I don't think you're the one-night-stand type. Or even a two-week stand."

"You're right. I'm not." Annoyed, with herself, with him, she sat up. The tablecloth slipped down and pooled in her lap. She was too angry to notice. She shoved her hair back with both hands, wishing that she'd never set foot on this damnable island.

Hunter's anger slipped away. His eyes were drawn to her full breasts covered only by a thin bra. He struggled for control. "I'm sorry."

Gaylan swiveled to face him, her eyes narrowed. "If you apologize one more time for kissing me, I swear I'm going to...to lift that cooler and hurl it against your thick head."

"I wasn't apologizing for kissing you."

"For what, then?"

"For not being all you want, all you need."

She felt her fists clench. "Suddenly you know what I want or need? Omniscient as well as thickheaded, are you?"

Hunter sat up slowly. "All right, then tell me. What is it you want? What is it you need?"

She was so furious she was trembling. "Right now? I need to get out of this cave and off this damn island. It's too close in here, too much togetherness. It makes me crazy. It makes me . . ." She stared at him, her chest heaving, awareness making her weak.

"What? It makes you what?"

"It makes me want you too much."

His eyes turned hot, hungry. "Well, the truth finally comes out."

"Yes." If she'd made a wrong choice, if she'd wind up hurt, so be it. She'd face that when the time came. "I'm tired of fighting this." She tilted her head back, challenging him. "What are you going to do about it?"

In answer, he pulled her into his arms and they fell back onto the blanket and the unforgiving rock beneath. Gaylan groaned against the impact as he pressed his mouth to hers, swallowing her protest. Her hands fluttered, then settled nervously on his back. Her hesitant touch gentled him and he eased back to look at her.

The ebbing candle reflected in her eyes as he framed her face with trembling hands. "You're so beautiful," he whispered.

She closed her eyes as his lips touched her lids. "Lie to me some more." She'd never thought herself beautiful, never been told as much by anyone. Surely the women he'd known had been more so.

"I'm not lying." He usually saw no need for words at moments like this, but she'd bared her feelings to him. He couldn't offer her forever, but he could offer her his own truth. "From the first day, I've wanted you." He pushed her straps down and stroked her smooth shoulders. His fingers moved around back, unfastened the hooks and tossed aside the satin bra.

When his hands touched her sensitive skin, Gaylan let the pleasurable sensations flow over her. When his mouth settled on one aroused peak, her body arched in response. Through half-closed eyes, she marveled at the contrast of his dark head against her pale skin.

Hunter's pulse was pounding. She smelled like rain and tasted like everything forbidden. His tongue on her flesh felt the flutter of her heart. Her small hands curling in his hair then trailing down his back had him dazed and aching.

She drew him back up to her. "I want you to kiss me. I feel so much when you kiss me."

Drowning. He was drowning in her, in her heated flesh, in her generous mouth, in her exotic taste. Control. He reached for the control that was his constant companion and found that it had fled like the sudden storm. Desire. It raged through him, clawed at him, had him mindless.

Gaylan felt his hand roam to the waistband of her silken panties and... And suddenly she heard the distant hum of an engine moving closer. Pulling her mouth from his, she fought her way out of the mists. "Hunter, wait. The helicopter."

He'd heard it, too, and decided that Jim's timing was rotten. "It'll take him a while to land." He dragged her mouth back to his and slipped his hand inside the swatch of silk that was the only thing she wore.

But Gaylan's passion had cooled at the thought of Jim catching them in the beam of the spotlight she could already see flashing about through the cave opening. Her hands pushed against his shoulders and she freed her mouth again. "No. We need to get dressed. I . . . I don't want him to find us like this."

Hunter was like a man obsessed, his goal in sight, unwilling to stop. "I want you *now*," he ground out, his mouth settling on hers, effectively silencing her. As his fingers found her, she struggled to sit up.

"No, please. Not like this." Her voice was strained, uneasy.

As if through a haze, Hunter heard the loudspeaker and Jim's voice calling his name. Lifting from her, he shook his head. What the hell was wrong with him? What had he been about to do, force her? With a rush of self-disgust, he got to his feet and grabbed his pants.

Trembling, Gaylan watched him pull on his slacks and duck outside. He called to Jim, who apparently saw him, for she could hear the copter setting down on the sand as Hunter came back in. Silently she reached for her clothes.

Hunter avoided her eyes as he finished dressing and stuffed the blanket and towels into the basket. He felt shame not for letting himself lose control, but for what he'd almost done. He couldn't leave without letting her know. "Gaylan, I'm sorry," he told her, a muscle in his jaw clenching.

It wasn't his usual apology for kissing her. She could tell by his tense manner that this was more. She needed to know what had made him want to continue their lovemaking when it was obvious they were no longer alone. She was fairly certain he hadn't been driven by uncontrollable passion alone. Not Hunter, who'd invented the word *control*. "What happened?" she asked softly. "Why did you do that?"

"It's not important. Let's go." He shoved their supplies out through the opening and made as if to leave.

She placed a hand on his arm, stopping him. "I want to know why. Tell me."

Hunter let out a shuddering breath. He studied her a moment, thinking again how lovely she was, even after weathering a messy storm. Her face was washed clean by the rain and more vulnerable than he'd ever seen it. He owed her the truth, but he just couldn't make himself say the words. Not now. "One of these days, when I figure it all out, I'll tell you."

Gaylan searched his eyes and knew she'd get no more from him until he was good and ready. "Okay."

He was relieved she wasn't going to push. Reaching for her hand, he crouched down. "Come on. I'll help you out."

Chapter Eight

Running offered many benefits, Gaylan thought as her shoes hit the hard-packed sand, spraying wet clumps with each step. It helped your heart rate, your circulation, your general health. It increased your lung capacity and kept your joints limber.

And it was a terrific way to escape.

She was tired, but she kept on moving. At eight in the morning, the beach section that was generally nearly deserted at six was already crowded with swimmers and sunbathers. She paid little attention to them as she ran.

Gaylan tried to concentrate on the glorious rays of the sun, the warm Pacific sea air, the magnificent ocean ebbing and flowing on her left. If she did that, she wouldn't have to think. And thinking was what she was trying desperately to avoid.

It didn't work.

Her mind kept returning again and again to yesterday and, most of all, the night she'd spent with Hunter on the deserted island in a storm. It had barely been drizzling when Jim had picked them up somewhere around two in the morning. Apparently Ross had informed him that Hunter happened to own the hotel and that the pilot needed to return for the two of them as soon as it was safe to take the copter up, not waiting for daylight.

It had been a tense ride back to the hotel landing pad, neither she nor Hunter feeling very talkative. She'd felt battered and bruised, and none of it had anything to do with the storm. Actually she had to admit he'd been great in an emergency, finding them shelter, keeping them safe through hours of uncertainty.

It was the last few minutes alone in the cave that had her feeling unsure and defenseless.

Their confrontation had been brewing for several days, the sexual tension between them sizzling beneath the surface, just waiting to explode. She'd been maneuvered into admitting she wanted him, come hell or high water. She wanted to make love with him and she'd face the consequences like an adult. She was a big girl now and knew that people had to take responsibility for their actions. Faced with that, Hunter had given in, breaking his own resolve to stay uninvolved.

And it had been something of a disaster.

She'd felt like a teenager caught parked in her boyfriend's jalopy on a deserted road with a police officer about to shine a flashlight into the car. Hunter had heard Jim's arrival, too, yet had chosen to ignore it and pushed on. She was sure he wasn't a man who just wanted a quickie, and certainly not a man who couldn't control his basic urges.

Why, then, had he tried to persuade her to hurriedly complete the act, thereby rendering it meaningless?

Slowing her pace, she stopped and bent over, placing her hands on her knees and catching her breath. After a minute, she unhooked her water bottle from her waistband and took a long swallow. Before starting off again, she tucked several strands of hair back into her ponytail. In moments, she was running at her usual stride.

He'd said he'd tell her when he'd figured it out. Gaylan was pretty sure he'd already figured it out. And didn't like his findings. At least, he hadn't lied to her, insulted her intelligence by brushing it off. And it was something that was far from unimportant or he wouldn't have been so contemplative afterward.

They'd walked wearily back to their suite after thanking Jim. Hunter had unlocked the door and, without a word, she'd walked toward her room. From the center of the living room, he'd quietly spoken her name. She'd stopped, turned and looked at him, her eyes questioning. Slowly he'd shaken his head and muttered, "Nothing." Fine. She'd hurried in, showered and curled into a miserable ball in her solitary bed.

He'd wanted her from the first day they'd met, or so he'd said. He'd struggled against his desire for her much as she'd fought her feelings for him. It had been a matter of time before those explosive emotions boiled over. Gaylan understood Hunter's reluctance to get involved with a woman whom he apparently regarded as a gold digger trying to entice him into a serious relationship.

Nothing could be further from the truth, she thought, running out of steam and stopping again to wipe her damp face. She didn't want his money, other than the legitimate salary she was earning. And she couldn't imagine being involved with a man who was with her against his better judgment, because he desired her physically, but had little use for her otherwise. There were names for women like that, and they weren't very nice.

He wouldn't believe her even if she made him listen to her explanation. Gaylan had to admit that she probably appeared to be a woman who'd do most anything for money, whose motivations were far from altruistic. Hunter didn't know about Mel's problem or her own fervent need to get started as an illustrator.

And she had no intention of telling him. Hunter was a man who dealt in absolutes, who saw things in black and white, whereas Gaylan was convinced there were many shades of gray possible.

She walked along now, too weary to run, cooling off. She needed rest but she didn't want to return until she felt certain Hunter was in his morning meeting in Taro's suite. Perhaps she was lethargic partly because she'd been with Hunter's party for only one week and it had already affected her deeply.

She hadn't all but asked him to make love to her last night merely because they'd been thrown together alone for hours; it had not been a simple case of proximity and opportunity. She'd never given herself lightly. It had been, despite the brevity of their acquaintance, because she was beginning to care for Hunter. Seriously.

And she must get over it.

He didn't want involvement and she didn't want heartbreak. Yet she couldn't seem to help herself. At first, she'd barely liked the man. He'd presented a dominant, unemotional, almost ruthless veneer to her as a newcomer. But in no time, she'd caught glimpses of the lonely boy he'd been and the vulnerable man beneath the facade. She'd seen the fun-loving side of Hunter emerge, though he fought it, tooth and nail. She'd seen that he was capable of feeling deeply, though he'd steeled his heart against it. And her own heart had gone out to him.

Gaylan sighed and brushed back wisps of hair with both hands. Dear God, she couldn't afford to fall in love with Hunter James II. He would hurt her, she felt certain, because he was determined to protect himself from involvements at any cost. She would pay the price for his resolve. She had to guard herself before it was too late.

But how did one *stop* caring?

Gaylan hadn't a clue. Turning around, she decided she'd take her time going back and . . . Glancing over toward a lone palm tree on a sandy rise just off to the left, she recognized Nari sitting underneath. On her raised knees was propped what looked like a large sketch pad. Walking over, Gaylan saw that Nari was so absorbed in what she was doing that she didn't notice her until her shadow fell across the young Japanese woman.

Surprised, Nari looked up, then smiled. "Hello. I see you made it back from the helicopter picnic, despite the rain. I'm sorry I had to back out. How was it?"

How, indeed. She needed to sugarcoat their stay. "The storm was a little frightening, but otherwise, it was fine." If you didn't count a small case of interrupted passion that had shaken both of them.

"When we heard, I was frightened for you. But then, I rather thought Hunter was very capable of taking care of you."

He'd taken care of her, all right. He'd sent her emotions spiraling and her thoughts whirling. "How's your headache?'' Gaylan asked, needing to talk about something else.

Nari dropped her gaze. "Better, thanks." She indicated a shady spot next to her. "Sit down, won't you?"

Gaylan eased onto the sand and glanced at Nari's sketch pad. "Working on some of your designs?"

"Yes." She looked at Gaylan hesitantly. "Would you like to take a look?"

"Love to." Gaylan took the pad and studied each of three pages filled with several sketches. The first focused on bathing suits, the second on robes and the top sheet showed a magnificent bridal gown exquisitely portrayed with scooped neck and puffed sleeves. "Nari, these are lovely. You're very skilled."

Nari's smile broke through, as if she'd been holding her breath. "I don't show my work to many. I have no idea if they're really good, by professional standards. I compare them to ads I see in newspapers, but..."

"But you don't want to draw for ads, do you? You want to actually design, to have your sketches made up by seamstresses and shown to prospective buyers?"

Nari shook back her long hair, shifting in the breeze. "That's my dream. But it's not so easy. You have to establish yourself, get some publicity that draws the attention of buyers, have showings by models. You need a lot of money and even more luck."

Gaylan thought of her work, the long road she'd already walked studying, learning, working with several other authors until she'd connected with Helen and found they complemented each other. "Rome wasn't built in a day, as they say. Of course, all that takes time. Couldn't you take sample sketches to some of the haute couture houses to begin with and see if you could get on staff? It would be a start."

Taking back her book, Nari closed the cover. "I've thought of doing that. I've hesitated because Hiroki would very much frown on my working."

A familiar problem faced by married women everywhere, no matter the country, Gaylan thought. Some men simply insisted on being the sole provider. "Are you so sure?"

"Yes." Nari's dark eyes were suddenly bright as they turned to Gaylan. "My headache yesterday was brought on by the quarrel Hiroki and I had."

Must be something in the Hawaiian air, Gaylan thought. "He isn't in favor of your pursuing your designs?"

Nari shook her head. "He said I should be happy with my baby and the good life my husband can give me. He pointed out that you are happy traveling and being there for your husband, and that I should be also."

Gaylan felt a rush of guilt, her deception adding to this poor woman's problems. "Oh, Nari, it isn't fair to compare us."

Setting aside her pad, Nari twisted a tissue in her hands. "I suppose he is right. I am ungrateful and—"

Gaylan touched her arm. "No, you're not. I'm sure you're a wonderful mother and a good wife. I can't believe it's wrong for you to want to do designs in addition to caring for your family."

"How is it you don't want more? Of course, you're newly married, but..."

"Let's not talk about me, but rather concentrate on you. Would you like me to talk with Hiroki?"

Nari looked skeptical. "I don't think he will listen."

She had to do something. This charade was costing Nari. She'd have to talk with Hunter or perhaps Ross, see how much she could reveal without going back on her word. "Let me think about this some." Rising, she dusted off her running shorts. "Want to start back? I need a shower."

"No, you go ahead. I'll be along later."

"If you're sure you're all right?" She hated leaving Nari in an upset state, but she had some things to take care of.

Nari picked up her pad. "I'll be fine. Thanks, for listening."

Planning what she'd say, Gaylan started back.

Hunter was having a bad morning. The meeting wasn't going well, and the fact that he'd had very little sleep and awakened to find Gaylan already gone didn't improve his mood. Yasu was looking at him expectantly. He was ready to throttle the niggling lawyer. "You're absolutely certain we can't continue until you get those figures?" he asked, barely hiding his irritation.

"I'm sorry, Hunter," Yasu answered, her voice quietly insistent. "I feel that without the comparative study of your East Coast affiliate shipments, we can't finalize. Our commitment hinges on feasibility."

Ross rushed in, trying to smooth over a potentially volatile situation. "I don't feel the request will delay us long. I'll get on the phone right away with our home office, tell them what we need and see how quickly they can fax us the figures. Shouldn't take more than a day or two."

Two days! Hunter looked first at Hiroki, then Taro, and saw that he'd get no help from them. He doubted if they'd have wanted to see the report if Yasu hadn't brought it up. That's what happened when you allowed women to sit at the negotiations table. He kept his expression bland, but inside he was seething. "Fine. You do that, Ross." He pushed his chair back and stood.

Evan rose as well. "We'll let you know as soon as we have the information." He acknowledged the quick bow from Taro and Hiroki's brief nod. "Coming, Hunter?"

Leaving Ross to verify the details with Yasu, Evan hurried Hunter out of the suite, well aware that his employer was highly annoyed. In the hallway, he walked alongside Hunter. "I have to tell you that I can't blame Yasu for wanting that report," he said. "In her place, I would have done the same thing."

Hunter's strides were long and agitated. He couldn't remember the last time he'd been close to losing his temper in a meeting. "Then why didn't she bring it up earlier? We could have had them here by now. Hell, we're going to be negotiating this agreement *three* weeks the way things are going."

Evan knew much of Hunter's irritation had to do with the fact that Yasu was a woman. The man simply hated doing business with women. Even though Evan knew the basis for Hunter's prejudice dated back to Jolene, he couldn't agree or approve. "I'm certain Ross will do his best to rush things."

At the door to his suite, Hunter turned to his attorney. "I'm not so sure. Have you noticed how he and Yasu are always together, and not just when they're working? I don't think Ross would mind if this went on all summer."

"That's not fair, Hunter," Evan told him. Their long association allowed him to speak his mind. "Ross works very hard. He wouldn't deliberately hold things up."

Hunter ran a hand over his face, then winced. He'd cut himself shaving this morning, which had started off his day just fine. Still, he had no business taking his lousy mood out on either Evan or Ross. "You're right. I just…well, I just want this *over*. I want to get back to L.A." Back to normal, where he wouldn't have to share his living quarters with a woman whose very presence made him long for things he knew he shouldn't want.

Guessing the path of Hunter's thoughts, Evan hid a smile. "Where's Gaylan?"

"She was gone when I left. It doesn't matter where she is as long as she's here tonight, dressed and ready, with every detail taken care of for dinner. In between, she can go fly a kite for all I care."

Evan's shrewd eyes narrowed. So that's how it was. Interesting. He'd felt the sparks between the two of them as far back as their plane ride here. By the look of him, Hunter hadn't realized he'd fallen for Gaylan yet. He wondered how Gaylan felt. "I'm sure she'll have everything under control."

Hunter ran long fingers through his usually neat hair. "I hope so. Damn but I wish this week was over."

Evan clapped him on the shoulder. "I know. Why don't you take the day off?" One of Hunter's problems was he took too little time for outside interests. "I've been thinking of going deep-sea fishing. Would you like to come along?"

He'd taken the day off yesterday and the whole experience had set his teeth on edge. "I have a business to run, in case you've forgotten. I didn't come here to play, Evan."

It was no use. The more Evan said, the more he seemed to get on Hunter's nerves. At times like this, it was best to leave him alone. "All right. I'll see you later." Evan walked to the elevators.

As the doors slid open, Gaylan stepped out, nearly colliding with Evan. "Sorry," she said. "My mind was elsewhere."

Evan studied her face. She was flushed from her run, but it was more than that. Gaylan looked worried. "Is anything wrong?" he asked, leading her over to a small lanai off the outdoor hallway. As the man who'd gotten her into this, Evan felt a responsibility. He knew how demanding Hunter could be. Their occasional lovey-dovey displays in public didn't fool Evan. He was certain that they were acting for the benefit of the Yamaguchis and that the pressure of their private time together had taken its toll on Gaylan.

"I have a problem," she said, deciding to confide in Evan. After all, he was the one person who knew her whole situation. Quickly she told him about Nari's quandary over her desire to work and Hiroki's objections. "Ordinarily I'd stay out of a marital difference of opinion, but Hunter's comments last week that, as his wife, I was content to travel and attend to his needs have put me in the middle."

Evan frowned, crossing his arms over his chest. "I don't see what you mean."

"The fact is, if I were *really* married to Hunter, I'd still want to try to sell the books Helen and I have been working on, as I told you on the day this whole situation began. In other words, like Nari, I'd want to work outside the home in addition to being a wife and homemaker. Knowing Hunter the little that I do, I know he'd never put up with a working wife, like Hiroki."

Thinking of the session he'd just attended, Evan had to agree.

"My point is that Hunter's statement has given Hiroki the ammunition he apparently needed to keep Nari homebound. And it's not fair to her, especially since he's using a premise that isn't so."

Evan shifted to lean against the half wall overlooking the lush tropical gardens seven stories below them. "If you're asking my opinion, I think you'll be opening a big can of worms if you draw Hunter into this problem. First of all, he's paying you to pretend to be his wife. Secondly, one presumes that you would have married him knowing how he feels about women in business—a fact that is widely known—and that you'd agreed to respect his wishes on the subject. So, if you reveal to Nari and Hiroki that *you* also want to work outside the home, it'll be conceived as going against your husband's wishes. Not exactly the marital bliss Hunter wants to convey. *And* you'll also have to reveal to Hunter one of your motivations for accepting this job, which you asked me not to disclose from the outset. I don't know why you wanted to keep that information secret. Apparently the reason no longer exists. Am I right?"

"Not exactly." Gaylan leaned her elbows on the railing, trying to think of a solution that would hurt no one. "I didn't want Hunter to know about my plans or about Mel simply because it's no one's business but mine what I intend doing with the money. I probably should have told him, since he obviously thinks I'm a gold digger out to fleece every rich man I run across."

"Oh, I think that's being a bit harsh."

"No, Evan, it isn't. Hunter's wife apparently did a real number on him. I don't know what he was like before his marriage, but I do know that now he hasn't a very good opinion of women in business or in his personal life.''

"You don't like him very much, do you?''

The sixty-four-thousand-dollar question. "My feelings aren't relevant. I think there's a lot of good in Hunter, a side of himself he rarely shows. He suffered a cold, indifferent upbringing, which has left him unskilled in the area of relationships. He has warmth and generosity, but he's suspicious of his own infrequent tendency to exhibit those traits. He distrusts the motives of everyone, except possibly you and Ross.'' She shook her head. "How do you get through to a man like that?''

Evan's eyes widened as the truth hit him. "You say your feelings aren't relevant, but they are. Especially since you've fallen in love with the man.''

Gaylan swung around to face him. "I certainly have not.''

Chuckling, Evan shook his head. "My dear, thou doth protest too much.'' Quickly he sobered. "Not the wisest thing you could have done, Gaylan.''

Struggling against the truth of it, Gaylan's chin moved up in defiance. "If I have, I'll get over it.''

Evan ignored that. "He'll hurt you.''

Gaylan's shoulders slumped, as if in sudden defeat. "I know,'' she whispered. The elevator doors slid open behind them and two people stepped out, chattering gaily as they strolled off holding hands. She moved closer to the potted fern, reaching for some shred of composure. She almost had herself together when Evan's arm went around her in comfort.

"I'm so sorry, Gaylan. If I'd known this would happen, I never would have come to you. I never dreamed of it because you're both so different.''

"Aren't we, though?" She blinked rapidly, holding back the tears that threatened to fall. "It's not your fault. I'm a big girl now, Evan. I know how to handle myself, or so I thought."

Divorced for years, Evan knew what it was to love someone who was impossible to live with. "We're seldom prepared when something like this happens."

Gaylan squared her shoulders, determined to pull herself together. "Back to my immediate problem. I'm going to tell Hunter about Nari and Hiroki's dilemma, hopefully in a way that I won't have to reveal too much about myself. After all, our marriage is only make-believe. Hunter wouldn't be compromising his position while playing let's-pretend. Perhaps together we can talk about working wives in a way that will convince Hiroki to let Nari try her hand in the workplace."

Evan looked doubtful. "I wouldn't do it right now. Yasu is demanding some papers from L.A. that probably won't arrive for a day or two. The negotiations are tabled until then, delaying everything. I just left him and Hunter is *not* happy."

Gaylan released a disappointed sigh. "I suppose he blames it on the one female at the table."

"It seems you know him well already."

How had she let this happen? Gaylan wondered. She'd been hired to do a simple job for two weeks at fantastic pay in one of the world's most beautiful spots. Why couldn't she have stayed uninvolved—with Hunter and with Nari's problem—and just put in her time, taken the money and run? Why was nothing simple when it came to Hunter James II? "I guess I'll play it by ear," she said, turning toward the hall leading to the suite.

Evan took her hand, squeezed it. "I hope you haven't forgotten that you're hostessing a dinner tonight."

Gaylan closed her eyes briefly at the reminder. She'd gone over the menu with the staff yesterday morning. With the tension simmering among all of them, wouldn't it be a night to remember?

"I really don't want to see you get hurt. Please watch yourself around Hunter."

Her smile was tinged with sadness. "Good advice."

He held on a moment longer. "Do you know the definition of a survivor, Gaylan? One who outlasts. I believe you're a survivor."

Gaylan went on tiptoe and kissed his cheek. "See you at dinner."

Evan watched her walk away, her back ramrod straight. She appeared in control and tough enough to handle things. But he'd seen her eyes and knew his warning to be careful around Hunter had come too late.

He was changing, Hunter thought as he fastened his cummerbund. And he wasn't crazy about the changes. Damn women were enough to drive a man crazy.

Yasu Shigeta was a nice enough person and without a doubt a beautiful woman. It was her business manner he disliked, the tenacious, ridiculously thorough, hair-splitting legal side. She'd taken a simple business transaction, one that had been roughed out by Evan and Ross and Hiroki weeks before they all met in Hawaii, and dissected every section, clause and comma.

Evan was a good attorney, one who'd seen to it through the years that Compu West was rarely involved in legal disputes and that if they were, they came out on top. He kept Hunter informed, honest, inviolate and he did it with a minimum of fuss and time expended. Yasu, by comparison, was a fanatic hell-bent on examining every word under her own microscope, and anyone else's timetable be damned.

To be honest, he could have left, Hunter told himself as he reached for his bow tie. He could have claimed that important business back in L.A. demanded his attention and flown home, leaving the details to Ross and Evan. After all, just because the Yamaguchis had decided to combine business with pleasure didn't mean he had to.

He was here to consummate a business deal, not to play volleyball in the sand and drink beer or to picnic on an uninhabited island or go fishing. He was the head of a multimillion-dollar conglomerate, not a figurehead who was basically a playboy. He could have returned and flown back for the formal signing of the final contracts.

But he'd stayed.

Why? he asked himself, studying his own gray eyes. It was damn difficult for a man to hide from the truth when he was all alone in his own room gazing into his own eyes. He knew the answer without speaking her name out loud.

Gaylan Fisher.

She was the one who was really changing him. Not the Yamaguchis and not Yasu. Gaylan with her huge eyes and her soft hands and her woman's body. Even thinking about her had his blood heating. He couldn't help remembering the feel of her silky skin, her ragged sighs when he'd touched her breasts, the way she kissed him.

He'd wanted desperately to join with her, to be inside her, to know her at last. But, for all the wrong reasons.

Hunter adjusted the tie, no longer meeting his own eyes in the mirror. He wasn't very proud of what he'd almost done. Although he'd figured out the reason, he had trouble living with the answer.

He hadn't seen her since their return in the middle of the night. She'd been gone this morning and he'd apparently been in his room when she'd returned. He'd knocked on her door about an hour ago and asked how soon she'd be ready. She'd called out that she'd be ready on time. That was the only contact he'd had with her.

Grabbing his tuxedo jacket, Hunter shook it out, then put it on. He was in no mood for a formal dinner party tonight, but he didn't know how to get out of it gracefully. He didn't know exactly what he was in the mood for instead. His emotions were in a turmoil and he was unused to the sensations. Not even with Jolene had he suffered such ambivalence.

Wearing a frown of disgust at his own indecisiveness, he walked into the living room and poured himself a drink, then sat down to wait for Gaylan to appear.

In her bedroom, Gaylan heard the clink of ice cubes dropping into a glass and was surprised. She'd rarely seen Hunter drink but an occasional glass of wine. But then, Evan had said he was upset.

She'd waited until she'd heard his shower running, then she'd snuck into the master bedroom and grabbed the clothes she'd need for this formal dinner. She'd made several calls from her room to the staff, finalizing the menu and flower arrangements, though she had little enthusiasm for the function. She'd much rather have stayed in tonight, dressed in shorts and a top, and have a shrimp salad sent up. But she had to earn her salary, smile all evening, put on a happy face.

Angling her head, she slipped the stem of a gold hoop earring into her earlobe, put on the back and shook out her hair. Studying her mirrored reflection, she decided the white cocktail dress looked pretty good since her tan had deepened.

Again, she forced her mind to replay the conversation she'd been rehearsing all afternoon. Ideally she'd be able to convince Hunter to help her help Nari. Taking a deep breath, she left the room.

He was seated in a leather chair with his back to the lanai. As she walked out, he rose, stunned anew at how lovely she was. Her dress had a high neck, yet the way it clung in all the right places made it look sexier than anything low-cut. "Can I fix you a drink?" he asked, giving himself a little time to get used to her presence.

"No, thanks." She sat down on the small settee and saw the quick hunger leap into his eyes though he hadn't commented on her appearance. "You look wonderful in a tux."

Trying to keep the mood light, Hunter sat back down and crossed his long legs. "Let's see now, I look terrific in sweats and wonderful in a tux. You should see me in grubby overalls."

She tilted her head. "I'd be willing to bet a tidy sum that you've never ever been in grubby overalls."

He smiled. "You'd win. You, on the other hand, are more beautiful tonight than I've ever seen you." He imagined the only way she could possibly look better would be wearing nothing at all. He coughed into his fist at that thought, realizing he'd have to rein in those flights of fancy.

"Thank you."

"Do you do it on purpose, to keep men edgy and off guard?" He sipped his Scotch slowly. Very slowly.

"Absolutely. Is it working?"

"It is with me. I imagine you'll probably steam Taro's glasses and make Hiroki forget he's on a second honeymoon."

Just the opening she'd been waiting for. "I have a favor to ask of you regarding Hiroki."

"What might that be?"

Again, she explained the situation of Nari wanting to work in fashion design as she had to Evan, going on to say she was very impressed with the young Japanese woman's sketches. Then she explained about Hiroki's reluctance to allow his wife to work.

"I understand that perfectly," Hunter stated.

"I thought you might. You may recall that at our first dinner with the Yamaguchis, you told them that I didn't work outside the home but rather traveled with you, which was all I had time for."

"I do remember that."

"The truth is, if we were actually married, I'd probably want to work at something." Gaylan looked at him as he silently studied her.

"Well, since we aren't really married, we don't have to address our differences on this subject."

"But don't you see, it would help Nari so much in trying to convince Hiroki to let her try her wings if you were to say that you wouldn't mind if I also worked."

"You want me to lie?"

Gaylan let out a huff of exasperation. "Hunter, this whole fiasco is a lie. What possible harm could it do to mention that you wouldn't disapprove if I wanted to work as, say, an illustrator of children's books?"

He took a rather long sip, watching her over the rim. "Do you?"

She hadn't intended to mention that, but had gotten caught up in her need to convince him. "As a matter of fact, I do. But that's immaterial. What's important here is that we would present a picture of a husband and wife who had a fifty-fifty marriage, each acknowledging that the other has needs and encouraging their partner to fulfill those needs."

"And you think the Yamaguchis would believe me after they've gotten to know me somewhat and know my attitude about working women?" Including their dear Yasu Shigeta?

She shrugged, trying for nonchalance. "People change their minds."

"I don't very often. Why are you interfering in their marriage and in their customs? Why are you encouraging Nari to go against her husband's wishes?"

"I'm not." Gaylan struggled to keep her voice calm. "I haven't encouraged her to do anything. I thought that together we could help her have her chance."

He felt a rush of temper. "Well, forget it. I'm not changing my mind or lying for you. You can't have every little thing you want, Gaylan. Life isn't like that." Hunter drained the last of his drink.

She saw red, literally. "Every little thing I want! What do you know about me, that you can say that? I'm not the one who was born with a silver spoon in my mouth. What do you know of struggle, of worries?"

In her fury, she jumped to her feet and began to pace, building a full head of steam. "You have no right to judge me. I've worked hard all these years with no outside help. I put up with a cranky old man and his often asinine demands and his idiosyncrasies for six long years while I struggled to deal with my own grief over the loss of my parents." She could have said more, so

much more. About Mel, his arrests, her disappointment and fears. But she was afraid she'd already said
too much.

Reaching the bar, she gripped it with both hands,
trying to calm down. "Have every little thing I want.
That's a laugh. If I could have just one thing right now,
it would be to be able to go home right this second." She
bit her lip, trying desperately not to cry.

Hunter set down his glass and got to his feet. He'd
been angry—with Yasu, with the delays, with his jum-
bled feelings. He'd accused Gaylan unfairly, judged her
unkindly. He felt an unexpected surge of shame. So
seldom did he spend enough time around a woman to
hurt her that he was shocked that he had.

Clumsily he touched her shoulder. "I'm sorry."

Still upset, Gaylan pulled away from his touch. In so
doing, her right earring back fell off and the gold hoop
dropped down. "Oh, damn." Blinking, she bent down
to look for it.

"Let me help." Hunter stooped and picked up the
hoop just as her hand closed over the back. They stood
up together.

Gaylan held out her palm.

"Let me put it in," Hunter said, and shifted her long
hair aside. Carefully he inserted the stem, took the back
from her and pressed it in place. Gently he rearranged
her hair, then took hold of her shoulders and turned her
to face him squarely. "I really am sorry."

She shook her head and stepped back. "Never mind.
I'm sorry I asked."

"Don't be. I think you're right. It can't hurt to give
Nari a little help. You bring up the subject at dinner and
I'll back you up."

She turned a suspicious look on him. She would have refused if it had been for her. But she didn't want to let Nari down. "Every time I think I have you figured out, you throw me a curve."

He stepped closer, wondering why he'd given in, wondering why the scent of her baby soap was more alluring than anything he'd ever smelled, wondering why he couldn't keep a single resolution he made about this woman. "I understand women find men of mystery very exciting."

"Do they?"

"The question is, do you?"

Gaylan knew he could read the answer in her eyes. She knew also that she was stepping closer and closer to the fire, and felt helpless to stop. "Yes," she whispered.

His arms crushed her to him and his mouth slanted over hers.

He kissed with too much passion and with that enticing hint of frustration. She'd never known anything like it. His assault on her senses was thorough, reckless, rapid. In seconds, he had her soaring, her hands bunching in the material of his jacket as she struggled with a feeling of panic that he could take her under so effortlessly.

Hunter backed her up to the bar, caged her hips between his thighs while his teeth nipped at her lips. When her mouth opened, his tongue moved inside and stroked hers with an insistence that had her responding in kind. As she unconsciously aligned her body with his and pressed closer, he dropped hot, wet kisses along the smooth column of her throat.

Floating. Gaylan was floating, feeling shivers of ice, then raging heat race along her spine. His clever hands had her trembling while his mouth returned to hers, seducing, arousing. Then suddenly, as if a sleepwalker shocked awake, Hunter was straightening, stepping back.

"We have a dinner to put on," he said, his voice not quite as steady as he'd have liked. But he'd had the strength to pull away. At last, his years of discipline came through. The incident on the island had been a momentary lapse.

Dazed, Gaylan met his eyes, locking her gaze with his for a long moment. "I wasn't sure you could put on the brakes."

"Don't think it was easy." But he'd done it. He'd proved he was strong, in control.

The mantel clock chimed the hour. The servers would be arriving momentarily with the food. She had only moments left to learn what she needed to know. "I know why you stopped tonight. I need to know why you wanted to keep going last night, with the helicopter almost at our door."

He should have known she wouldn't let it go. He supposed he owed her the truth, unkind as it was. "I thought that if I had you once, if I got you out of my system, I could walk away."

It hurt, but she wouldn't let him see. She raised her chin, challenging him. "And can you?"

The knock at the door was well timed for Hunter. He let the backs of his fingers caress her cheek ever so lightly. "I'll let them in."

She had her answer, Gaylan thought as she stepped into her bedroom to repair her makeup.

Chapter Nine

Hunter hated dinner parties, formal or informal. If he had his druthers, he'd have preferred a simple meal, which he'd have eaten alone at his table while reading one of the many reports being faxed or overnighted to him from his L.A. office. Or he might have skipped dinner altogether since he wasn't feeling all that well tonight. Perhaps it was the drink he'd downed too quickly or maybe the heat, he decided as he tried to concentrate on the talk around the table.

He disliked small talk even more than dinner parties. Gaylan, on the other hand, seemed to be an expert at it.

Seated at the head, across from her at the foot, he sipped the cup of broth the waitress had set on his plate and found the miso soup wasn't half bad. He'd been hesitant about serving a Japanese dinner to their Japanese guests when Gaylan had suggested the menu yesterday, mostly because he wasn't much of an experimenter when it came to eating. Ross and Evan had often chided him during their travels because he inevitably ordered from the American side of the menu even in the exotic restaurants that they occasionally found themselves dining in.

He'd been in the middle of studying a file when she'd interrupted to discuss the Japanese dinner, and in the interest of time, he'd given her carte blanche. After he'd had time to think about it, he'd feared tonight's dinner would consist of the currently popular sushi. The thought of eating raw fish and other concoctions of an unknown nature had had his stomach rolling queasily. He needn't have worried, he acknowledged as the waiters removed their soup bowls and others began serving the main course.

While Gaylan had been in reapplying her makeup after that stunning kiss, he'd asked one of the parade of servers about their dinner and been pleased at her selections. Not for the first time, he wondered how she managed to come up with choices he himself would have picked.

"Mmm, I love tempura," Nari commented.

"You love anything you don't have to cook yourself," Hiroki said, his smile taking the sting from his words.

"Some of us aren't good in the kitchen," Gaylan said, accepting a helping of chicken teriyaki.

They'd spent half an hour having wine and hors d'oeuvres, which she hoped had been long enough to put most everyone at ease. She decided to jump right in. "Our talents lie in other directions. Planning menus instead of cooking dinners. Sharing quality time with our families instead of quantity. Making a contribution outside the home that fulfills us and enriches our relationships." Gaylan saw Nari's surprise turn to hesitant pleasure.

Here it comes, Hunter thought, refusing the snowy-white rice. He'd always disliked plain rice, but he supposed it was almost a requisite in this particular meal.

Hiroki glanced first at his wife, then Gaylan. "Surely you don't subscribe to the working-wife theory. I've seen how devoted you are to Hunter, traveling with him, seeing to his every need. That leaves you very little time for anything else."

Gaylan toyed with her cucumber salad, choosing her words carefully. "Oh, I think it's possible to do both." She smiled sweetly at Hunter at the far end of the table. "We're living proof that a cooperative marriage works, right, darling?"

All eyes swung toward Hunter, each questioning, with the exception of Evan, whose expression was guarded.

He'd promised, Hunter reminded himself. He could just imagine Yasu's surprise at what he was about to say, after he'd been all but openly critical of her during their business discussions. He was equally as surprised that he'd agreed to go along with Gaylan's scheme.

Setting down his wineglass, Hunter assumed what he hoped would pass for an I-thought-you-knew look. "I was sure this must have been mentioned sometime during one of our get-togethers last week, but perhaps not. Gaylan does illustrations for children's books."

Taro and Yoshiko went on eating, but Hiroki lay down his fork and Nari's face lit up. "She does? How long has she been doing this?"

Hunter figured his part was over. "Gaylan, why don't you tell them?"

Her stomach muscles relaxed now that he'd come through. Gaylan smiled at Hiroki. "Actually I haven't found a publisher yet, but a writer friend and I have put together two manuscripts for submission. We're searching for an agent and the right publishing house. We're very hopeful we'll sell soon."

As he listened to Nari's interested questions bubble forth, Hunter wondered how much of what Gaylan was saying was the truth and how much she'd fabricated in order to help the young Japanese woman she'd apparently come to like. She hadn't alluded to career aspirations in any of their conversations prior to today, nor had Evan mentioned her interest in becoming an illustrator. Suspicious by nature of any new gambit, Hunter couldn't decide if her excitement as she discussed her drawings was genuine or if he was seeing another example of the good actress he knew her to be.

Hiroki looked a bit taken aback. "I guess I'd thought you mostly supported your husband by traveling with him and being there for him. You'd even mentioned wanting a big family. How can you be all things—a supportive wife, a good mother and a committed illustrator?"

Finished with her dinner, Gaylan patted her mouth with her pale blue linen napkin. "Haven't you heard, Hiroki? This is the nineties. Women all over the world are doing it all." She looked into his dark eyes and saw the hesitancy, the doubt. "It may seem as if a woman would be overwhelmed by all that, but in reality, most women I know are fired up by the challenge. And a wife who's allowed to do her own thing within the limits of the family is a very satisfied woman." She swung her gaze to Hunter's shuttered face. "I don't believe Hunter feels in the least neglected, do you, darling?"

She was carrying this a little far, but he had little choice except to agree. "Gaylan's very adept at all her undertakings," he managed, rubbing at a spot above one eye where a headache was trying to break through.

"I can vouch for that," Evan added, wondering what in hell was going on.

Ross found himself studying Yasu, who'd remained silent during the exchange. Had she not married because of this very thing, a prejudice among most men she'd known regarding working wives? He couldn't help wondering.

"It is true that times have changed," Yoshiko commented resignedly. "In our country, some young wives are pursuing careers."

"Change is not always for the better," Taro said, apparently unwilling to step away from centuries of tradition.

Ross spoke to the entire table, but his eyes were still on Yasu. "They say that the willow that doesn't bend will break." He saw her look up and try to assess his remark.

Enough, Gaylan thought. She didn't want to beat a dead horse. She'd done her best, perhaps opened Hiroki's eyes. The rest would have to be up to Nari. Quietly she signaled the headwaiter to begin clearing. "Everyone ready for tea? We have a very special dessert tonight."

"What is it?" Taro asked, his sweet tooth attested to by his thickening waist.

Gaylan just smiled. "It's a surprise. You'll see in a moment."

As the servers worked, Hunter watched Gaylan expertly change the subject, deftly including everyone in a discussion on the artful floral bouquets on the table

and throughout the suite. She'd had the hotel staff prepare them to her requirements, personally overseeing
each arrangement. She'd told Hunter once that she liked
working with living things, that plants thrived on love.

Poppycock, he thought. They thrived on sunshine,
water and fertilizer. But as she explained her theory to
the Yamaguchis, they seemed to look at her as if she'd
just reinvented the wheel. With no small amount of
surprise, Hunter heard Yoshiko invite Gaylan to visit
their Tokyo home and learn about flowers indigenous
to that area.

"Of course, Hunter-san, you also are invited," the
ever-polite Taro added, trying not to make the invitation sound like an afterthought.

Hunter's response was a try at a smile that resembled a grimace. He had to concede that he'd lost control of his own dinner party. But then, hadn't he hired
Gaylan so she'd charm the Japanese, so he'd be able to
complete his business deal? She was doing exactly what
she'd been required to do. She was a woman who
wanted something, as he'd learned today. A career as a
published illustrator. And she was willing to be involved in a masquerade for money, presumably until she
hit the big time. If she ever did.

Or was the career talk just another ploy? Hunter was
having trouble telling the difference between fact and
fiction lately. He had to keep in mind that Gaylan, like
Jolene, was out for herself. He mustn't think the soft
glances she sent his way, the almost shy way her hand
had reached for his on the settee earlier as they'd sipped
wine, meant anything more than that she was doing her
job.

Odd, though, there were times when he met her eyes
and saw something fragile there, something defense-

less. Once or twice, he'd glimpsed flashes of pain she'd then quickly covered up and not revealed to him. True, she'd lost both her parents at an early age, but that had happened eight years ago. Surely she still wasn't reacting to that. She didn't appear to be scheming, but hadn't he learned the hard way that women often had hidden agendas, camouflaging their motives until they'd won a man over? Her kisses, her exciting reaction in his arms, were undoubtedly a studied response. No matter how much he wanted her, how much his body yearned for her, he mustn't lose control again.

Not unless it would be on *his* terms—a mutually satisfying physical relationship without strings—which seemed highly unlikely.

Hunter watched the tea being poured and wished this interminable evening would end as he wrenched his attention back to the table talk.

"I've always admired the topiary gardens in Japan," Gaylan was saying. "Such a beautiful art form."

"Speaking of art forms," Nari went on, "you should see my mother-in-law do origami. She's a true expert."

Yoshiko smiled modestly. "Your praise is perhaps not deserved. I do it for my own pleasure."

Gaylan's interest was genuine. "I'd love to see a demonstration."

"And so you shall, then, my dear," Yoshiko happily agreed.

"The dessert is served," the headwaiter said as the servers set down two large cake plates, one at each end of the table.

Hunter's eyes widened as he realized what the surprise dessert was. Each dish contained a dozen chocolate cupcakes with white icing and sprinkles. His usually bland expression was replaced by a shocked pleasure. His gaze moved to Gaylan, but he was speechless.

"One of my husband's favorite desserts. Please, help yourselves." She'd managed to catch him off guard, not an easy thing to do. Gaylan felt a rush of warmth at his almost boyish enjoyment as he bit into one. For just a moment, she'd glimpsed a youthful vulnerability and guessed that surprises of this nature were not common in Hunter's life, despite his wealth.

Why, Gaylan wondered, did that fact only endear him more to her lonely heart?

"I don't think I want to go deep-sea fishing, Evan," Gaylan told him the morning after the dinner party. She had to smile at the blue cotton hat sporting a variety of colorful fish hooks that the attorney had jammed on his iron gray hair. In his new jeans and a plaid shirt, the man was hardly recognizable.

Evan looked honestly disappointed. "Are you sure? It's not as difficult as you might have heard. The guys that operate the boat help you reel them in."

Stretched out on the lounge chair on the lanai off the living room, Gaylan set down the book she'd been attempting to read. It was too beautiful a day to be hotel-bound, but she didn't think a fishing trip was the answer for her. "I sunburn too easily to be out on the ocean for too long, but thanks for asking."

He nodded toward the inside rooms. "Where's Hunter?"

"Holed up in his room working. He told me he'd wasted enough time with silly activities as it was." Her tone indicated how silly she thought that comment was since he worked all the time. However, he hadn't gone for his morning run, and the quick glimpse she'd had of him on the lanai when she'd returned, he'd looked distant and inscrutable.

Evan shoved his hands into his jeans pockets. "A hard man to understand sometimes."

"You've a way with understatement." Her glance fell on the binoculars lying on the small table. "See those glasses?" she asked, keeping her voice low. "Early this morning, I came back from my run and caught Hunter using them, staring right out that way to the left, so absorbed he didn't hear me come in. I was curious, so later, when he'd gone into his room, I came out and aimed the binoculars in the direction he'd been watching. I was hoping I wouldn't learn he was a Peeping Tom." She shook her head. "He'd been intently studying that sandy section where several young boys were playing a game of makeshift baseball." She looked up at Evan. "What do you make of it?"

Evan pulled up a wrought-iron footstool and sat down close to Gaylan's chair, torn between loyalty to his employer and this young woman's obvious desire to know more about this enigmatic man. Since he felt Gaylan was motivated by her growing feelings for Hunter, he would tell her a little. "Years ago, when Hunter was a youngster, his father refused to let him play with the other boys. He wanted his son in the library studying, in his office learning the business by observing, or pursuing cerebral activities, not merely leisure time-wasters."

"So he could one day take over the empire his father built?"

"Yes. Nothing could give a man a high like consummating a particularly tough business deal, Hunter, Sr., used to say. Not sports, not sex, not anything."

How sad, Gaylan thought. "And Hunter believed his father?"

Evan shrugged. "Outwardly, at least. But inside, he longed to be like the other boys. So he confiscated that old pair of binoculars and he'd watch the neighborhood kids play street baseball or ragtag football from his upstairs bedroom window, sometimes for hours. His mother once told me she used to cry at the sight of him looking so wistful. But when she'd try to persuade him to go out and join the boys, Hunter would adamantly refuse, afraid to displease his father."

Gaylan's heart ached for that small, lonely boy. "Why didn't his mother intercede with his father on Hunter's behalf?"

Evan gave a mirthless laugh. "She was as afraid of her husband as Hunter, maybe more."

"Yet she found the courage to leave him."

"After fifteen years. And it did take courage, because she also had to leave her son. Hunter was only fourteen and it nearly broke her heart. She knew he'd never let her have custody. However, I think she thought she'd lose her mind if she didn't get out from under her husband's control."

There was that word again, *control*. "Hunter's got the same hang-up on controlling." She remembered his remark yesterday, his need to be in charge even in lovemaking.

"No, not in the same way. Hunter can be very strong, especially in business dealings, but I've never known him to be unfair or ruthless for the sake of dominance. Perhaps you've never seen his softer side. For instance, he has a strong belief that every man deserves a second chance."

Curious, she frowned at him. "Such as?"

Evan glanced through the doorway at Hunter's closed bedroom door, then leaned closer, lowering his voice. "This is strictly confidential. Ross's father used to be the gardener at Hunter's family home when the two of them were teenagers. Ross had been in trouble, a couple of misdemeanors and finally a felony. He served two years in prison and when he got out, he probably would have continued his ways if Hunter hadn't looked him up."

"What'd he do?"

"Hunter asked Ross the question he asks nearly every employee he hires. *'Where do you see yourself five years from now?'* Ross was belligerent at first, then finally confessed he wanted to be an attorney. Too late. He had a record. But he could go to college, could train to be an executive assistant to one of the most powerful men in the country."

"Hunter put Ross through college?"

"Not exactly. He wasn't old enough, didn't have his own money yet. But he talked his father into paying Ross's way, one of the few times Hunter, Sr., ever gave in to his son. And Hunter kept an eye on Ross to make sure he didn't screw up. Ross would go to the wall for Hunter."

Gaylan was puzzled. "Yet they don't seem like close friends. Like trusted business associates but not *friends.*"

"Because Hunter holds everyone at arm's length, afraid to get too close. Even his own mother."

"Yes, he told me a little about his mother. He can't seem to understand why she prefers a Georgia peach farm over all that his father offered her. I do."

"Of course. So do I. And I think, inside where it counts, Hunter does, too. He understands the concept of love, but he's always viewed it from the outside looking in. He cares, but he's afraid to care. The proof is that he loves his mother despite the fact that she was little help to him as a child. Two years ago, when the peach ranch nearly went bankrupt, she called Hunter. He bailed them out without a second's hesitation."

Gaylan drew her legs up and hugged her knees. "A checkbook is an easy panacea for a man with money."

Evan stood, shaking his head. "You're wrong, Gaylan. I'm privy to all of Hunter's doings, and he does a lot of good no one knows about, not just getting Ross on track. He'd fire me if I told you more, so I won't. Don't be too harsh a judge before you know *all* the facts." He adjusted his hat. "Got to go before my fishing boat leaves without me. See you later."

"Have a good time."

At the door, Evan paused, turning back. "I've talked with both of you lately and it surprises me no end how little each of you know the other after living together over a week. Yet a blind man could see that there's an attraction just sizzling between the two of you." He gave her a paternal smile. "I have to warn you again. Be careful, Gaylan. No one who steps close to the fire comes away without some injury."

"I'll keep that in mind." She waited until he left, listening to Hunter moving around in his room. She didn't feel like another round just now, which would probably happen if she hung around and he came out.

Rising, Gaylan decided to go out onto the beach and walk for a while.

Two hours had passed before she returned carrying an interesting piece of driftwood she'd found far down the beach. Entering the suite, Gaylan wasn't sure what she'd do with her find, but it had caught her eye. Perhaps she'd put it in the sun after the damp wood dried out a bit more and, later, arrange it in a planter with some greenery around it.

The lanai off the living area was no longer sunny so she walked over to the open door of Hunter's room, thinking his balcony might still be in sunlight. What she saw had her nearly dropping the driftwood.

He was stretched out on the lounge chair wrapped right up to his neck in a dark blue blanket. A teapot and cup were on the table next to him. His eyes were closed and he was shivering. Quickly she set down her find and went to him. "Hunter?"

His eyes flew open and he shook uncontrollably as he looked up at her with dazed eyes. His lips trembled but he didn't speak.

"What's wrong?" She reached to touch her fingers to his forehead and found his skin hot and clammy. He had to be feeling miserable. "We need to call the doctor."

"No! I'm okay. Just getting a cold." His words came out ragged as he swallowed around a sore throat.

"I don't think so. You must have picked up a bug." She smoothed back his hair and found it damp as well.

"I'll be fine. Just need a little sleep." If only he could get warm and if this damnable shivering would stop. He'd called down for some tea, drunk two cups, and still he was freezing. "Could you get me another blanket, please?" He hated asking for help, but he had to set aside his pride. The thought of getting up and searching for more covers was enough to send him into spasms of quivers.

Gaylan had no medical training, but she'd spent a lot of time with an old man who'd become more frail by the day, and susceptible to a variety of ills. This had to be a virus at best, or at worst the beginning of a serious infection. She went to the closet, pulled down another blanket and arranged it around him. "It's eighty degrees out here, Hunter, and you're still cold. Whatever you have is not going away without medical assistance."

"Better. Better already," he mumbled.

"Sure you are." Without hesitation, she walked to his bedside phone and dialed the doctor's extension. When she mentioned she was calling for Hunter James, the doctor was on the line in moments. With her back to the lanai, she explained Hunter's condition and asked him to come up. Dr. Brewster said he'd be at the suite in ten minutes.

In the meantime, she fixed a cold cloth and took it out to him. Placing it on his forehead, she saw that he was still shaking despite the additional blanket. "Let's see if this helps," she said.

He kept his eyes closed, struggling with a weakness that threatened to take him under. Hunter hated weakness of any kind. Finding himself in this position had him trying to grit his chattering teeth. More than anything, he hated having Gaylan see him like this. "You . . . you can go now. Thanks."

Gaylan pulled up a chair. "I'm not going anywhere." She held the cloth in place, wishing the doctor would hurry.

"I don't need a baby-sitter," he said through gritted teeth, the effort all but exhausting him. "Where's Ross or Evan?"

She knew better than to take his dismissal personally. A private man, he didn't want anyone except perhaps his two trusted friends to witness his less-than-perfect state. "Evan's out deep-sea fishing and I believe Ross and Yasu went para-sailing down the beach. All four Yamaguchis rented a car and went sight-seeing early this morning. You're stuck with me, I'm afraid." She heard a knock at the door. "I'll be right back."

Dr. Brewster was short, stocky and very tan. He was also very professional as he listened to Gaylan explain that the patient would be less than cooperative.

"Not to worry, Mrs. James," the doctor said in a slight British accent. "Most men are reluctant to seek medical help until they're forced to by circumstances or their wives." Carrying his black bag, he followed Gaylan out to the lanai.

Hearing voices, Hunter forced his eyes open. Recognizing Dr. Brewster, he glared at Gaylan. "I told you I don't need a doctor." Then, as if on cue, his body betrayed him by causing a deep shudder to rumble through him. He almost groaned aloud.

Gaylan stepped back into the coolness of the dim bedroom as Dr. Brewster unwrapped his patient and began his examination over Hunter's mumbled objections. She'd known it was the right thing to do to call the doctor, the same thing she was certain Ross or Evan would have done. She'd deal with Hunter's temper later. Still, she called the front desk and left a message for Ross to phone the suite as soon as he returned. She knew that Evan would be gone till much later.

Dr. Brewster finished and rose to his feet. "You've got a bad case of influenza, Mr. James." He handed two containers of pills to Gaylan in the doorway. "See that he takes one of each of these every four hours. They'll help lower his fever and ease the achiness. Otherwise, he's to have lots of fluids and bed rest."

"I don't want those damn pills," Hunter stated, trying for an emphatic tone just before a fit of coughing took him. "I can get better on my own. Just need a little sleep."

It was the control thing, Gaylan was certain. He'd lost control of his body due to the illness and it was infuriating him. "Don't worry, Doctor. I'll get the medicine into him."

Dr. Brewster's brown eyes measured her, then he smiled. "I have no doubt you will. And be careful yourself. He's contagious right now."

"How long before he's better?" Gaylan asked, well aware of Hunter's impatience.

"If he follows directions, he'll be feeling better by tomorrow morning, but he won't really be himself for about eighteen to twenty-four hours." Snapping shut his case, he turned to leave. "You listen to your wife, Mr. James, and you'll be fine in no time." He didn't even flinch at Hunter's scowl. As a hotel doctor, he'd seen it before.

Gaylan thanked him, saw him out and returned with a glass of ginger ale over ice. She stopped to turn down Hunter's bed before she went to stand over him as he lay on the lounge chair, his eyes closed, deliberately ignoring her. "Come on. It's time to get into bed."

He felt weak as a kitten and mad as a bull. Why had this happened to him, especially now? He never got sick.

Slowly he opened his eyes. Even in his sorry state, he found himself admiring those incredibly long legs and that cloud of hair that shimmered in the sun. His anger dissolved. "Lady, are you propositioning me?" he asked in a voice he wished didn't sound so shaky.

"Certainly." She tugged the blankets from him. "See if you can stand up and I'll help you inside." Why hadn't she asked Dr. Brewster to stay long enough to get him settled?

The cooler air hit Hunter and he shivered. "So damn cold," he complained as he braced himself, struggling to his feet. He felt Gaylan's arm encircle him. "I can do it without help," he insisted.

Silently she stepped back, watching him. The white T-shirt and maroon briefs he wore were both damp. He'd need to change, and she wondered how she'd manage to help him when he was fighting her every step of the way.

His knees were trembling, but he forced himself to take a step, grabbing hold of the lanai door for support. How had he gotten this weak this quickly? Hunter wondered. He took another shaky step, then felt the room tilt. He dare not pass out. Slowly he turned to look at Gaylan.

She searched his eyes. He wasn't giving up and he wasn't asking for help; rather his look acknowledged that he'd accept her assistance this once if she'd care to give it.

Gaylan slipped her arm about his waist and walked with him to the bed. She moved out of the way as he sat down heavily. "You need to get out of these sweaty clothes."

Annoyed at the truth, he reached for the hem of his shirt and let her pull it off him.

Gaylan found clean clothes in his dresser and helped him into a dry shirt. She noticed her own hands trembling as she adjusted the smooth cotton over his chest, resisting the urge to run her fingers over the hard muscles, the soft hair. He was ill, she reminded herself and held out the paisley silk shorts to him. "Can you change into these on your own?"

"Yes," he said quickly, grumpily.

But first, she'd get the pills into him. She shook out two into her palm and offered him the ginger ale.

He eyed them suspiciously. "I'll take them later."

"Now," she said, "or I'll pour this over your head, ice and all."

That earned her his best scowl yet. But he took the pills. When she left the room to rinse out his cold cloth, he worked hard to remove his briefs, but just as he had them almost off, he was overcome with a wave of dizziness that had him falling back onto the bed, struggling to breathe. He couldn't ever remember being this tired.

Gaylan returned, startled at how pale his face looked against the dark blue pillowcase. She noticed he hadn't quite managed to undress and reached to assist him.

"No," Hunter groaned. "I..."

"Oh, cut it out," she said, irritated at his silly modesty. "Do I look desperate enough to jump the bones of a delirious man?" At last, she felt him relax and stop fighting her. She made quick work of getting his clean shorts on, trying to keep her eyes averted in case he was watching her face. Still, she couldn't help the heat that moved into her face.

Even ill and feverish, Hunter James was a mighty inviting specimen.

Gently she arranged the covers over him. Turning on his side, he pulled them tight around his neck, struggling to not let her see how badly he was shaking again. Carefully she lay the cold cloth on his forehead. She watched his eyes flutter shut.

"I'll be close by if you need anything," she whispered.

Quietly she pulled over a chair and watched him drift into a restless sleep. She realized she was witnessing something few people had seen: Hunter James II not in control. That's why he hated being sick more than the average man. He couldn't bear losing control of his body—not to illness, not to lovemaking, and certainly not to a mere woman.

However, there are times, my good man, Gaylan thought as she saw his breathing even out, *when every person finds himself out of control.* A hard thing to learn. She wondered if this timely lesson would be lost on Hunter.

It was evening before Ross came to the suite with Yasu in tow, the two of them looking tired, sunburned and happy. "Is anything wrong?" was Ross's first question.

Fresh from her shower, Gaylan brushed back her damp hair. "No, everything's under control. I just wanted you to know that Hunter's down with the flu, but I'm taking care of him."

"What? He never gets sick. Where is *he*?" Ross looked genuinely alarmed.

"In bed, sleeping." She explained about Dr. Brewster's visit and his diagnosis. "I've been checking him regularly. The fever hasn't broken yet, but he's taking his medicine."

From long habit, Ross went into motion, his concern for Hunter causing him to forget Yasu's presence. "Thanks for handling things till I got here, Gaylan. I'll take over now."

Gaylan's brows shot up. "Excuse me?"

"I'll go in and stay with Hunter, see to his needs, like I have in the past. He seldom gets sick, but..."

She'd put up with too much to cave in. Drawing her robe more tightly about her, she squared her shoulders. "That won't be necessary, Ross. He's my husband and I'll take care of him."

Ross was taken aback. Then, remembering their situation, he glanced at Yasu and saw her watching him intently. Recovering, he sent Gaylan a sheepish look tinged with apology. "I'm sorry. I only thought to help. If you're tired, I could—"

"I'm fine, thank you." She *was* feeling fine, if a little annoyed. She'd agreed to pretend to be Hunter's wife and now, suddenly, she felt as protective as if she were. As concerned as if they were truly married. As shielding as if he were hers. Shaken by the realization, she moved to the door, anxious that Ross and Yasu leave. "If you'd like, you can phone later and I'll update you."

Yasu got the picture first. She took hold of Ross's arm. "Yes, we'll do that. Give Hunter our best when he wakes up." She looked pointedly up at Ross, easing him toward the door.

Ross glanced worriedly at the door to Hunter's room. "May I just look in for a moment?" he asked, unable to leave until he was certain his friend was sleeping peacefully.

Swallowing her irritation, Gaylan nodded. She watched him walk in, then return in moments. She bit back a sarcastic remark that came to mind as he smiled down at her.

"He seems awfully hot," Ross commented, his hand on the doorknob.

"Of course. He has a fever." Gaylan stood her ground, waiting.

"Right." Ross opened the door. "I'll call later."

Gaylan closed the door after them, wondering if Ross was on his way to verify all she'd told him with Dr. Brewster. Let him, she decided.

She was determined to keep watch over Hunter herself, and she'd like to see anyone try to stop her.

Chapter Ten

It was turning out to be a very long night, Gaylan thought as she finished changing the bed for the third time. She'd called down for extra linens and had done the changing herself. That she didn't mind. It was managing Hunter that was the difficult part, getting him into a chair while she quickly freshened the bedclothes.

At least he was no longer fighting her about taking his medicine or letting her help him in and out of a change of clothes. And she'd been able to get a cup of chicken broth down him as well as a variety of soft drinks. He'd made it to the bathroom alone and had stumbled back to bed, refusing help.

Gaylan brushed back her hair and saw that it was two in the morning this third time she'd resettled him. Moving to the bed, she felt his forehead and found it to be slightly cooler to the touch. She hoped that it wasn't just wishful thinking and that his fever was actually breaking.

Restlessly she wandered out onto the lanai. Moonlight splashed on her upturned face as she let the night breezes caress her. She was wearing only a nightshirt over cotton shorts, yet she felt warm from grappling with Hunter, who outweighed her by a good sixty pounds.

Evan had stopped in when he'd returned and heard about Hunter from Ross. But he hadn't offered to take over, apparently noticing that Gaylan had things well in hand. Taro and Hiroki had phoned and asked her to give Hunter their best. Ross had called only once and she'd told him that Hunter was about the same, wrestling with the fever and chills.

About seven, she'd had a sandwich sent up and tried to read while eating. But she'd heard Hunter moaning and had gone in to freshen his cold cloth.

Now, through the open door, she heard him turn over yet again and went back inside. She'd left a lamp on low so she wouldn't stumble around in the dark. She leaned down to touch his face.

His eyes opened and for a moment, he seemed disoriented. Then he remembered and tried a weak smile. "Sorry," he murmured. "So much trouble."

Gaylan sat down on the edge of the bed and smoothed back his disheveled hair. "No, you're not," she assured him and found she meant it. Silently she stroked his face, rough from his day's growth of beard.

Eyes closed again, he leaned into the caress, settling his face against her open palm. "You feel so good, so cool." His voice was raspy, heavy with sleep. He was drifting, hating the fever that tossed him around, loving the touch that seemed like an anchor.

She'd sponge-bathed his hot body before this last change of clothes, doing it dispassionately, like a mother tending a small boy. But now, as she leaned close, she couldn't help remembering how her hands had felt brushing over his very masculine limbs. Her own body softened at the mental image she conjured up of a well Hunter, of the freedom to touch him at her leisure.

Hunter shifted slightly as he dozed, shoving the top sheet down around his waist. Gaylan waited until he was breathing evenly again, then put her other hand on the soft cotton of the shirt that covered his chest. In that hazy state between sleep and wakefulness, he brought his hand up and covered hers, holding it fast over his heart. At the same time, he pressed his lips to her other palm so briefly that she wondered if she'd imagined it. She wondered also if he was aware of the gesture or had moved instinctively.

In the dim light, Gaylan felt her heart reach out and her mind come to a sudden realization. She'd stepped over the line. She loved him.

It was a mistake, her practical brain reminded her. Evan had said she'd get burned if she stepped too close to the fire, and she knew he was right. Most likely, Hunter would hurt her. Watching him sleep, his face open and vulnerable as she'd never seen it in wakefulness, she saw the trust he couldn't give when fully aware. Well again, he'd inevitably move away, need his space, distrusting one and all.

How sad, she thought, raising her hand from his cheek to trace his strong brow. Only here and now, with him stripped of his control and lost in sleep, could she view the real man. Here his defenses were peeled away, his paranoia hidden from her, his need for her seeping out of his every pore. He wanted love, just like everyone else. He just didn't know how to go about getting it, or giving it.

So he stayed huddled in the isolated tower that he'd built for himself—impervious, immune, immovable. Gaylan would wager few had ever seen him as he was now, and if he was aware of her intense scrutiny, he'd hate it. How was she ever going to get him to willingly leave the secluded haven of his studied indifference? How could she bring him to admit he needed love, needed her? How could she teach him to accept her love and want to give his in return?

A shiver raced along Hunter's spine and he hunched in, reaching for the blanket. "So cold," he murmured.

Coming to a decision, Gaylan rose and walked around the other side of the bed, then crawled under the covers, turning toward him as he lay on his side. She stretched her arm out to encircle him, drawing him up tight against herself. She heard him make a low sound in his throat, then felt him put his hand over hers. Snuggling into him spoon-fashion, she shared her body heat with him and heard him sigh contentedly.

Little did Hunter realize that she was also sharing her heart with him.

The mists were swirling around him, trying to drag him under deeper, making his eyelids seem impossibly heavy. With no small effort, Hunter opened his eyes, waking slowly. He lay still, getting his bearings, becoming aware of his surroundings.

Memory rushed back and he recalled the doctor's visit, the liquids Gaylan kept forcing down him, the cool cloths to his head. His body came alive inch by inch and he became aware of a small hand under his own in the area of his heart. Against his back he felt the unmistakable softness of breasts, and a rush of pleasure suffused him. Lower still, a very feminine leg was somehow twined with his.

Hunter blinked, trying to clear his foggy brain. How and when had she come into his bed? He'd been sick, he knew, and feverish. But no amount of fever would have made him forget making love to Gaylan, something that his restless body had been longing for for days now. Had she lain with him because he'd been so cold, simply to warm him? Or had she fallen into an exhausted sleep after watching over him for hours?

Moving slightly, he saw by the digital clock that it was a little after four. Through the curtained lanai doors, he could see the sky barely beginning to lighten. He could feel Gaylan's warm, deep breathing against the back of his neck. The best guess was that she'd probably considered him no threat and had decided to get some rest alongside him instead of in the other bedroom.

Slowly, trying not to wake her, he curled his fingers around hers more tightly. Instinctively she returned the pressure, then relaxed again. He closed his eyes, absorbing her nearness. She felt so damn good against him. While it was true that he wanted her sexually, this was a feeling very different, very new. This was a feeling of comfort, of rightness, of sharing.

He'd never known anything like it, Hunter acknowledged. His mother had not been a cuddler when he'd been a small boy. Jolene had preferred twin beds and he hadn't protested. He'd never spent an entire night with any of the women he'd known since, never wanted to. Apparently he'd missed out on one of life's greatest pleasures, snuggling with a woman who freely shared her body with him.

She'd been tending him since about noon yesterday, nearly eighteen hours, a long time. She'd fed him, bathed him, changed his clothes and his bed. Every time he'd groaned or called out, she'd been right there. It puzzled him.

What would she get out of being his nursemaid?

He'd like to think she did it because she cared, but he knew better than to fall into that old trap. People always wanted something from you. You just had to wait and figure out what, then decide if the price was worth the payoff. Admittedly Gaylan was the first woman he'd met that he had difficulty pinpointing.

It didn't matter what she wanted, for now, for this moment in time when he was weaker than usual. He wouldn't admit it out loud to a soul, but he needed her just now. Needed her comfort, her feminine warmth, her softness.

He also needed to be in more control of their positions. Taking great care, Hunter turned over, shifting Gaylan onto her other side. She didn't waken but instead adjusted her position and snuggled her little bottom tight up against him as he curled around her. Hunter swallowed hard, wondering if he could keep his body from reacting to such intimacy and undoubtedly spoiling the moment. The urge abated and he slowly maneuvered his arm upward until he was able to fill his hand with one of her breasts. Again she sighed softly as her flesh grew accustomed to his touch.

In the dim light, he gazed at her hair spread out on the pillow like a golden cloud. He moved his face into it, inhaling her fresh scent mingled with the wondrous aroma of woman. Hunter closed his eyes with a feeling of contentment such as he'd never known.

His arms wrapped around Gaylan, his body intertwined with hers, he slept.

He awoke with sunlight streaming in and his arms empty. Hunter rubbed his eyes, watering from the glare, and struggled with a surprising sense of loss. He looked over and frowned at the unoccupied side of the bed. Had he been dreaming? he wondered.

If so, it was the best dream he'd had in a long while. He could still feel Gaylan snuggled into him, and this time his body's reaction was unavoidable. Shifting uncomfortably, he heard running water being turned off and realized she was in showering.

He let out a relieved sigh. At least she hadn't abandoned him. Another new feeling, Hunter realized. Never before had he wanted to awaken with a woman. Instead he'd wanted to get on with his day, to forget the night before. But now, he lay remembering. And was unaware that a smile formed on his face.

"Well, I guess you're feeling better," Gaylan said as she walked in from the bath wearing the Japanese robe the hotel provided. Wrapping a towel around her wet hair, she moved closer, a little nervous about her patient.

She hadn't meant to fall asleep. She'd intended to warm him enough so he'd stop shaking, then leave him. But the long day and night had caught up with her. Not only had she slept, but she must have slept like the dead, for she'd awakened to find herself wrapped in Hunter's arms. His hand on her breast had started a fire deep inside her, one she knew she had to put out.

He'd probably turned restlessly in his sleep and, finding her there, instinctively reached for her. She hoped his memory would be fuzzy and he wouldn't recall the intimate hours they'd slept together. Trying for nonchalance, she stepped closer and touched his forehead.

"Not exactly cool, but certainly on its way to normal, I'd say." His eyes as he watched her were clear and free of the fever. She tried a small smile. "How do you feel?"

I feel like pulling you back into this bed and seeing if we can heat things up again. "Like I've been run over by a semi," he said out loud.

Carefully she sat on the edge of the big bed, down toward the vicinity of his knees, which were bent with the sheet tenting them. The blanket lay bunched at the foot. "Do you remember yesterday at all?"

He could see a hint of nerves, in her eyes, in her restless hands. So she did remember lying with him. He decided to let it go, for now. "Not much. I remember you ordering me around like a top sergeant."

Gaylan relaxed. He didn't recall the rest, thank goodness. "For your own good, mister. And I had to fight off both Ross and Evan." She told him briefly of everyone's concern as she glanced at the clock and saw it was eight. "They'll probably be calling any minute or pounding on the door, insisting on seeing you."

Hunter looked over at his desk, the silent fax machine. "I'm surprised there've been no calls from L.A."

She met his direct gaze. "I turned off your business phone. The doctor said you needed rest."

"You what?" Hunter shot up to a sitting position, then flinched as he felt the room sway, the pain shoot into his temples.

"And you're not out of the woods yet, big shot," Gaylan said, reaching for the medicine bottles. "Not for at least another eight to twelve hours." She poured water from the iced carafe and held out his pills.

He wanted to send her packing. He wanted her to stay by his side. He felt angry and frustrated and . . . and vulnerable. He didn't like the way he felt. Moving slowly since quick actions made his head hurt, he took the pills and reached for the water. Unable to prevent a slight moan, he lay back down, feeling his energy supply sadly depleted.

"The trouble with influenza is you think you feel better, then it whams you again."

"Thank you, Doctor." He wasn't so much annoyed with her as with this damnable situation he found himself in.

"Do you feel up to a shower? It might make you feel better."

Hunter ran a hand over his unshaved face and knew he must look like hell. "Give me a minute and I'll go in."

"Shall I order breakfast?"

"No."

She rose, sticking her hands in her pockets. "Hunter, you have to eat a little something. You're weak as a kitten."

She couldn't have said anything that would have angered him more. "All right, dammit." He turned his scowl on her. "You sure as hell are bossy."

"You sure as hell are grumpy." Now that he was on the mend, perhaps she should just turn him over to someone he'd feel more comfortable with. Sick and sleepy, she'd managed just fine. But feeling better obviously made him feisty as well. "Would you like me to get Ross or Evan in to take over?"

He thought that over and knew he wanted Gaylan and not either of his two friends. It wasn't an easy admission to make, even to himself. His face changed and he almost smiled. "If I have to have someone help me take a shower, I'd rather it be you."

She blushed, immediately and deeply. She'd been wrong. He did remember. Flustered, she stepped back. "I'll go order breakfast."

Watching her scurry away, he smiled.

Hunter was amazingly resilient, Gaylan discovered. Even Dr. Brewster, who stopped in to check on him after lunch, thought so. His fever had indeed broken in the early hours of dawn, and although he was much better, it still was two degrees higher than normal.

Although she knew the dizziness kept recurring, he shaved himself and showered while she changed the bed and straightened the bedroom, telling the morning maid she needn't bother with that room. She could tell he had little appetite, but he forced himself to eat a little breakfast and lunch, knowing his body needed fuel. And he insisted on meeting with Evan and Ross to go over several pending business transactions.

But by late afternoon when the two men finally were preparing to leave, Gaylan could see that Hunter was tired and in need of rest. She tilted the blinds on the windows and closed the lanai doors in the bedroom, throwing the room into a golden haze from the sun drifting in. She set the air conditioner to cool and turned down his bed. She heard him close the front door and join her, his footsteps slow.

"All set for you," she said, and stepped aside as she looked up at him. His denim shorts rode low on his hips and his face seemed pale against his navy knit shirt. She saw his gaze settle on her face, his eyes a dark pewter. Uncertain of his mood, she felt her heart start to hammer. "What is it?"

"I want you to lie down with me." He said it softly, not a command or a demand. Merely a request.

He wasn't a man who asked easily. She saw the invitation in his eyes and something more. Something dark, intense, inevitable. It was the throb of desire she knew was reflected in her own.

She wanted him; of that she was certain. She loved him, another realization she'd acknowledged in the wee small hours of the morning. Her hesitation didn't stem from lack of need, but from fear. The fear that if she stepped even closer to the fire, she might never recover.

"I'm not sure that's such a good idea," she said, her voice husky with repressed emotion.

"I won't touch you, if that's what you want." Hunter found his own voice none too steady. He was unused to asking; begging was totally foreign to him. "I find I sleep better when you're near me." Another hard admission.

She knew what it was costing him to ask. He wouldn't touch her if that's what she wanted. The trouble was she wanted him to touch her so badly she ached with the need. She also knew that if she passed up this opportunity, she might regret it the rest of her days. How could she deny herself the one thing she wanted more than the air she breathed?

"All right," she said, walking around to the other side of the king-size bed. "But just for a little while." Who was she kidding? Gaylan wondered as she nervously slipped off her sandals and lay down on the pale peach sheet. She settled her trembling hands at her waist.

Hunter felt light-headed, and knew it had nothing to do with the flu or his medication. He'd never wanted a woman like this, never yearned quite like this, never longed for someone's touch to this extent. He pulled his T-shirt off over his head and tossed it aside, then lay down on his back, turning his head to face her. He saw that she had her eyes focused on the ceiling.

Long moments passed while he waited for his heart to stop pounding in wild anticipation. But his heated blood only continued to race through his veins. He'd seen the latent passion in her eyes and knew if he leaned over and kissed her, she'd probably respond. But that wasn't how he wanted this to go. Not this time. Not quite sure why, he wanted her to come to him.

"Can I hold your hand?" he asked, unable to think of a better beginning.

Gaylan kept her gaze on the overhead ceiling fan turning lazily as she reached her hand over to him. She felt him thread his fingers with hers, then scoot his body closer so he could place their joined hands on his chest. His heartbeat under her hand was erratic, much like her own.

His fingers caressed her smooth skin, his thumb stroking her sensitive wrist, feeling her pulse pounding. Inching upward, he touched the delicate inside of her elbow and saw her begin to shift restlessly.

He was driving her slowly crazy, Gaylan decided. She wanted him to stop. She thought if he stopped she'd die. "Hunter, I..."

He eased onto his side and looked at her. "Do you think I'm still contagious?"

She hadn't even considered that. "I don't know."

"Are you afraid to take a chance, to kiss me?"

Lord, yes, she was afraid, but not of germs. "You need rest, not—"

"I need something else more. I need you." He wondered if she knew how difficult it was for him to say those words.

He'd said *need,* not want. Dare she believe him? She remembered the scene in the cave on the island, his confession later about his feelings. "You mean you need to get me out of your system? You want to have me once so you can walk away?"

He supposed he deserved to have those words thrown back into his face. "I did feel like that. Then. I no longer do." He reached over to caress her lovely face with the backs of his fingers and saw that his hand was trembling. No woman had ever made him tremble before. "You're different from any woman I've ever known, Gaylan. You've made me rethink some things."

Perhaps she was making some headway. "Such as?"

"Such as the fact that I admire you and respect you. I...no one's ever done for me what you have, taking care of me, the way you got in bed with me last night." Things had shifted for Hunter when he'd realized what she'd done. Shifted irrevocably. "Why did you do that?"

"You were so cold, shivering. You couldn't get warm so I decided to help in the only way I knew how."

He absorbed that slowly. Could it be that she really didn't have a hidden agenda? "I haven't known many women who didn't have ulterior motives. That's why I've had such trouble believing you."

"And now? Do you believe me now?"

"I'm trying to. But why? Why would you be so good to me?" Hadn't they had a strictly business arrangement? Surely taking care of him for twenty-four hours through an illness was above and beyond what she'd been hired to do.

She looked at him, wondering how much he could see in her steady gaze. "Don't you know?"

There was something in her eyes, a warmth that reached out and wrapped itself around a heart he'd never thought lonely until recently. "What I know is that from the start, I've wanted you. I just didn't know until yesterday that I needed you." It was the most he was able to offer. He hoped it was enough. His hand curved around, cradling her face, loving the feel of her.

Gaylan sighed as she turned into the caress, unable to fight this fierce attraction another moment. He hadn't said all she'd wanted to hear, but it was a start. "I need you, too," she said, knowing she'd never spoken truer words.

Hunter leaned down and pressed his lips to hers. As always, she opened to him, returning the kiss with a passion that sent his senses reeling. Needs deep inside him, dormant way too long, rushed to the surface, all but overwhelming him.

All patience fled as he gathered her to him, then took her mouth with a savagery he hadn't known he possessed. His hands moved to frame her face, tilting her head back as his tongue began a slow dance with hers. He devoured, he consumed, he drank from her. His fingers thrust into the thickness of her hair, massaging her scalp as his lips continued their assault.

He felt her hands insinuate themselves between them, roaming his chest, tracing his muscles, threading through the hair there, causing deep shivers to shudder through him. Pulling back, he bent to taste the long, slender column of her throat. He was drunk on her hot female flavors, heady with the freedom to explore her, wild with the need to know her.

Gaylan burned for him in a way she'd never thought possible. Her restive hands skimmed along his ribs, over his strong, wide shoulders, down his smooth back. She felt him shiver at her touch and gloried in his reaction. He was so solid, such sleek male perfection. Needing to be flesh to flesh with him, she straightened to tug off her shirt.

In seconds, Hunter disposed of the rest of her clothes, then pulled her into another fierce embrace. He closed his eyes as her full breasts brushed against his chest, and the lower half of her came in intimate contact with the hard evidence of his desire. Holding her close, he felt her trembling reaction and savored his own.

Her body a riot of sensations, Gaylan watched his eyes open and lock with hers. In them she saw that hint of vulnerability he tried so hard to disguise in so many ways. But she'd found him out, discovered how deep his needs ran, and wondered if he knew that finally someone saw through him. She could tell he felt in control, something very important to Hunter.

And it made her want even more to see him lose that control, become helpless in the act of love, to trust her enough to let himself go completely.

His hand sidled between them and caressed her breasts. He saw her eyes darken as her arousal deepened. "I've wanted so long to make love to you," he confessed.

"*With* me," Gaylan corrected. "Make love *with* me. Two people each surrendering to the other."

"Semantics again," he answered as his hand slipped lower, past her flat belly.

"No. There's an important difference." Her body jerked in response as his fingers slipped inside her, then relaxed as he gentled her. She took a breath, trying to concentrate. "*With* means we're together. *To* means one is giving and one receiving."

"I intend to do both." Hunter kissed her then, long and lazily as she arched against him. Wanting to watch, needing to see, he leaned back to look at her while his fingers worked their magic. "I want to watch you climb. I want to see if I can make you soar."

She had little breath left with which to tell him. "I know you can." Seconds later, she lost focus, a blush suffusing her face as she murmured his name, her hands curling into fists.

"You're so beautiful," he told her, pulling her close and kissing her hard, swallowing the soft sounds she made as she came back to herself.

Recovery was slow and she savored every second. Easing back, she gave him a satisfied, womanly smile. Then her hands moved to the waistband of his shorts.

Quickly he stopped her. "No. I want to be inside you." Again he took her mouth with a stunning kiss, trying to remain in charge.

Gaylan pulled free. "Mmm, I want that, too. But first..." Though he struggled against her determined hands, she was too fast for him. In moments, she had his shorts on the floor and her fingers around him. His sharp intake of breath told her all she wanted to know. At last, free to touch him as she'd yearned to, she quickly drove him to the edge.

"Gaylan," he groaned, squirming away from, then closer to, her clever fingers. "Go easy. It's been a long time."

"I'm glad to hear it." With very little effort, she shoved him onto his back and lay across his chest, stretching to kiss him deeply, her touch slowly driving him wild. She could feel it in the way he shifted about under her ministrations, hear it in the way his breathing became labored. He was close, she knew. Close to wanting her as desperately as she wanted him, close to losing control.

Hunter struggled to survive her onslaught, realizing she was the first woman who'd reduced him to this, the only one who could bring him to his knees. She'd made her point, now he'd make his. In one swift movement, he rolled her onto her back.

He took his mouth on a reckless journey of her, skimming along her throat, her breasts, her belly and lower. He tasted her, nibbled her, plundered her. He had her sighing, then sobbing, finally reaching to bring him back up to her waiting mouth. Always he returned to her mouth and the kisses that fed his soul.

Gaylan was drowning in him, soaring with him, shuddering against him. She welcomed wherever his hands and teeth and tongue touched. Her body hummed, her skin shimmered, her blood heated to boiling.

Hunter was frantic to meld with her, his body sweaty with his need, his heart thrumming with passion. But he had to stop for a moment, to be sane and sensible. "In the drawer," he managed. "I have to get something from the drawer."

Her arms drew him back to her. "No, it's all right." Simmering with impatience, she urged him on. Poised above her, he watched her eyes as he slowly joined with her. She sighed her welcome, then felt him begin to move as she wrapped herself around him.

She saw his face glisten with the sheen of his desire, watched his eyes close as passion took him over. She tightened her arms, reaching for the unreachable, straining, the summit in sight.

For once, she admired his control as he held on until she felt the world slip away, felt herself shatter, sensation overshadowing all else. She cried out in his arms, unaware tears trailed down her cheeks, as she felt him follow, shuddering his release.

She held him then as their hearts beat in unison and their bodies, still joined, began to cool. She stroked his hair and along his passion-dampened skin, savoring the masculine feel of him, the quiet strength of him.

He'd come through, not just for her but for himself, and she'd watched it happen. He'd let go, surrendered all control, losing himself in her, trusting her. She knew without a doubt that he couldn't have stopped a few minutes ago, not if his life had depended on it.

And she could tell he knew, too, as he lifted to look at her. The knowledge was in his eyes and she wondered how he felt about it.

Deeply moved, Hunter smoothed the trace of tears from her cheeks. He'd let his body take control and it had been all right. Always before he'd remained a little outside himself, afraid to relinquish power over his emotions to another. But with this woman—this *one* woman—he felt safe.

"Was that *with* enough for you, Gaylan?" Hunter asked, his voice still thick. "Did I make love with you or to you?"

She smiled up at him, a lazy, womanly smile. "With and it was wonderful." His expression didn't change. "At least for me, it was. How about you?"

"It was all right," he said, then gave in to a grin at her startled expression. He caught her arm just before her fist would have connected with his shoulder. "Okay, so maybe it was more than all right." Suddenly he sobered. "Maybe it was even better than I'd thought it would be."

"Is that so terrible?"

He eyed her warily. "I never meant to get involved with you, Gaylan."

"It was the furthest thing from my mind when I agreed to this job. I wasn't even sure I liked you." What a difference a couple of weeks could make, Gaylan thought.

He smoothed her hair, remembering. "You stood up to me like no one has in a long while. That made me mad, but it also intrigued me."

"You annoyed me with this thing you have about controlling every aspect of your life. After that incident on the island, I was afraid you'd carry that over into lovemaking."

He cocked his head to the side. "You think I'm such a control freak that even in bed I need to be in charge?"

She met his eyes. "I did, yes. I feel that you have to trust your partner when you make love, to let yourself be vulnerable to them. I wasn't sure if you'd be able to do that."

Being totally, soul-searchingly honest with a woman was something else he was unused to. Hunter was surprised to find he wanted to tell her the truth. "I wasn't, either. It's hard for me to take risks like that." He rolled over onto his back, taking her with him, keeping her within the circle of his arms.

She settled her head on his chest, one hand playing with the soft hair. "It's hard for me, too. Intimacy's always a risk. I've never been one to take it lightly."

Hunter cupped her chin, tilting her face so he could look into her eyes. "I know that. Are you sorry you did with me?"

She felt her heart swell with love for this man who needed so much reassurance, who'd never really known love. Yet she'd never met anyone who needed it more. "Sorry? How could I be sorry when you make me feel so much? When just looking at you makes me want you?"

He'd never known anyone who wanted him like that and was unafraid to admit it. "It's the same with me. All you have to do is touch me with those soft hands and I want to drag you off to bed, to make love with you until neither of us can move."

Gaylan's heart was soaring with hope. He'd come so far. She smiled seductively at him as she raised an arm and waved it about. "It seems I can still move," she challenged.

He laughed out loud, something Hunter couldn't remember ever doing in bed with a woman before. "Let's see what we can do about that." And he pulled her to him, kissing her soundly.

Chapter Eleven

By sundown, after a light dinner for two in the suite, Hunter felt well enough for a stroll on the beach. Matter of fact, he felt more than well. He felt happy and just a little giddy, something brand-new to him.

Wearing a blue-and-white aloha shirt Gaylan had given him, and white pants rolled up to his knees, he walked barefoot in the sand just on the edge of the lapping waves, holding Gaylan's hand and wondering at this odd new feeling. He couldn't figure out if it was due to his recent illness and medication or the time he'd spent in bed with Gaylan, either making love or just holding her while this unique contentment flooded his being.

The former possibility he knew would be short-lived. The latter was another thing.

He was seeing her in a different light. She seemed secure within herself, comfortable with her own sexuality, a warm and loving woman. She pleased him in bed, in the shower they'd shared afterward—another first for Hunter—and as his hostess. She was fun to talk with, to laugh with, something he hadn't done enough of, he now realized. She amused him, interested him, aroused him.

Why hadn't he seen it before? He supposed he was too busy fighting his desire for her, afraid to give in for fear she'd get a stranglehold on him. But she wasn't like that. She was her own person.

After a great deal of convincing, she'd finally shown him the one sketchbook she'd brought along. Her drawings of children were damn good. He'd told her so and mentioned a publisher he knew whom he could call and ask to consider her work. She'd gotten all irate and said she didn't want that kind of assistance, that if she and her story-telling partner couldn't make it on their own, then they just wouldn't make it at all. He thought that was pretty silly, but he said he'd honor her wishes.

Beside him, Gaylan strolled along with a lightness to her steps that she'd never had. She was here on one of the most beautiful beaches in the world at sunset and she was in love. The fact that Hunter hadn't said he loved her didn't matter right now. He would, she was certain. He was just a cautious man who took his time coming to important realizations.

"Is that music I hear?" Gaylan asked, dodging a rather high frothy wave. "Sounds like drums and guitars."

"Probably a sunset wedding up ahead. They often have them on the beach."

"Hawaiians, you mean? Or visitors?"

"Could be either." As they rounded the bend, he saw the tiki torches and the colorful costumes with plumed headdresses. "There it is."

Excited, Gaylan pulled him along. "Oh, let's watch. Do you suppose they'd mind?"

"I don't see why they'd mind." Hunter hadn't been to a wedding in years, much less a Hawaiian one. But Gaylan's exhilaration was contagious. Moving close enough to watch without being obtrusive, they stopped in the shadow of a palm tree.

Gaylan inhaled the pungent aroma of the smoking tiki torches held by the young men and women who formed a long aisle leading toward a white-robed minister, who stood with his back to the sea. The honor guard, if that's what they were, wore Hawaiian sarongs, aloha shirts and muumuus, each decorated with a different lei of native flowers. The guests knelt or sat in the dry white sand on either side. The sun was like a huge orange ball in the blue sky as it slowly lowered over the shimmering water. The drumbeats picked up in rhythm as from under an airy canopy, the bride stepped forward.

"Isn't she beautiful?" Gaylan whispered, admiring the ankle-length white dress, contrasting with the girl's golden skin. In her sleek black hair, she wore a garland of delicate plumeria and she carried a bouquet of orchids. On the arm of an older man with gray hair dressed in native dress, she waited, her bare feet shifting nervously.

Hunter stood behind Gaylan and slipped his arms around her, letting her lean back against him. He had an inbred disdain for ceremonies, thinking them foolish and trivial in the overall scheme of things. But it was pleasant to stand here holding the only blond woman on

the beach, feeling her anticipation. Her romantic nature was eating this up, he thought with a smile. He also
thought Gaylan, in her peasant dress with its full skirt
falling to mid-calf, looked more beautiful than the
bride.

The air was ripe with the smells of the sea mingled
with the scent of the many flowers. The drumming drew
to a close and then the four guitars took over, beginning the wedding march. The bride and her father
started forward. Near the front, silhouetted against the
darkening sky, a lovely young woman swayed and
danced, using the ancient Hawaiian language, her slender hands telling a story. Gaylan felt her eyes fill as the
men and women along the aisle each waved huge feath-
ered plumes over the heads of the pair as they passed.

She placed her hands over Hunter's arms as he encircled her, needing more contact. Angling her head, she
saw that he was watching with a hint of amused toler-
ance in his eyes. How could he not be touched? she
wondered as she turned back to see the handsome
groom accept the hand of his bride.

The actual nuptials didn't take long. As they ended,
someone released two white doves from their cages. The
freed birds circled over the newlyweds for several moments, then flew off together. "I suppose that's sym-
bolic of these two starting their lives together from this
day forward," she said softly.

"They'll need more than white doves to help them
through the days ahead," Hunter commented. "You
ready to go back?"

The guitars moved into "The Hawaiian Wedding
Song" as the two lovers embraced. The guests got to
their feet and began singing. Despite his annoying re-

mark, Gaylan wanted to stay a bit longer. "Can we listen to this before we go? Unless you're tired."

Hunter shook his head. "I'm fine. Let's listen."

They did and Gaylan struggled with her emotions as she heard the sentimental song, the many voices joining in. Finally the wedding party retraced their steps along the aisle and stood at the back, accepting congratulations. At last, Hunter took Gaylan's hand and they started back toward the hotel.

"That's the most romantic wedding I've ever witnessed," she told him, brushing aside a tear, still so filled with the beauty of what she'd seen. "When I get married, I'd love it to be like that, in the outdoors with music and perhaps candles, in a natural setting. Churches are fine, but you can't beat Mother Nature."

"Ever the romantic," Hunter commented as they walked on. "I should think someone as intelligent as you would realize that romance is a trap, one that will snare you and confuse you. When your head's full of romance, you can't think clearly and sort out the real issues."

She stopped in her tracks and turned to face him. "You're a card-carrying cynic. I think that's awful. Cynicism can only make you hard and cold."

"Men in business need to be hard," Hunter added defensively.

They strolled in silence until they were back in the suite, both wrestling with their own thoughts. Once inside, Hunter felt it necessary to make his point. "I'm not so much being a cynic, Gaylan, as being self-protective. A man in business who keeps his head in the clouds will soon lose everything."

"Perhaps you're right, when it comes to business. But in a personal relationship, a man has to soften that hard edge, to share himself, to trust the woman he loves."

He dropped the keys on the table and turned to her. "I don't believe in love. Love is a foolish risk. I never take risks unless I'm almost a hundred percent certain of the outcome. With love, there are no certainties. Whenever love enters the picture, someone gets hurt."

"Not always. Not if there's trust and—"

Stepping close, he pulled her to him. "Face it. Love is a delusion. Or maybe an illusion. In any case, it doesn't last and it's not real." He tightened his arms and felt her hands flutter at his back. His mouth a breath from hers, he gazed into her shadowed eyes. "*This* is real, the way we make each other feel."

His kiss was urgent, demanding, almost bruising. It went on and on, penetrating her resistance until finally she responded, unable to fight her reawakened desire. Then, sensing her compliance, he gentled, as if remembering who he held in his arms, as if realizing he had no need to conquer this woman.

Breathing hard, he picked her up in his arms and carried her into his bedroom. Pausing at the bedside, he captured her gaze. "I don't want to control you, Gaylan. Between us, in this bed, there is no winner and no loser. There're only two people who want each other, who have something special between them. Do you agree?"

She could say no now and she knew he'd put her down and let her walk away. It came as no real surprise to her that he didn't believe in love. Or thought he didn't. In her heart, Gaylan believed she could make him happy, get him to admit he loved her in time. He'd already changed in many ways.

She'd always believed that miracles were possible. This would be the biggest miracle of all.

"Yes, I agree."

"I can't offer you what you want, the romantic wedding, love and a vine-covered cottage with a white picket fence."

Trembling, she tried to keep her emotions in check, to put her own feelings on hold until he was ready. "I'm not asking for anything more than you're willing to give."

He'd won, Hunter thought. He'd finally convinced her. His eyes turned smoky as he lowered her to the mattress and followed her down, his mouth claiming hers.

"Yes, operator, I'll accept the call," Gaylan said into the phone. It was the next morning and, while Hunter was meeting with the Yamaguchis to discuss the report that had finally arrived, she'd called the attorney she'd hired. But Avery Woods hadn't been in so she'd left a message that he call her collect as soon as he was able. She was pleased he'd phoned before Hunter's return.

"Hello, Miss Fisher?" Avery Woods asked.

"Yes, Mr. Woods. You've probably guessed that I'm calling about my brother. How are things going by now?" She'd spoken only briefly to him a couple of days after her arrival in Hawaii, but he'd had nothing to tell her at the time. Naturally she couldn't speak directly to Mel since he was in jail. She was getting anxious to know something. Anything.

"Things are coming along. The preliminary hearing is set for a week from next Wednesday at nine a.m."

She'd be back in California by then. "Good. I'll be there. How's Mel?" She waited, her nerves jumpy.

Avery cleared his throat, trying to think of a way to explain things without unduly alarming the boy's sister who was too far away at the moment to do anything about Mel's state of mind. "Naturally he's not happy. I've had several talks with him and I think we're seeing more eye to eye these days." But Mel Fisher had a long way to go in improving his attitude.

"I know he's headstrong and can be difficult, Mr. Woods," Gaylan went on, twisting the phone cord in the fingers of one hand. "But inside, Mel's a good person."

"Yes, well, jail isn't a pleasant experience. He's having some time to think things over. I've told him that he's going to have to make some changes in his life or plan on spending a lot of time behind bars. And next, we have to convince a judge that he's well intentioned to do so."

"Do you think they'll be lenient on him?"

Avery lit a cigarette and blew smoke toward the ceiling. "Depends on what you mean by lenient. We've got Judge Michaels presiding. I know he's fair-minded, but he's no pushover."

Her heart was sinking. "But it's Mel's first real offense."

"He has a juvenile record the court won't easily ignore. I've talked with the prosecutor and we're trying to work out a plea to present to the judge."

A small hope flared. "What does that mean?"

"Simply that the prosecutor will require that Mel be subject to several stipulations to satisfy the state that he's paying for the crime he committed, and getting the help he needs so he won't be a repeat offender. If the judge agrees, then we can wrap up the whole case at the preliminary hearing."

"What kind of stipulations?"

"There's a broad range here, from some prison time or possibly suspended sentence with probation for *x* number of years along with community service. And, of course, drug counseling. He may get some or all." He drew deeply on his cigarette, recognizing the near panic in Gaylan's voice, wishing he could give her more hope. He'd been impressed with Gaylan's devotion to her brother at their one meeting. "At this point, it's hard to say. I'll know more in a week or so."

"All right." Gaylan knew she sounded as low as she felt. Dear God, more jail time? It would harm Mel irreparably, she feared. "I'll call you as soon as I get back to California," she told Avery.

"Fine. And try not to worry."

"Thanks." Gaylan hung up the phone wearily. Trying not to worry was like trying not to breathe. It worked only for a very short while. Sighing, she walked to the dining room table, where she'd been working on making out a menu. They were having another dinner tonight since Hunter was feeling much better.

She wondered how she'd be able to keep her thoughts on meaningless table chatter when her mind was constantly churning over Mel and her newfound feelings for Hunter.

"So then, the report meets with your approval?" Hunter asked Yasu, careful to keep even a hint of sarcasm out of his voice.

"Yes, yes. This is exactly what we needed and it checks out just fine." Yasu turned to Taro and Hiroki. "Based on this last bit of information, I recommend we proceed with the merger."

Hallelujah! Hunter wanted to shout. But he didn't let his face betray his thoughts. He'd felt all along that there wouldn't be a problem since he knew all aspects of his company were on the up-and-up. The delay had irritated him at first; then he'd become ill and had no choice but to postpone things.

"Good," Ross commented, smiling at Yasu. "How long before the final paperwork is completed and ready for signatures?"

She turned to him. "A day, two at the most. If we work together to incorporate all the changes, that is."

Under the table, Ross slipped off his loafer and slid his stockinged foot up along Yasu's bare leg. He saw that her facial expression didn't change; she worked hard at not revealing her emotions in public. But he had the satisfaction of seeing her lovely eyes darken. "I'd be happy to work with you night and day if necessary, Counselor."

"I'm sure the daylight hours will be sufficient, *Mister* Weber." Pointedly she returned to her paperwork.

They hadn't discussed their affair, had simply drifted into it. Yasu was the first woman Ross had been interested in in years, and he was surprised how good he felt about their alliance. As he turned back to the others, he decided perhaps she wouldn't want anyone to know of their relationship just yet. "If that's all for now, gentlemen, then Yasu and I will move on to her place or mine and get busy finalizing things."

Taro missed very little, and though his face revealed nothing as he nodded and rose, there was a stiffness to his bearing that had Ross wondering if the older man disapproved of his getting close to his trusted assistant. Hiroki, on the other hand, winked at him as he got up to leave. Ross tried to keep from smiling, but wasn't sure if he'd managed.

"Hunter," Hiroki said, falling in step with him as they all left Taro's suite, "my wife has reason to thank you."

"Really? Why is that?"

"Your acceptance of Gaylan's need to do her own thing has convinced me to let her try her hand in the workplace. On a trial basis, you understand."

Hunter nodded at the tall, handsome young man. "Can't hurt to try."

"That's what I thought." He shook his dark head. "Keeping women happy is sometimes a full-time job."

Hunter clapped him on the shoulder. "You can say that again." Walking away with Evan, Hunter found himself smiling.

"You seem to be feeling awfully good since your illness," Evan commented. "I'm wondering if your best medicine wasn't your nursemaid?"

Ordinarily Hunter never discussed his personal life. However, going back as far as they did, he knew that no one knew as much about him as Evan Porter. Besides, apparently when it came to Gaylan, he no longer had a poker face. He stopped in the deserted hallway and turned to his old friend. "I'm thinking of inviting her to live with me."

Evan frowned, truly surprised. That wasn't the answer he'd been expecting. "Live with you?"

"Right. What do you think?"

Evan shook his head slowly, sadly. "I don't think she'll go for it. Gaylan's far too independent." *And she's in love with you, you idiot.*

Ah, but Evan hadn't seen the way Gaylan's eyes lit up when he walked into the room, the way she softened when he touched her, the way she opened to him when he kissed her. She was his, no mistake about it. "I think you're wrong. She needs someone to take care of her."

How could he make Hunter understand without revealing what Gaylan had asked him to keep private? Evan wondered. "She's been taking care of herself and . . . others even before her parents died. She doesn't need to be taken care of. She needs to be cared *for*. There's a huge difference. She needs a partner, not someone to take over."

Growing annoyed, Hunter jammed his hands in his pants pockets. "I don't intend to take over. I intend to support her, to introduce her to people who can get her published. Isn't that what she wants?"

Evan didn't often let Hunter see how he felt about things because in business he rarely disagreed with his employer. But this involved a woman Evan thought highly of and he couldn't keep his disappointment from showing. "That goes to show how little you know her, Hunter. She'll never let you do that."

He hadn't even told Evan that Gaylan had turned him down once on that offer already. It didn't matter. She'd come around. Evan wasn't the one living with her. Perhaps the older man didn't know Gaylan nearly as well as he thought he did. Certainly not as well as Hunter did.

"I believe she will." Turning on his heel, he strode down the hall toward his suite.

Hunter shifted her body until she was above him, her satin skin damp from their lovemaking. He was rock hard with desire for her. But he would not rush, would not allow himself the satisfaction his throbbing body screamed for until he'd shown her more and still more.

"The woman astride," Hunter murmured. "Isn't this the position men who demand to always be in control are afraid of, the position of female dominance?"

Gaylan shook back her thick hair, her breathing ragged. "So they say."

"I want you to know, I'm not afraid." Slowly, with excruciating care, he eased her onto him until they were deeply joined. He heard an involuntary sound of pleasure come from her as he filled her to the fullest. His arms wound around to bind her to him, and then he stretched to take her mouth.

He began to move, slowly at first, then a little faster. He felt her chest heave against his as her passion built. Faster still he drove her, and himself. Then they were climbing together, racing at top speed. In another moment, he felt her convulse delicately around him.

Only then did he allow himself to follow.

Recovering, he kissed her again, swallowing the soft sounds of satisfaction she made. Never had he been able to bring a woman to quite these heights. Never had a woman been able to make him feel so much so easily, almost as if she'd been made for him.

When she could once again breathe normally, Gaylan eased from him and lay back on the tangled sheets. As always, Hunter shifted to hold her to him, his one hand lazily cupping a breast, as if to feel her heart still beating rapidly. Beating for him.

She felt suffused with heat, not just from lovemaking. She felt warm with her love for him, this love she wished she could confess. For it burned inside her, needing to be free. Love had to be shared or it withered from loneliness. Yet she hesitated.

Hunter was the lover she'd always dreamed of. In public, he was considerate, thoughtful, caring. In private, he was teasing, loving, sensual. But without words. He couldn't bring himself to say the words she knew he was feeling. Would he ever?

The moon ducked behind a cloud, throwing the bedroom farther into shadow. She felt too good, too sated, to think more on it tonight. Perhaps, in the days and nights that still remained, she'd be able to get him to speak his heart.

Her arms lay on top of his as he held her, his breathing slow and even. He'd fallen asleep quickly tonight. She angled back to look at his face, so peaceful in sleep. "I love you," she whispered very softly. Arranging herself comfortably, she closed her eyes.

His face half-buried in her hair, Hunter opened his eyes. He'd heard and knew she meant what she'd said. Odd how, although he didn't believe in love, hearing her say those three little words had warmed him to his very core. But he mustn't let her sentiments take over his practical nature.

Yet he couldn't lose her, Hunter decided right then and there. She was everything he needed, everything he wanted.

And then it came to him, the perfect answer, for both of them. Why hadn't he thought of it before? First thing in the morning, he'd tell Gaylan his idea. She'd jump at it, he was certain, for it would give both of them what they needed.

Sighing, he snuggled her closer, closed his eyes and invited sleep.

Gaylan was humming as she poured two cups of coffee and took them out onto the lanai. It was a gorgeous morning, or was it simply in the eye of the beholder?

Sitting down, she crossed her long legs and took a sip. She and Hunter had gone for their run this morning, then returned to clean up. She'd just finished shampooing her hair under the shower when the door had opened and Hunter had stepped in. Since she'd introduced him to making love under running water, he'd become an addict. Their long session had delayed things considerably, but she hadn't minded a bit, Gaylan thought with a smile.

Wearing white shorts and yellow top, she waited for him to finish dressing before joining her. He had to attend a meeting in Taro's suite in twenty minutes. She planned to take her sketchbook and stroll around the grounds, hoping to find a shady spot to add a few more drawings to her Hawaiian collection. She already had an idea for a book that she was anxious to share with Helen. If all went well with the Yamaguchi business deal, they'd be flying back on Sunday, four days from today.

Four days left to enjoy being with Hunter, sharing herself with him, loving him. Four days to convince him he loved her, too. She let out a deep breath, wondering if she could pull it off.

Hearing him walking toward her, Gaylan smiled her welcome as he came out onto the lanai, sat down and picked up his cup. Lord but he looked good this morning, the sun shining on his dark head. His eyes as he sat back and turned to her were more alive than usual, sparkling with an excitement that piqued her curiosity.

"I've been thinking," Hunter began. "We're going to have things wrapped up pretty quick now. Sunday's almost here." He reached over and took her hand from where it lay on the chair's armrest. "I don't want to say goodbye."

Gaylan swallowed around a lump, hardly daring to breathe. Could it be that her wildest dreams were about to come true? "I don't, either."

He smiled, looking relieved. "I'm glad to hear you say that." His thumb stroked her soft skin. "At first, I'd thought of asking you to come live with me. But then, I decided that you wouldn't want to do that. You're much too independent." He realized he was repeating Evan's words, having thought them over long and carefully. Perhaps the attorney did have some insight into Gaylan.

"You're right," Gaylan answered, beginning to get a little nervous. "I wouldn't be interested in that."

"Fine." He hadn't lived with a woman on a day-to-day basis since his ill-fated marriage, and he wasn't sure how well he would have adapted. However, the thought of not having Gaylan available to him when he returned from his office or business trips was unthinkable. That's why he'd thought of a compromise. "Evan told me you have a house in Glendale, I believe, and that you drive a Volkswagen that isn't exactly brand-new."

Gaylan pulled her hand free, not comfortable with the slant of the conversation. "Yes, that's right. I'm confused as to what that has to do with you and me."

"Hear me out. You can sell your house and car and keep the proceeds."

He was a business man, Gaylan forced herself to remember. He approached everything from a business angle, even marriage. She would force herself to be patient. "Go on."

He leaned forward, his excitement growing. "There's a high rise not far from my L.A. office. Luxury apartments. We can go see them together and you can pick out the one you want. I'll buy you furniture, a new car, whatever you want. And, although I know you've turned me down once, I want you to know my offer still stands to introduce you to some important people in publishing. I wouldn't push, just ask them to look at your work and decide for themselves. In the meantime, I'd provide you with a monthly income, of course."

She looked to be in shock, Hunter thought, which brought a smile to his face. Obviously she hadn't expected him to be so generous. It felt good to surprise her. "And, of course, we could see each other as often as we like—when I'm finished at the office evenings or return from a business trip or simply take the day off." Something he'd rarely done before meeting Gaylan. "There'll also be times when I'll want you to come with me on my trips, so we can be together and you can act as my hostess, like on this business venture."

She just sat still, not moving, eerily silent.

Hunter frowned as he glanced at his watch and stood. "Look, I've got to get to that meeting. We can talk more about all this when I return." She looked so pale. Surely, given their last few nights together, this couldn't have been that much of a shock. Could she have reservations about his suggestion? No, he decided, she was just vastly surprised at how much he'd changed. No less than he himself was. "Will you at least say *something* before I leave? How do you feel?"

"Stunned," Gaylan managed, her voice shaky.

Hunter smiled down at her. "Yeah, me, too. I never thought I'd ever get involved again." He reached down to touch the ends of her hair. "But you're very special, Gaylan." Quickly he planted a kiss on her cheek and turned. "I'll be back in a couple of hours. Wait for me and we'll go someplace quiet for lunch and talk over the details."

His stride confident, Hunter left the suite.

Staring after him, Gaylan struggled to hold back the tears that burned the back of her eyes. Her emotions in a turmoil, she found herself trembling uncontrollably.

She'd behaved like a romantic fool, thinking that if she loved Hunter, he'd surely love her back, although he'd be slow to admit it, even to himself. While she'd been thinking of love and marriage, he'd been planning to set her up as his mistress. Shame and disappointment flooded her face with heat.

Gaylan had been basically alone for so long since the shock of losing her parents, and even before that since her folks spent so many hours working. She'd had Mel, but, facing hard facts, she had to admit that she and her brother had never been close confidants, carrying the burden of their loss separately.

Since her teens, she'd longed for someone she could truly share life with, the good and the bad. Getting to know Hunter these past few days, falling in love with him, she'd hoped that deep inside, he wanted that, too. That he wanted her, too. She'd gambled and lost. He wanted her, all right. In his bed, not in his heart. At his beck and call, as his mistress.

Rising slowly, her heart heavy in her chest, Gaylan had to admit the hardest fact of all: he would never love her.

Walking inside, she looked at the clock. She knew exactly what she must do. There was no time to waste. She would have to hurry.

Once again, she was alone, having to face a difficult decision. But she'd manage somehow. Hadn't Evan called her a survivor?

Hurrying, Gaylan went to her room.

Chapter Twelve

Thank goodness she'd been able to reserve a seat on the next flight out, Gaylan thought as she hung up the phone. Charging the ticket was a bit of a strain on her credit card; however, she'd had no choice. She had to leave and leave quickly.

Finished dressing, she hurriedly looked around the suite. She'd placed the rented jewelry on Hunter's desk and packed only her own things. Satisfied, she closed her suitcase and hefted it off the bed, pulling it by its handle to the door. She had only to scribble a short note, one that would explain her feelings enough so that he wouldn't bother following her. Face-to-face with him, she just might weaken, for already the thought of never seeing him again had her aching.

Gathering her thoughts, she reached for a sheet of paper and hurriedly wrote, wondering if Hunter would understand what she meant. What did it matter? she thought, moving into the living area and propping the folded note on the hall table. Since he didn't understand her, chances were he wouldn't understand her reference in the farewell note.

Just as she was about to pull open the door, she heard a knock. Groaning inwardly, she hesitated. Whoever it was might go away if she didn't answer. She couldn't spare the time to talk with anyone, nor did she feel up to explaining why she was obviously dressed for travel alongside her packed suitcase.

The knock came again, louder, persistent. She'd get rid of them in quick order, Gaylan decided, opening the door.

"Hello," Nari said, balancing her tennis racket on her shoulder. "I thought I'd try to talk you into a game." Her dark eyes swept over Gaylan's outfit. "Oh. Are you going somewhere?"

Of all the Yamaguchis, Gaylan felt she could relate to Nari best. She wouldn't lie. She'd done far too much of that already. "Yes. I'm going to L.A. My flight leaves shortly so I haven't much time."

Nari looked confused. "Leaving without Hunter? Is something wrong? That is, I know it's none of my business, but..."

"No, it's all right. I can't explain right now, Nari. It's just something I have to do." From the open doorway, she leaned out and glanced down the hallway nervously. "I really have to go."

Nari looked about, wondering who Gaylan was apparently watching for. "Is there anything I can do?"

"Yes. Please don't mention you saw me. I...I have your address. I'll write you later to explain everything. And I'm sorry, Nari. Sorry for everything." The weight of her deception had her shoulders sagging. She should have known from the beginning that if you lived a lie, even for a short while, you simply couldn't escape paying for it.

Nari was confused even further by Gaylan's apology. What on earth was she apologizing for when she'd been such a big help to her? "But I haven't even thanked you for talking about your work at dinner that evening. Hiroki was so impressed that he's allowing me to pursue my dream."

Tossing her key onto the table, Gaylan stepped out into the hallway, set the lock and pulled the door closed. She grabbed the handle of her suitcase and flung the strap of her purse over her shoulder. "I'm so glad for you." She started toward the elevators, hating to be rude but fearful that the meeting in Taro's suite would end early and someone would come along demanding explanations.

Trailing after her, Nari looked worried. "Is someone ill? Is that why you need to leave so quickly?"

"No, nothing like that."

"This doesn't seem like you, Gaylan. Running away. I don't know you very well, but it seems out of character."

Gaylan punched in the elevator button and sighed. No, she'd never been one to run from situations or problems. But there were times when there were no other viable alternatives. "I suppose it is." The elevator doors slid open soundlessly. She dragged her bag aboard. "I'm sorry, Nari. Goodbye."

Watching the doors close on Nari's frowning face, Gaylan felt tears forming, but choked them back. As she descended, she remembered the Hawaiian legend that if you left something of importance on one of the islands, you would return.

She was leaving her battered and bruised heart behind, but the possibility of her returning was slim to none.

"We've made excellent progress, Ross and I," Yasu said to the table at large. "We need only another day to revise the legal language and we'll be prepared for signatures."

"That's great," Hunter said approvingly. That would give him and Gaylan Saturday to just sit in the sun and relax before flying home Sunday. He glanced at his watch and saw it was nearly noon. This session had lasted longer than he'd hoped. He was anxious to get back to Gaylan and go over their plans for the future, which suddenly looked rosy to Hunter.

"Yes, that is very good," Taro agreed. "Perhaps, if you don't need us this afternoon, Hunter-san and I can get in a round of golf after lunch."

Hunter was searching for a way to politely refuse when there was a quick knock at the door and Nari burst in, without waiting. "Hiroki," she called out, her face very white, her eyes battling tears.

Hiroki jumped to his feet. "What is it?"

"It's little Taro," she said, her voice trembling. "My mother just phoned our room. They've taken him to the hospital and the doctors say he has pneumonia." Her hands flew to her mouth in disbelief.

"How can that be?" the frightened father asked. "We just talked with him two days ago."

"Yes, I know. Mother says he took ill very suddenly."

Taro rose and walked to them. "Children often become ill very quickly." His arm slid around his daughter-in-law. "He will bounce back. You will see." He looked up at his son. "We must fly home immediately. Call for reservations."

Still stunned, Hiroki nodded, then hurried with his wife to the bedroom to phone.

"Does Yoshiko know?" Taro asked.

Nari nodded. "I phoned her. She's in the bedroom packing. She knew you'd want to leave right away."

"Is there anything I can do?" Hunter asked Taro.

Taro turned. "I don't think so, but thank you. As soon as our little one is out of danger, I will phone you and we can discuss the final papers. Yasu, you may remain here and work with Ross for as long as it takes."

Childless, Ross wasn't sure he understood this mass exodus. "The papers are nearly complete. We could rush them along and have them ready for your signatures, if you would delay your return by one day, Taro. I'm sure your grandson is in good hands and—"

Hunter touched Ross's arm. He'd been watching Taro's face and could see that Ross's request didn't sit well with the older, very traditional man. "I don't think so, Ross."

Taro bowed to Hunter. "I thank you for understanding. Our child is in danger. We can think of nothing else just now. Family, our loved ones, come first, before business."

Hunter nodded. He'd come to know and understand the Japanese and felt that insisting just now would squelch the whole deal. But more important, it was the right, the humane, thing to do. "We will wait to hear from you."

Pleased at Hunter's intervention, Evan stood. "If there's anything we can do, Taro, please let us know."

"Yes, of course." Taro saw them to the door.

Ross fell in step with Yasu. "We might as well get to work. Your place or mine?" Smiling, they left the suite.

Evan and Hunter shook hands with Taro, then left to walk down to Hunter's suite. "Do you want to stay or shall I call and have our plane ready to go tomorrow morning?" Evan asked.

Hunter slipped the key in the lock and swung open the door. "Might as well go home." He was ready. He and Gaylan could spend the weekend together in his house, then get her apartment squared away next week.

Evan followed him inside. "What time do you want to leave?"

Spotting a folded paper with his name on it propped on the entryway table, Hunter walked over and picked it up. It was probably from Gaylan, telling him she'd gone for a walk and where to meet her for lunch. Pulling out the single white sheet, he quickly read the note.

Hunter:
I'm sorry, but, like your dog, Gypsy, I need to be free.

Gaylan

P.S. You don't owe me a cent. I'll just chalk this one off to experience.

Unable to keep the surprise from his face, Hunter looked around as if expecting her to pop up and tell him it was a joke. "Gaylan?" he called out.

"Is something wrong?" Evan asked.

"I don't know." Hunter hurried to his bedroom. Her clothes and cosmetics were gone. The jewelry lay in a pile on his desk, their brightness mocking him. A cloud shifted outside, blocking the sun, throwing the room into shadow. Shadow that seemed to darken his heart.

Dazed, he walked back to where Evan waited, a puzzled frown on his face. Why? he asked himself. Why had she left when he'd offered her the world on the proverbial silver platter?

"What's happened?" Evan persisted, though he thought he knew. After the conversation he'd had with Hunter yesterday, he could only guess that he'd asked Gaylan to live with him after all, and that she'd left him.

Hunter reached for the anger that was so much easier to bear than the hurt. "She's gone." He thrust the note at Evan, then walked to the lanai to stare out at the sea.

Evan read the note, not pleased that his prediction had come true. Slowly he followed Hunter outside. "You asked her to live with you?"

"No! Better than that. I offered to set her up in her own apartment. New furniture, new clothes, the car of her choice. *And* a monthly income whether she ever sells a book or not." He thrust his hands into his pockets angrily. "What kind of woman walks away from that kind of generous offer? I thought you told me she was needy."

"Not *that* needy. She has a lot of pride."

"Well, let her take her pride to the bank and see how much bread it puts on the table." He hurt inside, deeply, and even venting his anger wasn't making the pain go away. He felt betrayed. Against his better judgment, he'd fallen for Gaylan. He'd opened to her, become vulnerable to her. And this was the thanks he got.

Wearily Evan sat down on a chair. "I told you you didn't know her." He held out the note. "I could have predicted this."

Giving his rage free rein, Hunter whirled on him. "What do you mean by that?"

"I overheard the two of you talking on the flight over, when you told her the story of your dog. Do you remember what she told you?" When Hunter continued to scowl silently, he went on. "She said that the fastest way to kill love is to put restrictions on it."

"Love?" he yelled. "Who's talking about love here?"

"I am. She loves you. Don't you know that?"

Suddenly Hunter ran out of steam. Feeling drained, he sat down and leaned forward, his elbows on his knees, his hands dangling. "She told me that one night. I told her I didn't believe in love."

"She had the guts to go ahead and love you anyway. And you threw it back in her face."

"I don't need her to love me. I just need her to... to..."

"To be there to warm your bed, to play hostess when you decide to take a trip, to nurse you when you're ill, to listen to you when you want to talk, to be quiet when you don't."

Hunter flinched. "You make me sound pretty heartless."

"You have been, to Gaylan."

He scrambled to find some way to defend himself. "I'm still going to pay her, you know, even if she says she doesn't want the money. She's earned it."

"I rather thought you'd be fair. And yes, she's earned it, and then some." By living up to her end of the bargain until he'd humiliated her, by humanizing Hunter while he fought her every step of the way. Evan thought of Avery Woods, the lawyer she'd hired to defend her brother. "Besides, she really needs the money."

"*Needs* the money or merely *likes* money, like all women?"

Evan seldom lost his temper, but he found it slipping away now. "Dammit, when are you going to stop judging every woman by Jolene? Gaylan's one of a kind and you're a damn fool to have let her get away."

"Now, you listen here..."

"No! *You* listen. I was asked not to tell you this, but I've decided it would serve no purpose to remain silent under the circumstances. Gaylan's never had much because at an age when she should have been a carefree college student, she undertook to look after someone who's squandered every cent she could scrape together." Quickly, unemotionally, he told Hunter about Mel Fisher and all he'd put Gaylan through so far. "And it's not over yet. The lawyer I recommended doesn't come cheap, and still there's no guarantee that that reckless kid won't serve time. Which will just about kill Gaylan."

"She should let him." He knew his anger was tainting his viewpoint, but he felt little sympathy for Mel Fisher.

"But it's not in her. Gaylan has so much love in her that she can't give up on someone she cares about. Not unless that someone wounds her so deeply she sees no way out."

Restless, Hunter rose and walked back inside. He looked around at the silent, shadowed suite. He was alone, the way he preferred it. The way it was best. He *liked* being alone. Correction. *Had* liked being alone.

Until Gaylan had bulldozed her way into his life.

She was everywhere he looked. In the piece of driftwood she'd arranged in one of the planters, the greenery artfully draped around it. In the completed menu for tonight's dinner that she'd left on the sideboard. In her special scent that he could smell everywhere—on his sheets, in his closet, in his memory.

Meaning. She'd given his life so much meaning. Before, he'd gone through the motions, thinking he was happy. With her, he'd tasted his first true sampling of happiness.

Empty. The rooms were as empty as his heart. She'd brought him to life and he'd managed to chase her away.

Failure. It wasn't a word he was familiar with in connection with himself. He'd seldom failed at anything. Others failed, but he did not. Or did he?

Hunter had never considered his short marriage his failure, but rather Jolene's. Had he been wrong about that, unfair to his ex-wife because of his disappointment in her?

The thought was sobering. And this time, with Gaylan, he'd failed because of fear. He'd been afraid to care too much, to give control of himself over to another. Afraid to love and then, when he finally suspected he did love her, afraid to admit it even to himself.

He felt a hand on his shoulder and turned to see deep concern in Evan's eyes.

"Be careful, Hunter. Don't become like your father. He didn't know how to enjoy life or accept love. Remember that he died alone, a sad and lonely man."

Hunter blinked, wishing the truth was easier to handle.

"It's not too late," Evan went on. "Go after her."

A firm knock at the door prevented Hunter from answering just then. He went to see who it was, stepping aside as a worried Taro strode in.

"I need your help, Hunter-san," the man stated without preamble.

"Certainly," Hunter answered. "What can I do?"

"We can't get four passages to Tokyo on commercial flights until Saturday. Nari is very upset and my wife is also. I would be willing to pay if—"

Hunter stopped him with a wave of his hand. "Say no more. I'll contact my pilot right away. How soon can all of you be ready to leave?"

Relief shone on Taro's usually unemotional face. "Two hours."

"Done." He turned to Evan. "Would you call for me, make sure everything's in order?"

As Evan went to the phone, Taro reached to shake Hunter's hand. "I am most grateful. You are a good man, Hunter-san."

Hunter wished he agreed. It would seem that today was a day of reckoning in more ways than one.

"Taro, I hope you have a few minutes before you leave because there's something I need to tell you." It was time. Perhaps past time. He was having more than a little trouble facing his eyes in the mirror most mornings as he shaved. He'd agreed to the deception. The buck stopped with him and it was time he faced the music. Funny thing about being dishonest, even in small ways. You always paid for the deception sooner or later. Compu West would undoubtedly lose a very lucrative contract and weeks of work would go down the drain, but he'd sleep better.

Provided he could sleep at all without Gaylan wrapped around him.

"I've not been completely honest with you," Hunter began. He told him everything, sparing himself nothing, taking full blame for the deception. He was aware that Evan had returned and was listening intently. Finally he finished.

"I can only apologize sincerely. It was wrong of me and I know I've violated your trust. If it's any consolation, the whole thing's blown up in my face. I'll understand if you no longer want to do business with me."

Taro took a moment to respond. "In my country, we are not so much concerned about truth as we are about people. I give you an example. If you had a son and he was accused of a crime, which would concern you most, the truth or your son? To us Japanese, the important thing is relationships between people. That's what we consider the actual truth."

He paused a moment, looking from one man to the other. "The factual truth is not as important. The fact in this case is you lied about your marriage. The truth is you did it to cement our relationship, to comply with our traditions. You meant us no harm in doing so."

Hunter felt humbled, a feeling he was unused to. "You're very understanding."

"I had you checked out before coming here to meet with you, as I do all key men we do business with. We had found no record of your marriage and were surprised when you showed up with Gaylan. I assumed you had just married. Whatever the case, she is a charming woman and you are a most honorable businessman. When my grandson is well again, we will finalize our agreement and sign the papers." He stood, looking about. "I would like to say goodbye to Gaylan, if she is here."

Hunter was through with lies, with deception. "She left me, Taro. It's not been an easy couple of weeks for her."

The older man studied Hunter for a long moment, seeing more than surface things. "The rewards of business are cold and often fleeting. A life's partner and children are what is important, a reason for getting up each morning. I wish you good fortune in reconciling your differences."

Hunter walked to the door with him. "Thank you and thanks for accepting my apology."

Taro bowed. "We will not speak of this again." And he left.

Leaning on the open door, Hunter drew in a deep breath as Evan walked over. "You have a lot to think over, son." With that, he walked out, leaving Hunter alone with his thoughts.

Gaylan stepped out of the courthouse into bright sunshine after a rainy morning. She drew in a deep breath of air and let it out, releasing her tension with it. It seemed as if every day of the two weeks she'd been back from Hawaii she'd been tense, holding her breath. Now, it was finally over.

She hurried down the three steps on her way to where she'd parked her Volkswagen. The hearing hadn't gone too badly, considering everything. Avery Woods had said it could have been a lot worse. The experienced attorney had worked out a deal with the prosecutor, which the judge approved. Mel received one year mandatory stay in a nearby drug rehabilitation facility and then two years' probation. During those two years, he had to get a job and steer clear of drugs and anyone who used them. He also had to do fifty hours of community service, working with youngsters, telling them from firsthand experience what happened when you got involved with drugs.

Climbing into her car, Gaylan sighed. She'd hated to leave him, but she could visit often. One of the things that pleased her most was that Mel seemed oddly subdued instead of surly, repentant instead of rebellious. *Maybe this time,* she prayed as she started the car.

She'd been in for another shock. As she'd tried to explain to Mr. Woods that the original arrangements for his fee had fallen apart, but that she knew she'd have a job very soon and would pay him every cent, he'd stopped her. It would seem his fee had been paid in advance in full by an unidentified source.

But she knew exactly who'd paid the attorney, Gaylan thought as she headed for her small house. Evan must have arranged it. Well, she'd accept it. For now. But just as soon as she got a job or sold a book, whichever came first, she'd start a special bank account and pay him back every cent. She didn't want to be beholden to anyone.

She was a little surprised that she hadn't heard from Evan, since she knew they were probably back by now. Ah well, Gaylan thought as she turned onto her street. Perhaps Evan wasn't pleased at the way she'd left without an explanation. She couldn't blame him, yet . . .

Automatically she slowed the car as she neared home. There in front was a most unusual sight. A shiny black carriage with a restless white horse harnessed to the front stood at the curb of her house. Pulling into her drive, Gaylan turned off the engine and stepped out, her curiosity taking her closer.

Much to her surprise, Evan stepped out wearing a black tux and carrying a large plastic bag that hung to the ground.

"Don't say a word," Evan said, taking her arm and leading her up the front walk. "We mustn't be late."

"What is going on?" Gaylan wanted to know.

"It's a surprise. Open the door."

Inside, she turned on him. "Are you going to explain now?"

"Later. Think of this as a sort of progression affair. First, you get into this dress. Next, we get into the carriage and I drive you somewhere."

"Somewhere?"

"I can't tell you the location, but once you're there, you'll understand it all." He thrust the bag at her. "Now, hurry."

"Evan, I don't know. I—"

"Gaylan, where's your sense of adventure, your romantic spirit? I promise you, no harm will come to you. Have you ever known me to lead you wrong?"

Maybe once, she thought. But he looked so earnest, almost pleading with her. She took the bag into her bedroom.

It contained the most gorgeous long white dress she'd ever seen. It looked vaguely familiar, but she wasn't sure where she might have seen it before. As Evan had requested, she hurried to change, then paused to check her mirror image.

Hundreds, perhaps thousands of tiny pearls and white sequins were sewn onto the bodice of the scooped neck. The sleeves were puffed at the shoulders, then hugged her arms, coming to a point at her hands. The waist flared in and the long, flowing skirt fell to swirl around her ankles, trimmed at intervals of six inches, alternating pearls and sequins. The overall effect, Gaylan couldn't help thinking, had her looking breathtaking for the first time in her life.

"I'm ready," she said, and saw in Evan's eyes a deep male appreciation.

"You're lovely, Gaylan, my dear," he said as he led her out to the carriage.

The ride was long and they garnered quite a bit of attention through the residential streets until they were out on a country road, jogging along. Evan would answer no questions about their destination or the reason for her going with him. She didn't want to talk about Hunter. So instead she told him about Mel's court appearance and the outcome. He was genuinely pleased.

They'd run out of small talk about the same time they ran out of road. As if the horse had been trained to follow a certain route, although Evan held the reins, he turned down a small path that led through a thicket of woods.

"What on earth?" Gaylan murmured as she recognized nothing. If she hadn't trusted Evan as she did, she'd be getting quite frightened about now.

It was another ten minutes before she saw a clearing, cars parked off to one side and finally, an open-air chapel. As Evan pulled the carriage to a halt in front, she recognized the assemblage of seated guests, and gasped.

Many of her girlhood friends were present on one side, a few shyly waving. And up near the front were Taro and Yoshiko Yamaguchi alongside Nari and Hiroki, who was holding a small dark-haired boy of about four. Behind them were Ross and Yasu holding hands. She could only smile through her surprise.

"The dress," she whispered to Evan. "I thought I recognized it as the one in Nari's sketchbook."

"She had it made for you in Tokyo, at Hunter's request, of course."

A white-robed minister stood in front of the altar, facing the guests. Candles burned all around in a semi-circle and finally two guitarists stepped forward and began to play. Gaylan felt the rush of tears as she watched Hunter, startlingly handsome in a white tux, step forward and stand waiting for her.

She turned to Evan. "I can't believe this."

"It's a little nontraditional, I'll admit. But then, Hunter seems to have abandoned his ultra-conventional ways. And it's perfectly legal." He signaled to a dark-haired man standing off to the side who stepped up to the carriage. "This is Tom Fuller, a clerk from the Marriage License Bureau. He's been kind enough to come out here and notarize your signature. If you wish to be Hunter's bride, that is."

Gaylan looked at him, still in shock. "Are you sure that's what he wants?"

"Why don't we walk down there and find out?"

She did. Shakily Gaylan signed the license, then waited while Mr. Fuller notarized her signature before handing the paper to Evan and moving aside.

Evan stepped out of the carriage and helped Gaylan down. As they paused at the back, the guitarists began the wedding march. Slowly he led her down the white runner past the smiling faces of their guests to the man waiting for her. Finally they stopped and Evan hugged her, then handed her over to Hunter.

Her face radiant, Gaylan looked up at him as he leaned down to her.

"Is this romantic enough for you, Gaylan?" he asked softly, for her ears only.

"I thought our relationship was strictly business," she answered.

"It was," Hunter said. "Until you taught me to believe in love. You changed me, all for the better. I love you, Gaylan Fisher. Will you marry me?"

Her heart had never been so full. "I guess I'd better or all these people will have dressed up for nothing."

He reached into his pocket and pulled out the ring she'd last seen on his plane weeks ago. "Now, will you wear my ring?"

Eyes shining, she smiled. "Oh, yes."

"And that land I have up in Big Sur. Do you think you'd like to help me design our house for it, so we could live near the sea? I have fond memories of the ocean."

"That sounds wonderful. I left my heart in Hawaii, with you. But you brought it back to me."

"I think we should return to Kona for our honeymoon." He squeezed her hands. "I'll never be careless with your heart again, Gaylan."

Hearing the minister clear his throat, they both turned to face him.

There'd be time enough to talk later, Hunter thought. Years and years of time—together.

* * * * *

BABY BLESSED
Debbie Macomber

Molly Larabee didn't expect her reunion with
estranged husband Jordan to be quite so explosive.
Their tumultuous past was filled with memories of
tragedy—and love. Rekindling familiar passions left
Molly with an unexpected blessing...and suddenly a
future with Jordan was again worth fighting for!

Don't miss Debbie Macomber's fiftieth book,
BABY BLESSED, available in July!

She's friend, wife, mother—she's you! And beside
each **Special Woman** stands a wonderfully
special man. It's a celebration of our heroines—
and the men who become part of their lives.

TSW794

Take 4 bestselling love stories FREE

Plus get a FREE surprise gift!

Silhouette

SPECIAL EDITION ™

MEN OF COURAGE

COUNTDOWN
Lindsay McKenna

Sergeant Joe Donnally knew being a marine
meant putting lives on the line—and after a tragic
loss, he vowed never to love again. Yet here was
Annie Yellow Horse, the passionate, determined
woman who challenged him to feel long-dormant
emotions. But Joe had to conquer past demons before
declaring his love....

MEN OF COURAGE

It's a special breed of men who defy death and fight
for right! Salute their bravery while sharing their lives
and loves!

These are courageous men you'll love and tender
stories you'll cherish...available in June, only from
Silhouette Special Edition!

Silhouette

SPECIAL EDITION™

THE Jones GANG

by Christine Rimmer

**Three rapscallion brothers. Their main talent: making trouble.
Their only hope: three uncommon women who knew the way to
heal a wounded heart! Meet them in these books:**

Jared Jones

hadn't had it easy with women. Retreating to his mountain cabin, he found willful
Eden Parker waiting to show him a good woman's love in MAN OF THE MOUNTAIN
(May, SE #886).

Patrick Jones

was determined to show Regina Black that a wild Jones boy was *not* husband
material. But that wouldn't stop her from trying to nab him in SWEETBRIAR SUMMIT
(July, SE #896)

Jack Roper

came to town looking for the wayward and beautiful Olivia Larrabee. He never
suspected he'd uncover a long-buried Jones family secret in A HOME FOR THE HUNTER
(September, SE #908)....

**Meet these rascal men and the women who'll tame them,
only from Silhouette Books and Special Edition!**